Praise for the Hamptons Home & Garden Mysteries

"The dazzling houses showcased in the Hamptons Home & Garden mysteries aren't without skeletons in their closets. Fortunately, interior designer Meg Barrett has the golden touch when it comes to solving murders. Cozy mystery fans will adore the characters, stunning setting, and mouthwatering recipes in Kathleen Bridge's delightful series."

— Ellery Adams, *New York Times* bestselling author

"A delightful sneak peek into life in the Hamptons, with intricate plotting and a likeable, down-to-earth protagonist. A promising start to a promising series."

— *Suspense Magazine* on *Better Homes and Corpses*

"*Ghostal Living* is a marvelously entertaining tale of revenge, murder, quirky characters—and disappearing books! With a clever protagonist, wonderful details of life in the Hamptons, and plot twists on top of plot twists, Kathleen Bridge will have mystery readers clamoring for more."

— Kate Carlisle, *New York Times* bestselling author

"An excellent read."

— *RT Book Reviews* on *Hearse and Gardens*

"The descriptions of furniture and other antiques, as well as juicy tidbits on the Hamptons, make for entertaining reading for those who enjoy both antiques and lifestyles of the rich and famous."

— *Booklist* on *Better Homes and Corpses*

Books by Kathleen Bridge

Hamptons Home & Garden Mysteries

Better Homes and Corpses
Hearse and Gardens
Ghostal Living
Manor of Dying
A Design to Die For
A Fatal Feast

By the Sea Mysteries

Death by the Sea
A Killing by the Sea
Murder by the Sea
Evil by the Sea
Buried by the Sea

A Fatal Feast

Kathleen Bridge

BEYOND THE PAGE
PUBLISHING

A Fatal Feast
Kathleen Bridge
Beyond the Page Books
are published by
Beyond the Page Publishing
www.beyondthepagepub.com

Copyright © 2021 by Kathleen Bridge
Cover design by Dar Albert, Wicked Smart Designs

ISBN: 978-1-954717-56-5

I dedicate this book to Lon Otremba in gratitude for supplying all the recipes included in here and in all ten of my previous mysteries. You are not only a great friend, but also an exceptional home chef. I have so many fond memories of sitting around the Otremba table with you and Michelle, sharing not only great meals but great conversation and tons of laughter.

As Julia said, *"I think careful cooking is love, don't you? The loveliest thing you can cook for someone who's close to you is about as nice a Valentine as you can give."*

Lon, thanks for all the Valentines. Hugs, Kathy.

Acknowledgments

As always, thank you to my fabulous agent, Dawn Dowdle at Blue Ridge Literary Agency, not only for her encouragement but also her friendship. To Bill Harris at Beyond the Page Publishing for his excellent editing and wonderful suggestions. And to my mom, my partner in vintage and antique crimes of a *fun* nature, thanks for being my eagle-eye beta reader. Thanks again, Michelle Mason Otremba, for your research and suggestions when I call you in a panic. Congrats to Howard Rudolph for his generous charity bid, which won him a chance to be a character in *A Fatal Feast*. To Ellen, Nancy, John, Josh, Lindsey, and Amy (you know why). Lastly, to all the bloggers and the entire cozy mystery community for supporting me from day one and beyond. I am incredibly grateful for your unwavering encouragement and support.

Chapter 1

"I'm sorry, Mr. Seaton. You're welcome at the winery," Bethany Garnier said, clutching a corkscrew in her right hand. "But you, Meg Barrett, *certainly* are not!" There was a definite edge to her voice that my hearing aids had no problem picking up.

"But . . ." I said, confused.

Then, Bethany, the owner of Garnier Vineyards, one of the Hamptons premier Long Island wineries, cleared things up *tout de suite.* "You've got a lot of nerve showing your face. I heard it was *your* construction guys who renovated my former family home into some posh A-list restaurant, and it was *your* company, Cottages by the Sea, that did the restaurant's interior design. Maison Garnier was constructed stone by stone to be a replica of my family's centuries-old farmhouse in Bordeaux that the Nazis destroyed. I was under the impression that a family with three small children bought it. Not some conglomerate. My real estate agent must be on the take."

Bethany took a step toward us.

I took a step back. Patrick held tight to my hand and pulled me forward. He was right. I was never one to shy away from a confrontation. Lately, I'd been trying hard to mind my own business by focusing on my blissful existence in Montauk, which entailed living in my small oceanfront cottage, junking and rehabbing vintage finds to use in my clients' cozy homes, helping the set designer find items from the 1930s for the streaming mystery series *Mr. & Mrs. Winslow,* and enjoying my budding relationship with Patrick Seaton, a formerly reclusive writer who'd moved to Montauk following the tragic deaths of his wife and child. I used the word *formerly* because in the past when Patrick and I'd exchanged classical poetry in the sand, he'd only select gloomy verses. Now, ever since we'd started dating, some of his verses were downright sunny. I prayed that I'd been the catalyst to his metamorphosis, just as he'd been to mine.

Glancing at Bethany's angry face, I said meekly, "I wouldn't call the three owners of Privé a conglomerate. As far as I know they're all local business owners. And, from my understanding, Privé's not

1

really a restaurant, it's more like an exclusive gourmet dining club."
I added, "You have to be a member to get in the door."

"Sounds like a restaurant to me," Bethany said, raising her thin
upper lip in a sneer. "Does our mutual friend, Elle, know about your
treachery?"

"Sure," I said. "Elle knows all about my assignment at Privé.
Half of the interior décor came from Mabel and Elle's Curiosities.
However, I'm pretty sure, like myself, she had no idea the
farmhouse had been yours." *Or why it should matter,* I thought.

Elle Shoner was my best friend and partner in crime involving
anything having to do with vintage décor. Elle had told me that she
and winery owner Bethany's friendship dated back to when Elle's
late Great-Aunt Mabel and Bethany's grandmother were friends. I
only knew Bethany from my visits to Garnier Vineyards
accompanied by either Elle or Patrick.

"Well, I'll be sure to give her a call about all of this," Bethany
snapped.

I felt my cheeks warm, then looked beseechingly at Patrick,
whose handsome face was probably the same shade of pink as my
own. Bethany had always been friendly, even sending out special,
on-the-house tapas plates to go with our wine flights. Noticing her
clenched jaw, it looked like the word *friendly* no longer applied.
Trying to appease her, I added, "The construction team did a great
job on the exterior of Privé. I think if you came over to see it, you'll
like what's been done."

"Like it. Like it . . ." she stuttered. She took a few more menacing
steps toward us.

She raised her hand as if to push me away. I held my ground.
"Bethany, I swear, I didn't know the farmhouse used to be your
family's home." We were about the same height, five feet seven, but
I had ten pounds on her—a moot point judging by the expression on
her face and the bulging vein at her temple. *Hell hath no fury like a
woman scorned.* I didn't think I was the one Bethany should be upset
with. I was just the hired help, as Jackie, one of the partners at Privé,
reminded me of on more than one occasion.

Tears glistened in Bethany's usually smiling, vibrant eyes.
"*Grand-père* was born there."

Then why had she sold it? I reached in my handbag, grabbed a package of tissues, and handed her one. Bethany took out a few and blew her nose.

Bethany's customers, who were sitting on the patio under a white slatted pergola, had all eyes trained on us. I'm sure, like myself, they'd never seen usually mellow Bethany in such a state. But I was innocent. All I'd known before this evening was that her Sagaponack vineyard and wine-tasting operation was across the pond from Privé.

Now, glancing at Bethany's quivering chin and gritted teeth, I wished that Patrick and I had opted for a quiet night home. It was the Thursday before Labor Day weekend and we'd planned on having a farewell and good-riddance toast to summer, knowing that soon the seasonal Hamptons crowd would be heading due west. We were just days away from having the East End of Long Island all to ourselves.

Hallelujah.

And what a summer it had been. There'd been campfires and clambakes on the beach and gourmet meals at Patrick's kitchen counter, which he'd made in the workshop behind his oceanfront cottage. I wasn't allowed anywhere near his stove due to my lack of culinary skills and tendency to overcook, okay, burn things. Then there was the simple bliss of twilight evenings when we'd sit side by side reading on his or my screened porch, both of us trying to convince the other of our favorite genre's merits. Even though Patrick wrote fiction, he enjoyed reading historical biographies. I read mostly fiction, preferring whodunit mysteries. But there was one thing we both loved to read—classical poetry.

"Sorry, Bethany. I truly am," I repeated ad nauseum. "You must believe me. Privé will never compete with Garnier Vineyards. Everyone loves it here."

It would be a lie if I'd said I would have given up the assignment knowing that Bethany was the former owner of the building that housed Privé. *Former* being the key word. The money I'd been paid to transform the interior of the renovated French farmhouse into an elite dining club was the most I'd made in a year since moving to Montauk and close to the salary I received as editor-in-chief of *American Home and Garden Magazine* before fleeing Manhattan and a cheating fiancé for the serenity only the salt life could offer. I admitted that the two-timing fiancé story was cliched, and my exodus on the wimpy side—but my move to the easternmost tip of Long Island turned out to be the best thing that ever happened to me. And Patrick was just the icing on the cake.

Bethany looked from me to Patrick, her hands at her sides as she tried to hold down her gauzy boho caftan from the stiff breeze blowing in from the ocean, only a half mile away. She and I weren't besties like my newly married bosom buddy Elle and I were. However, we'd always been friendly, chatting about things like local charity events, Bethany's wine recommendations, and Garnier Winery's delicious farm-to-table tapas plates that came with each wine-tasting experience. A sip and bite and you were off to gastronomic heaven.

She pointed the corkscrew in my direction. Her red-wine-stained fingertips matched the color of her long, wild hair. "I suppose you and these partners, more like thieves, didn't know that next spring I have plans to open a full-service restaurant. It would be easy enough for anyone to look up the architect's plans that I filed at the courthouse. It's obvious one of those traitors must have the zoning commission in their pocket. How else can you explain the property going from residential to commercial in a blink of an eye."

"As I said, it's not really a restaurant, more of a gourmet club. If you want, maybe I could put in a word with Chef Kelsie about ordering some of Garnier Vineyards' wines for Privé?"

"Kelsie Stevens from Pondfare in Montauk?" she asked, surprised, her countenance softening.

"Yes," I answered. "She's the chef de cuisine. And someone named Sasha is her sous chef.

"I know Kelsie. She's great," Bethany said, lowering the corkscrew. "An amazing chef. I'll call her myself. And please, don't tell me you're referring to that tramp Sasha Morgan as being the restaurant's sous chef. Good luck on that one. She worked here for a brief time. Very brief. Then we got rid of her."

"It's not a restaurant," I repeated for the last time. My involvement in Privé was over. All that was left to do was to attend the small dinner the partners were throwing tomorrow night. Duke and Duke Jr. Construction had done their job of renovating the exterior of the stone farmhouse to its former glory, and I'd completed my contract by filling Privé with upscale French farmhouse/cottage décor.

"You know what, there's nothing to worry about," Bethany said. "I'll just wait until Privé fails because of Sasha. Then I'll buy the place for a fraction of the price they bought it for. What an ostentatious name. Who came up with it?"

"I'm not sure," I mumbled, "but I do know that translated from French to English, Privé means *Private*."

"My family's French. I know what the word means," she snapped.

I didn't like being talked to in such a condescending manner and was ready to tell her so. But then I looked up at Patrick. He squeezed my hand, which I took to mean, *just let her vent*. I repeated a few mantras I used when meditating on my beach, took a deep breath, and exhaled to the count of four.

"No one will come in the off-season, anyway," she said. "It'll be fun to watch pretentious Privé's ruin. Meg, maybe I will stop by for that tour you offered. Catch a peek before it goes belly up. My new restaurant will be available to everyone. Not just the Hamptons elite. We'll see who the victor is."

"Hmmm, sounds like a plan," I said. *A bad plan.*

Bethany looked at Patrick, who up until now hadn't said a word, then she broke into sobs. Patrick let go of my hand and went to her, placing the palm of his right hand on her shoulder. "It can't be that bad," he said softly. "Garnier Vineyards has been in the Hamptons for decades. I've never been here when it hasn't been packed. Even in the winter."

His words seemed to calm her.

"Patrick," I whispered, "maybe we should go?"

"No," Bethany said, drying her eyes. "Please don't. I'm fine. Meg, I'm sorry for taking things out on you. It's been such a struggle now that Tom is gone. He was the business part of our marriage. I should have held out for a better price for the farmhouse. All I wanted to do was sell it to a family that could restore it to its former glory, then I would move on to build the restaurant Tom and I always dreamed of. Patrick, you can relate to my loss because of your Catherine and Lucy. I'm not sure if you knew this, but early in their careers, your wife and my Tom worked together as newbie chefs at one of Daniel Boulud's restaurants in Manhattan. Tom always said Catherine was a better chef than he was."

"I didn't know that," Patrick said in a barely audible voice. Then he turned his head and looked off into the distance.

I was floored that Patrick's late wife had been a chef. I was the worst cook on the planet, which Patrick had witnessed on more than one occasion. It also explained why he was such an excellent home chef, on par with my father—he'd learned from his deceased wife. I felt warm tingling as the Barrett blotches started up from my chest, traveled to my neck, then burned my cheeks.

Patrick's tragedy had not been something we'd discussed, though he knew everything about my recent breakup with Cole Spenser. Not that I could compare the two losses. Patrick won. Hands down. Before I could ask if he was okay, Patrick strode away and went to stand at the wood railing overlooking the pond. A breeze blew back his light brown hair highlighted with sun streaks of gold from surfing at Amagansett's Ditch Plains Beach. He'd confessed at the beginning of June that he usually fled the Hamptons during the summer tourist season. It was obvious he'd stayed because of me. Now I wondered if at the mention of Catherine, he might have regretted our time together.

I knew I never would.

I glanced back at Bethany. Had she mentioned Catherine on purpose, as payback for my involvement at Privé?

"Now I've done it," Bethany said, looking over at Patrick's stiff stance. "It must be hard dating him with all that baggage. Tom told me Patrick was despondent after the accident—or should I say vehicular homicide by that drunk driver. So tragic. And his little girl . . . I must give him credit for dating again. I know I'll never find anyone like my Tom. I don't even plan on looking. Tom was irreplaceable."

Bethany was my age, in her early thirties. It seemed a little young to give up on finding someone else. And didn't Patrick deserve some happiness?

Patrick must have known we were talking about him. Or at least Bethany was. He turned and smiled at us.

As if reading my thoughts, Bethany said, "You better go to him. You don't want him going down that slippery slope of depression.

Did you happen to read that last book he wrote? *The Sting of the Sea.* A wonderful book but so-o-o sad." Then she walked away to greet some regular customers.

I felt gutted. I stood there, not knowing whether I should take her advice or give Patrick time alone. I had read *The Sting of the Sea.* It had been a departure from his thrillers, and I understood where he must have been coming from because it had come out a year after the tragedy. But Bethany had been wrong that it was his last work of fiction because he'd recently released another thriller and had a contract to write two more. And besides that, his screenwriting for the *Mr. & Mrs. Winslow* television mystery series was certainly upbeat and occasionally laugh-out-loud funny. Why was I second-guessing our relationship? I knew why. Catherine. I took a few steps in his direction and he did the same toward me.

When he reached me, he put his arm around my shoulder and gave me a kiss on the top of my head. "Everything okay with Bethany?"

"I think so."

"Let's have that toast we talked about. Then go home and make a bonfire. You burn the most perfect marshmallows," he said, adding a mischievous grin.

I smiled up at him, happy for his cheerful banter but wishing at the same time that there was something I could do to make it all better. But I couldn't. He needed to find his own peace. In his own time. I wasn't going anywhere, and I wasn't about to give up on happiness. Our happiness.

Or so I told myself as we walked toward our high-top table and a nagging green-eyed monster hopped onto my shoulder and whispered, *Megan Barrett, how can you compete with a ghost?*

Chapter 2

I'd wanted to bring Patrick to Friday night's pre-opening dinner at Privé, but Chef Kelsie made it clear that we were to be a closed group: the three partners, head chef Kelsie, sous chef Sasha, and myself. Not even the waitstaff was allowed inside. Hence the reason I was in the kitchen, acting as combination busgirl and server — bringing in our dirty dishes, then taking out the next course. If the food wasn't so darn good, I would've complained about my servitude.

With the final payment for my design services safely in my handbag and an amuse-bouche in my belly that had lived up to its name of being the chef's choice of a teaser — a one-bite hors d'oeuvre consisting of a marinated smoked oyster, crème fraiche, and a smidgen of caviar atop a sterling silver tablespoon — I was happy to help. The faster the service went, the faster it would hit my belly. Plus, I was curious to find out the partners' first impressions of how I'd done designing the interior of Privé.

Ever since yesterday, when Bethany had gone off the rails about her family's former home, I couldn't help but look at Privé in a different light, wondering how long it had sat unoccupied. Judging by its original ramshackle condition it must have been uninhabitable for at least a decade — maybe two.

So far, the only partner who'd been a thorn in my side during the interior design process was Jackie, or Mrs. Putnam-Fairchild, as I was ordered to address her. She'd wanted me to go with a more formal, over-the-top, drenched in gold, French chateau aesthetic. The two male partners, one of them her husband, wanted Privé's furnishings and décor to be more on the masculine, rustic side. I'd thought I'd done a good job compromising on both décor styles, refusing to let *Jackie's* jabs get to me, even if she was, as she claimed, a cousin twice or thrice removed from Hamptonite Jacqueline Bouvier Kennedy Onassis's father, Black Jack Bouvier.

Thinking about family ties, my mind wandered again to last night's scene at Garnier Vineyards. Why had Bethany been so upset? As far as I knew, the winery business was flourishing. Last year, during the Hamptons garden tour, I'd visited Bethany's magnificent oceanfront home in Bridgehampton. By its opulence, she hadn't looked like she was hurting for cash. Maybe money had nothing to do with why Bethany had been so distraught. It was more a matter of losing her grandfather's home and all the memories that went along with it. I understood a love for nostalgia (an understatement), which was one of the reasons my cozy cottage's screen porch was a replica of my grandfather's in Michigan.

Maybe Elle could convince Bethany to come take a peek at what I'd done to the farmhouse. Bethany would see that I'd kept to the original floor plan of the old farmhouse, only knocking down one wall that wasn't load-bearing. I'd left the wood-stained rafters on the ceiling untouched, then painted the rough stone walls and ceilings a clean linen white. For the exterior of the farmhouse, my construction guys had sandblasted the stone façade, then whitewashed it, making it appear older than its seventy-five years. Cracked windowpanes had been replaced with thick hurricane glass. And in the old cottage at the rear of the property, I'd made a serendipitous discovery—the farmhouse's original ten-foot-tall cedar shutters. I'd touched them up in a paint shade close to their original color by mixing duck egg blue with pale smoke gray. The best part was that all the shutters, even the pair on either side of the front door, were functional and could be closed during a nor'easter or hurricane. Seeing it was the last week in August, I knew foul weather was still a possibility. Never underestimate Mother Nature when living near the Atlantic Ocean.

"Sasha, when the hell are you going to get it right!" Chef Kelsie shouted and my left hearing aid buzzed with static. "Sasha, look at that plate!" Kelsie pointed over to the Carrera marble island where her sous chef sat on a bar stool, sipping a glass of wine.

Kelsie, Privé's head chef, had used the same tone that a mother might use on her naughty child, but she wasn't old enough to be Sasha's mother. Maybe an older sister. "Is your work on that plate aesthetically pleasing to you? It isn't to me," Kelsie admonished. "Do you see anything wrong? I wouldn't give that to my dog, and she'll eat anything. We're serving this meal to the owners of Privé, the same threesome who can hire and fire us at will." She rolled her eyes in my direction. "Sasha! Are you even listening?"

"Thought you were one of the partners?" Sasha said, not in the least ruffled by her boss.

"Who told you that?" she asked. Kelsie was attractive in a healthy, wholesome way: clear skin, no makeup, except a light dusting of mascara on her long lashes above large, expressive dark brown eyes that matched the color of her naturally curly short hair.

"A little birdy," Sasha said, taking another sip of wine. On the other hand, Kelsie's sous chef wore expertly applied makeup that brought out her high cheekbones and startling blue-violet eyes that she'd lined in thick black eyeliner. The color of her eyes was reminiscent of those I'd seen in photos of the actress Elizabeth Taylor. Unlike Kelsie, there was nothing understated about Sasha.

"I'll only receive a small percentage of the business," Kelsie said. "And that won't be for a year. As if it's any of your business, *sous* chef." She opened one of the refrigerated drawers next to the sink and took out a lemon. "I'm not an equal partner. Not even close. But you're right, Sasha. I do have a stake in Privé. So, get your act together before it's too late."

Kelsie's former boss, Pierre Patou, the head chef and owner of Pondfare in Montauk, had been the one who'd recommended my one-woman design business Cottages by the Sea to Privé's partners. Not that he advertised it but Chef Patou had earned a Michelin star and was recently the winner of television's *Top Chef Challenge*. He was from the old school of fine dining, more concerned with his food than basking in the notoriety of winning the competition. His recently published six-hundred-page cookbook, *Nouveau French-American Cuisine*, was now at the top of every nonfiction bestseller list, here and abroad.

I'd known Kelsie from my frequent visits to Pondfare when she'd been Chef Patou's sous chef. We'd also bonded over lessons at Karen's Kreative Knitting in Montauk. Sometimes those lessons turned into group therapy sessions. At one of our classes, I'd shared a few things about Cole's and my breakup. Then Kelsie trumped my story by telling our small group about her divorce and three miscarriages. Apparently, she'd blamed the hormones taken during her IVF treatments for the anger and resentment she'd directed at her innocent husband. Her single-minded goal had only been to conceive. Then one day, her husband just walked out the door and never came back. The next thing Kelsie knew, he'd opened a tech company on the West Coast. "I have no regrets," she'd said, sniffling. "In a way, Pondfare saved my life. The restaurant became the child I couldn't have." Each of the women warriors in our knitting group had rushed over to her side and gave her consoling hugs. Then, after tea and lavender scones were served, the afternoon ended with more smiles than tears.

"I don't see why you're in such a tizzy," Sasha said. "It's only dinner for five. And her." She nodded her head in my direction.

"We have to get these ten courses perfect for tomorrow for when potential club members arrive." Kelsie's jaw was clenched as she gazed angerly at Sasha. I wondered if she might have been better off staying at Pondfare. I'd never once heard her raise her voice in Pondfare's kitchen or elsewhere. On the other hand, Chef Patou's shouting and berating of his staff could be heard all the way to Pondfare's usually packed dining room.

Kelsie's face was as red as the plum tomatoes she slid into a simmering copper pot. "I don't have time to babysit, Sasha. Get your act together, or else." Then she marched over to the center island and tossed the cutting board from the tomatoes into the double farm sink, managing to decapitate the top of a champagne flute from its stem.

I cringed. Not from the sound of shattering crystal. My hearing aids didn't pick up the high-pitched sound. It was that one of the set of forty I'd found on an online French antiques shop had been destroyed. The cost for shipping the glasses had almost exceeded the cost of their purchase. Not that I'd paid for the set out of my pocket. It was one of the perks of my design assignment at Privé. Money didn't seem to be an issue.

The chef de cuisine didn't notice my distress because she was too focused on her assistant. I went to the sink, picked up the two pieces of glass, wrapped them in paper towel, then threw them in the trash. I didn't want anyone to cut themselves, or worse yet, for Kelsie to grab a shard and use it as a weapon against her sous chef.

Sasha clapped her hands. "Good going, Chef. You broke a glass. Lee won't be happy when I tell him." She turned her head toward me and said, "And, I can tell you've upset her, too. Who are you again?"

"Maybe if you spent more time at Privé during the past two weeks, you would have met Meg," Kelsie answered. "Meg, this is Sasha Morgan, my supposed assistant chef. Sasha, Meg Barrett,

Privé's interior designer."

"Oh, yeah. Good job. Place looks great. Should have known chef here had nothing to do with the kitchen's flawless design."

Kelsie mumbled a warning under her breath, then turned and strode over to one of two wall ovens. She cracked open the oven door, then quickly shut it. A yeasty aroma escaped and mixed with the other heavenly scents coming from assorted simmering pots on the eight-burner stove. "Needs another minute and a half," Kelsie said to herself.

"I'm the one that should be doing the baking," Sasha said, sticking out her pouty lower lip. Unlike Kelsie, Sasha wore a white chef's toque and white chef's coat that fit her in all the right places. Her sleek raven-black hair was fashioned into a single braid that trailed down to the middle of her back. "Outta my way." Sasha pushed back her bar stool, which made a scaping noise against the tile that my hearing aids did pick up, stood, and charged over to the ovens. "Baking's my job. Not yours. I went to pastry school, remember?"

Kelsie laughed. "That's funny. Then where were you when I was making the pastry? I'm executive chef and you'll do as I say. Finish plating the first course. I won't tolerate insubordination. It's been a trying two weeks since you showed up."

"How can it be trying? You just said I was never here."

"Sasha, I think you'd be better off working at one of the other hundreds of restaurants in the Hamptons. Lord knows, we have enough of them."

"I thought this wasn't a restaurant, it was a *club*." Sasha put quotation marks in the air.

"Semantics. If things don't go well tonight, I'm going to have a talk with the partners. See if I can hire someone more experienced."

Now it was Sasha's turn to blow a fuse. "Try it. You won't like it."

I moved to the other side of the kitchen and backed up to the door of the walk-in combination refrigerator-freezer, wishing I had a reason to go inside and get out of the line of fire. Although, I wasn't the one that needed to cool off.

"Is that a threat?" Kelsie asked.

"Chill lax, Kel. What's the big deal? You'll never be able to fire me. So, let's be pals. At least for tonight."

Kelsie ignored her, grabbed two oven mitts from a drawer, put them on, then opened the oven and removed a metal sheet pan topped with six mini bread bowls. She put the pan on the granite counter, picked up a spatula, then transferred each bread bowl to a wire cooling rack. "I apologize, Meg," Kelsie said, nodding her head in my direction.

"No apologies necessary. I can't imagine the stress you're under. I mean, both of you are under. It's like how I feel when I show my interior design clients their cottage for the first time." I didn't want Kelsie to know that I was worried about her. This was a side of her that I'd never seen before. "So, what are you going to fill those cute little bread bowls with?" I asked, trying for some mundane chitchat but curious at the same time.

"Why don't you ask my sous chef? If she's even read the menu that I gave her last night." Sasha had gone back to her stool and was looking down at her phone.

Kelsie shook her head. "Sasha, or should I say *I*, will be filling these brioche bowls with rum-soaked apricots, foie gras, then spoon a fig and burgundy wine sauce on top. But the timing may be off because of her!"

"Don't blame me for your poor time-management skills," Sasha said, putting down her phone, getting up, and pouring herself another glass of wine.

I'd counted three since I'd been in the kitchen.

"I knew I should have followed up on some of your references," Kelsie said, taking the bowls off the cooling rack, then placing them on a sheet of parchment paper. "But apparently you have a guardian angel in one of the partners. Lee, I'm sure. I was told to hire you—no questions asked."

"Keep it that way," Sasha said, going back to her stool. When Kelsie turned to get something from one of the glass-fronted cupboards, Sasha aimed her middle finger at Kelsie's back. Then she winked at me as if I should keep her secret. Which I did. But only because when I looked over at Kelsie, it was obvious she didn't need any more ammunition against Sasha. Unlike Sasha, who was dressed in chef whites, Kelsie had on a soiled apron, and in lieu of a chef's toque she wore a sweatband that up to now had been keeping the beads of perspiration from dripping into her eyes.

"I left the menu at home, because I had to get here at such an ungodly hour," Sasha whined. As Kelsie and I looked on, Sasha dipped a pinky finger into a bowl holding a pale green liquid. She brought it to her full, glossy lips, tasted it, then scrunched her perfect nose in distaste.

Kelsie stormed over to where Sasha was sitting. Chef Patou's huge cookbook was splayed open in front of her. Next to the cookbook were six ivory gold-rimmed appetizer plates topped with paper-thin slices of meat.

"You're doing it wrong!" Kelsie growled. "We went over this days ago! Sasha, I think this might be your last day in the kitchen, guardian angel or not. Here." Kelsie flipped angrily to a different page in Chef Patou's monster cookbook. "Read it and learn a thing or two from a master."

"I agree Chef Patou is a master, you on the other hand . . ." Sasha said, then smiled.

"Chef Patou always collaborated with me on his recipes. Adding this or that when needed." I was waiting for Kelsie to add a "so there," like the pair was fighting over a toy in the sandbox.

I'd never met Sasha before, but I could tell she knew how to push Kelsie's buttons while still remaining calm. I was sure the wine helped. "Hmmm, don't see your name mentioned anywhere in here. Just his wife, Bella."

Ignoring her jab, Kelsie said, "We're running behind, Sasha. Do as I say." Then she pointed to the page with the recipe.

Sasha glanced at it, then used her green fingertip to keep track of the words, moving her lips as if reading the recipe. I knew, because I was an expert at reading lips, that Sasha was just saying gibberish.

"Watch what you're doing. Look at the stain you just left on the page!" Kelsie shouted. She went to the sink, wet a paper towel, then came back to the counter. Then she gently patted the page with the paper towel. "It's not coming off. You better get me a new cookbook, Sasha. One that's autographed like this one."

"You can't have it both ways, Chef," Sasha said with a smile, then rolled her eyes in my direction. "First you tell me to read it, then you go haywire because of a little smudge."

"It doesn't matter," Kelsie said, moving the cookbook and stand out of Sasha's reach. "You won't be messing up any more cookbooks, or anything else. Because you will be long gone as soon as I find your replacement. Do you know how many other young chefs would love your job?"

Sasha reached next to her wineglass and removed a knife from the knife block, then pointed it at her boss. "You try to get me fired and you'll see that it won't be so easy-peasy. I'm here for the long haul, Kels. You'd better change your 'tude and find a way to work with me. You could hire me an assistant?"

"That's rich. My assistant wants an assistant. Meg, what do you think?"

"Uh, I—"

Not waiting for my answer, Kelsie said, "Put the knife down, Sasha. Like you said, I own a percentage of this place, and I will get you fired if you ever threaten me again."

Sasha laughed. "Yes, Chef. Thank you, Chef. I wasn't threatening you, silly goose. As per that recipe, I need a knife."

"No, you don't. You only need a spoon."

Sasha returned the knife to the wood block and picked up a spoon.

Kelsie reached over her and ripped the spoon out of Sasha's hand. "This is the last time that I'm showing you how to execute this." She dipped the spoon into the bowl that held the opaque grass-green liquid. "Just dip the tip of the spoon into the artichoke aioli, then drizzle it in a zigzag motion above the paper-thin slices of raw Kobe beef. After that, you get a clean spoon and do the same with the beet aioli. Only start on the other side of the plate so that the lines crisscross." She did as she'd instructed, then said, "See? Not so hard."

The finished product was like a piece of art. I wished my gourmet home chef father could be here to see Kelsie's masterpiece. Plus, at this rate, my retired Detroit PD homicide detective dad might also come in handy if either chef decided to hone their knife skills by stabbing each other.

"Yes, Chef," Sasha answered. "Whatever you say, Chef." Then Sasha added a military salute and grinned.

"You're incorrigible. And exasperating," Kelsie said. "Right, Meg?"

I was Switzerland. My only goal was to get the show on the road and devour the next course. I still couldn't believe this was the same

Kelsie I'd known from Pondfare. I walked over to Kelsie and asked, "Can I do anything to help?"

"Not unless you have a culinary degree and can take over for Sasha. What am I saying?" Kelsie said with an evil chuckle. "Meg, you could take over for Sasha without a culinary degree."

I raised an eyebrow.

Kelsie laughed. "You're right, I forgot about your fear of baking."

"And fear of frying."

She laughed at my joke and I glimpsed a return of the old Kelsie that I knew from knitting class and Pondfare. "Well, you and Patrick aren't shy about eating. You guys are regulars at Pondfare. By the way, how's that going?"

"Things are going just fine," I said with a huge grin. But at the mention of Patrick, I was reminded that his deceased wife had been a chef. Which in turn reminded me of how despondent he'd been yesterday at Garnier Vineyards following the mention of his wife's name—Catherine. A name straight out of the pages of *Wuthering Heights*.

I wasn't one to wallow in yesterdays, so I was happy when Kelsie said, "Meg, if you want to lend a hand, I guess you could go into the walk-in fridge and bring me the foie gras. It's on top of the steel cart and covered in plastic wrap. Even though you've never prepared it yourself, I'm sure you know what uncooked duck liver looks like."

She was right. It was one of my father's favorite menu items. Just from growing up with an excellent home chef for a father, living in Manhattan for ten years, and now residing in the Hamptons, where fine dining was the order of the day, I could probably recognize most of the gourmet items in Privé's larder.

Little did I know how wrong I would be on that assumption.

"Got it," I said, hurrying to the walk-in, not wanting to get caught in the crosshairs of another spat. I glanced over at Sasha, who didn't seem to care that I was taking over her job as sous chef. She'd completed plating the carpaccio and was pouring herself another glass of wine. I was beginning to lose count.

I opened the door to the combination refrigerator-freezer. It closed behind me with a whoosh and a click. "There it is," I said, my words coming out in icy puffs of frost.

In front of me was the stainless steel trolly topped with the plate of duck liver.

But, beyond the trolley, hanging from a hook, was something so disgusting that I nearly lost my amuse-bouche.

Chapter 3

It was the carcass of an animal that I literally couldn't make heads or tails of. A skinned animal. Or at least I thought it was an animal. Its body was wrapped in plastic, but its head wasn't. Sightless eyes looked back at me in terror. I snatched the plate of liver and hurried to the exit, my hand fumbling with the latch. For a moment, I envisioned what it would feel like to be stuck inside with that *thing*. The shiver that coursed up my spine had nothing to do with the cold. I felt terror, just like what I'd seen in the thing's large unblinking eyes.

I burst into the kitchen and the door hit something solid.

"Kelsie!" I whimpered. "What is that awful creature hanging from a hook?"

Lee Cutler, one of Privé's partners, stumbled back against the counter. Apparently, he was the something solid that I'd walloped with the walk-in's door.

"What the hell!" he shouted, rubbing his nose. "Am I bleeding?"

"Oops, sorry," I said. With a shaky hand I placed the plate of duck liver on the counter.

Kelsie rushed to Lee. "No blood," she said.

"Well, that's a relief. I came to see what the holdup is." He gave me a dirty look, then said to Kelsie, "Why are you standing there. Ice. Before my nose bruises."

Before I could stop myself, I said, "That thing in there scared the bejesus out of me!"

"You're frightened of a butchered llama?" Lee asked. "Wait until you taste it. You'd be surprised how lean and delicious it is. Keep an open mind, darlin'. It'll serve you well."

Taste it? "Do people really eat them?" My mind went to my favorite flannel pjs with a pattern of pink prancing llamas on them.

"Llama isn't on our menu," Kelsie said, looking confused.

"Yum," Sasha said.

"That's my girl." Lee went to Sasha and wrapped his arm around her shoulder, then pulled her in for a big smooch. She gave in at first, then pushed him away. "Leave me alone. You know why." I'd been working on the farmhouse for two months and had no idea that Lee Cutler was dating Privé's sous chef.

"What's wrong, Sasha?" he asked. "Is meanie Kelsie working you too hard?" Lee stood about six feet four to Sasha's five feet ten. His dark looks, muscular build, and tanned face (which brought out his amazing pale green eyes), made him one of the most attractive men I'd ever seen in the Hamptons. And that said a lot because we had tons of them, including Patrick Seaton.

"You know what's wrong, Leland Cutler. Don't pretend you don't." Sasha went back to her stool, where she picked up her glass of wine from the counter, then downed it.

Kelsie handed Lee a bag of ice. He held it to his nose and said, "You're right. Llama's not on tonight's menu. I meant to put it in my truck, but my idiot employee got a flat tire. One of tomorrow's specials for my Hampton Classic horse show food truck will be llama sliders."

I felt my stomach acids churning. Cutler's Meat Wagons food trucks were famous nationwide. Their simplicity was in the fact they offered only cooked red meat. No seafood. No veggie burgers. And no chicken or foul. The only nonmeat item on the food truck's menu was potato spears smothered with your choice of cheese, bacon, chili con carne, onions, sour cream or Cutler's BBQ Meat Sauce. His tagline was: *Only real men & women eat red meat.*

Lee glanced over at the counter, his gaze resting on the completed dishes of carpaccio. "Kel, baby. Let's get a move on. Bring out our first course, and then we can make a toast to Privé's success. I've already poured the Veuve Clicquot." He clapped and said, "Chop-chop."

Wow. Was I glad my job at Privé was finished.

Or so I'd thought.

He turned his gorgeous green eyes on me. "You're the girl who did the interior, right?"

"Uh, yeah." But I wasn't a girl, I wanted to add.

"I have a project for you. I want to make that old cottage out back into a private space where certain members of our club can meet to smoke a cigar, have a nip of brandy, and shoot the bull. No crystal chandeliers, or for that matter, the color pink. Think upscale hunting cabin in the woods. I've already talked it over with Noah and Jackie. They're on board."

I opened my mouth to speak, then closed it.

19

"We'll give you fifty grand for your services and carte blanche on the spending. And before you start, I want some kind of drawing, or something. You know, whatever you interior design gals scribble on paper before you start a project."

Lee Cutler was a condescending jerk. But a jerk willing to pay me the big bucks just to decorate a thousand-square-foot building.

Jerk vs. fifty thousand.

Jerk wins.

"I'd love to, Mr. Cutler." No matter what directives he planned on giving me for the cottage, I would add a few soft touches, not just for Jackie's sake, but because I believed comfort and simplicity were genderless. So far, my Cottages by the Sea clients hadn't had any complaints. But there was always a first time, I thought, looking at Lee's piercing stare. "But what do you want me to do with the stuff in the cottage that I haven't used in Privé?"

"You can toss it in the dump for all I care. And call me Lee. But only if the next time you open a door, you don't hit me with it. Oh, and there's one caveat . . ."

"Yes?"

"You've only got a week to complete it."

My mouth fell open. *A week?*

"Is there a problem with that?" he asked arrogantly.

I saw Sasha roll her eyes. "Of course not," I managed in a squeaky voice, thinking of the llama.

"You don't seem convinced," he said. "I'm sure there are others who would jump at the chance."

"I would love to. Count me in." I held out my hand and he shook it.

I'd wanted to say, *Hell yes!* Not only because of the money, but also the fact I could take home whatever was in the old saltbox cottage that had been on the property long before Bethany's grandfather built the post–World War II farmhouse. My fingers tingled at the thought of all the things inside that I might be able to use in my clients' cottages. I'd get Elle to help. When it came to anything of a vintage or antique nature, Elle, who'd once worked at Sotheby's in Manhattan, knew her stuff. For once I'd be able to give Elle a percentage of my fee like she'd done in the past when she'd been on retainer for a local insurance company, and I'd helped her inventory the art and antiques at the Seacliff estate. Also, I had to admit that Elle was a voice of reason when I stuck my nose into things that didn't concern me. A frequent occurrence, in her and her cop husband's opinion.

"Good. Glad that's settled. Why don't you step out into the hallway and I'll give you the key," he said with a wink.

We left Kelsie and Sasha in the kitchen. As we exited under the open stone arch leading to the hallway, I could feel their eyes following us.

Lee stopped, reached into his pocket, and pulled out a single key. Something else came with the key and flitted to the floor. A business card. I bent to pick it up, but Lee swiped it from my hand before I had a chance to take a good look. Then he stowed it back in his pocket. There'd been a single word printed in the middle of the card, *Exotica*. Underneath there'd been a phone number with a 631 area code.

Lee handed me the key. As I took it from him, he grabbed my left hand and examined it, zeroing in on my empty ring finger.

"How about Monday. Dinner," he said. "Bring your plans for the cottage. Wait. I can't do dinner. I forgot it's the last day of the Hampton Classic horse show. Make it Sunday."

He shoved the bag of ice at me. "See if you can get them moving any faster."

I went back inside the kitchen and put the bag of ice in the sink.

Sasha chugged the last drop of another glass of wine and said to me, "If I were you, I would run for the hills. You want nothing to do with that guy. I can handle him, but as a precaution, make sure you're never on the grounds after sunset—this place has its own kind of hauntings going on."

"Vampires?" I asked jokingly, trying to break the serious look on Sasha's face.

"What the hell are you talking about?" Kelsie said. "You heard Lee. Get moving, Sasha."

Sasha just laughed, and I shivered.

I waited for Kelsie to admonish Sasha, but no such thing happened. She just glanced nervously out the window, worry lines creasing her forehead.

Chapter 4

We were seated in the Burgundy Suite with our tenth course in front of us. Petits pots à l'absinthe. After the previous nine courses, which hadn't included the amuse-bouche, I was so full I didn't think I could manage a spoonful. Plus, wasn't absinthe the tainted liquor that killed people back in the day?

Trusting Kelsie's culinary skills, I took a taste. Then another. It wasn't until I was scraping the bottom of the pot that I noticed all eyes were on me. Even Sasha's blurry ones. I placed the small dish down on the twelve-foot antique farm table and dabbed demurely at the corners of my mouth. I wasn't fooling anyone that I had a demure bone in my body after the way I'd devoured the previous nine courses. But who cared. I'd probably never set foot in Privé again. Certainly not as a guest at any of its six dining room tables.

Naturally, wine had been served with each dish. French wine. And champagne. French champagne.

I didn't think I'd ever seen anyone consume so much alcohol as Sasha in the three hours it took us to finish the tasting menu. She'd even made her way over to the suite's well-stocked bar. Apparently, a huge fan of the Rémy Martin cognac. She'd taken off her white chef's coat and toque and was wearing a stunning, iridescent low-cut minidress in the same shade of violet as her eyes. When she'd stumbled into the suite, I'd also noticed that in her sandals she was around the same height as Lee. I'd also noticed that when he'd tried to help steady her, she'd pulled away, revulsed.

Not that I knew Sasha well, but ever since Lee had walked into the kitchen, something seemed off with her. And it hadn't been just the amount of booze coursing through her veins. After Lee gave me the key to the cottage and I'd stepped back into the kitchen, Sasha had been more subdued. Even obeying orders like a true sous chef. Not that she offered to help me clear the dishes and put them in the dishwasher, that still remained my job.

Even Kelsie had softened her countenance a bit. Instead of barking orders to her assistant, she had almost whispered them apologetically, like Sasha had been Kelsie's chef de cuisine, not the other way around.

It seemed Lee Cutler, owner of the Cutler's Meat Wagons food truck dynasty, sure had a hold on them.

"So yummy, Chef," I said, nodding my head in Kelsie's direction.

"I would have preferred to have had a food critic at our table instead of a layman," Jackie Fairchild snapped, obviously referring to me. "The food is okay. I don't know if it's on par with what we will be charging Privé's members for dues. And I think it's ridiculous that the help is sitting at the table with us."

"Oh, Jackie, are you forgetting that I also have a stake in this enterprise," Kelsie said. "And if we did have a critic at the table, I'm sure I would pass with flying colors. There were just a few small bumps in the kitchen."

"Don't blame me for your menu," Sasha slurred. "I'm the one who gives you 'spiration to think outside the boxes-s-s. Up to you, you'd make everything from that huge cookbook you live by. You're no Chef Pierre Patou. Not one fres-s-sh idea 'cept from those pages."

Kelsie stood, about to say something, looked at Jackie, then sat back down.

Sasha tried to stand. But even with Lee's shoulder for support, she couldn't make it. Giving up, she slunk back into her chair. "I'll call a friend I know," she said. "Food wine editor at *News-s-s-h-day*. One word. This-s-s sinks ships." By the look on everyone's faces, her arrow had hit its bull's-eye. Sasha turned her head and looked at Lee, Noah, Jackie, Kelsie, and me in order of how we were seated. I think the reason I was included had more to do with her blurred vision. "Don't worry," Sasha said, lapping at the inside of her petits pots à l'absinthe like my cat Jo after a hunger strike, "all your secrets are safe with moi."

"I've never!" Jackie Fairchild said, nudging her husband, Noah, who up until now might have been a figure from Madame Tussauds Wax Museum. If I had to choose his look-alike, it would be a cross between James Stewart and Harry Potter. His round tortoiseshell glasses gave him an owllike appearance. So maybe James and Hedwig, Harry's owl?

"S-s-s-hut-up, Jackie," Sasha said. "You know I'll come out on top. I haven't invested millions like you have in one of Noah's projects." Sasha tried again to stand. Lee grabbed her by her long braid to keep her chin from hitting the table.

If they were a couple, why didn't Lee try to save her? Maybe whisk her away for a timeout in another suite. Instead, he wore a grin on his face, like he was enjoying the show.

"Enough," Jackie interjected. "Decorum at all times is Privé's motto. Lee, can't you take care of her?"

"Motto, we have a motto?" Lee said, throwing his napkin on his plate. "I didn't get to vote on that one. Leaving me out as usual, I see."

"Put a sock in it, Lee. No votes are needed between the three of us. Noah and I always vote together. You will have to get used to being the odd man out."

Noah reached over and took his wife's hand in his. Even though he looked to be twenty years her junior, he was completely gray. It was obvious by Jackie's taut face that she'd had more than her share of procedures involving a needle. She looked to be in her fifties, but judging by the crepey skin and raised veins on her wrinkly hands, I'd guess mid-sixties. She had shoulder-length blonde hair with side bangs and wore classic clothing and jewelry straight out of the fashion pages of *Town & Country* magazine. Her skinny-girl physique was a testament that she'd only taken one bite from each of our ten courses.

When I'd first come to work at the farmhouse, Kelsie had told me that Jackie owned a premier horse stable and equestrian center in Bridgehampton that visiting royals frequented whenever they were in town. Jackie was also a professional horsewoman who'd won the Grand Prix tournament at the Hampton Classic horse show. Her equestrian prowess explained her perfect upright posture, but if I saw her with a riding crop in her hand, I'd be sure to stay out of her way. Even though I'd had carte blanche on my purchases for the interior of the farmhouse, Jackie's constant questioning had been a constant source of irritation.

"We've discussed this," Noah said firmly to his wife. "What better way to give constructive criticism than to have the chef de cuisine and sous chef at the table."

Jackie, who sat at the head of the table, pulled her hand away from his. "I suppose it was you, darling, who offered Sasha Morgan the job as sous chef. I've seen you two, whispering together. If so, you've made another poor choice. Just like that last teenage slasher movie you produced. By the way, your ex-wife called. Said she had something to tell me that I'd want to know about. Wonder what it will be?"

Noah picked up his wineglass and chugged it down. "I'll talk to her."

"See that you do," Jackie said. "I want nothing to do with that woman. Probably wants more money for your two darlings. She won't get it from me."

There seemed to be a pattern here. Two dysfunctional relationships. Wait. More like three if I included the dynamic between Kelsie and Sasha. I was thrilled Patrick hadn't been allowed to join me. Looking back, I'd trade one of his home-cooked meals for tonight's ten courses in a heartbeat. And before a food fight started, one that I would probably have to clean up, I planned to vamoose as soon as I could.

"Why is she dining with us?" Jackie nodded her head in my direction and the others looked my way.

A wedge of truffled brie fell from my open mouth. I'd been thinking the same thing. *Why was I here?*

"She's invited," Kelsie said, "so we can give her accolades for the job she did decorating Privé." She clapped her hands, and everyone joined in except for Jackie. Even woozy Sasha tried to make the palms of her hands match up.

"Terrific job, Ms. Barrett," Noah said, glancing at his wife's pursed lips. "Jackie, don't you agree?"

Jackie murmured something under her breath that my hearing aids couldn't pick up. Then she turned to Kelsie and said loudly, "You would say that Kelsie, seeing you're the one who suggested we choose Ms. Barrett over dozens of high-end Hamptons decorators who were more qualified to take on a project of this scope."

"Chef Patou recommended her, Jackie," Kelsie said, smiling sweetly. "And you can't argue that the interior of Pondfare is one of the best in the Hamptons. No. Wait. It is the best."

"Lee," Jackie said, directing her gaze across the table, "I suppose you offered Ms. Barrett the job of fixing up the cottage into some kind of primordial man cave."

"As a matter of fact, I did, Jackie. And Meggie agreed to do it."

Meggie? I squirmed in my chair and wished I could morph behind a flower branch on the room's hand-painted chinoiserie wallpaper that I'd commissioned from a design house in Paris. I sat up straighter and told myself that Jackie was a bully. I didn't have to put up with bullies. Having been paid for my design work, the only thing to worry about was working with Lee Cutler on the cottage. And I'd not only dealt with bullies before but also misogynistic men like Lee. Then I remembered the sightless eyes of the llama hanging in the walk-in.

"Look at her," Jackie said, referring to Sasha, whose eyes kept opening and closing as she swayed from left to right like someone sitting next to you on an airplane who kept nodding off. In this case, it was her boyfriend Lee's shoulder that Sasha's head finally rested on. Or was that ex-boyfriend?

Jackie pointed at Sasha. "She'll be the ruin of this place."

I glanced up at the crystal chandelier hanging over the pine farm table. Even though I was happy the conversation had veered away from me, I wished I was anywhere but where I was.

Sasha lifted her head from Lee's shoulder and mumbled, "Not feeling sh-o-o good."

"Lee, you better take her home or Kelsie won't have a sous chef for our membership drive," Jackie demanded.

Lee was busy looking into the mirror on the wall behind me and didn't respond to Jackie's directive. When I'd first sat down to the table, I thought he was flirting with me, but soon realized he was just enamored with his own handsome reflection in the faux Louis XVI mirror I'd found at an estate sale. Like handsome Narcissus in Greek mythology, give Lee a reflecting pool and he would probably fall into it and drown.

Sasha was irritating, but as I looked over at her, I could see she was in no shape to defend herself. I was always one for the underdog, so I said, "Maybe Sasha should go rest in one of the other dining suites. There's a nice chaise in the Provence Suite."

"And what if she vomits all over the blue-and-white toile fabric?" Jackie asked. "We open our doors tomorrow. No. Just call her a car. Lee, Noah, and I have some business to discuss in private."

Lee pried the glass of cognac out of Sasha's hand. "I've never seen her drink this much. I'm sure . . ."

"Well, here everyone is!" a female voice said. Standing under the threshold, haloed by the light from the hallway, was Bethany

Garnier looking, for want of a better description, frazzled. "What's the problem? Surprised to see me?" she asked.

I glanced around the table, and judging by everyone's open mouths, including mine, yes, we were definitely surprised to see her. Even Sasha startled in her chair from Bethany's booming voice.

"Well, let me give you all a warning," Bethany spat. "I have my own resources at city hall and plan to close your butts down. And, I've hired a lawyer to investigate how you finagled your way into getting my property zoned commercial. Meg told me that you plan to open your doors tomorrow. Don't count on it."

Everyone turned their gaze to me. Jackie said under her breath, which I was able to lip-read, "Figures."

Bethany stepped inside the suite. "Sorry, folks. I don't think Privé will stay *private* for too long." Then she laughed, more like cackled, as she looked from me, to Jackie, then to Noah, Kelsie, and Lee, finally resting her crazed hazel eyes on Sasha.

"This is private property," Jackie said. "If you don't leave immediately, I'll call the authorities and tell them you're trespassing."

"I'm the one making the threats here," Bethany said. Then she stomped over to Kelsie and looked down. "I don't like the way you brushed me off earlier this morning when I asked if your little club could carry Garnier Vineyards' premier wines. I thought we were friends, at least business acquaintances. If you were more accommodating, I wouldn't have had to call my attorney."

"That wasn't my decision," Kelsie protested. "I'm the chef de cuisine, not an equal partner, or even the sommelier. Bethany, you know that."

"You silly woman," Jackie said, picking up her wineglass and tipping it in Bethany's direction. "Privé only serves *French* wine and spirits. We don't need your domestic wannabes. And if we did serve domestics, they would come from the Napa Valley, not Long Island."

"I think Garnier wines are equal to if not better than most California wines," I said in a low voice. Here I went again, defending the underdog. "Bethany's won numerous awards . . ."

"Enough from the peanut gallery," Jackie said, giving me dagger eyes, then she turned them on Bethany, who'd reached over Sasha's shoulder and grabbed her full glass of wine.

"Doesn't look like Sasha needs any more of this," Bethany said. "What a surprise."

"Time for you to scoot, Ms. Garnier," Jackie hissed. "Lee, do you want to escort her out?" Owing to his height and gym-honed muscular body, I could see why Jackie turned to Lee instead of her husband. Lee had about five inches on Noah and an extra thirty pounds of pure muscle.

Bethany ignored Jackie, then raised the wineglass in the air. Speaking in French, she said, *"Voici à votre échec."* Then she took a sip of the wine and spit it back into the glass, as if spitting into a bucket on one of her wine-tasting tables. "Blech! Tastes like vinegar."

"Here's to failure," Kelsie said, translating Bethany's toast to English. "How unkind. Why don't—"

Noah interjected, "Bethany, we haven't even opened up yet. Why don't we all take a deep breath and see how things go? I'm sure once we open that there will be room for negotiations on the wine selection. No need for lawyers."

Lee stood. "Shall I escort you out? We aren't scared of your threats. We purchased this property fair and square. It's too late for seller's remorse."

Sasha glanced up at Lee, tried to stand, but fell back into her chair with a thud. "Yesh . . . Get outta here . . . Your husband was the only reason Garnier Vineyards was a successh. You probably killed him with all your demands and whining. Like you're doing now."

Sasha's words were apparently Bethany's last straw. "How dare you! You little tramp."

Bethany flew to Sasha's side, reached out her hands, and we all watched in horror as she clasped them in a chokehold around Sasha's delicate neck.

Chapter 5

"Well, that was quite an evening," I said to Kelsie, hanging the last pot on the brushed-copper rack above the stove.

"You're telling me," Kelsie said. "If I didn't have a contract, I'd go back to Pondfare. I thought this was going to be an easy gig. A way to get my name out there without being overworked."

"You don't think you'll be overworked preparing ten-course dinners for Privé's members? You really are a superwoman."

After chugging a bottle of water, she said, "Privé's not like a country club. Gourmets only. We aren't just talking foodies; we're talking about some of the best palates in the world. Not to mention the richest. If the members prefer, Sasha and I, along with a small waitstaff, will be on hand to cook and do the shopping. But in most cases, the members reserve blocks of time. Then they take over the kitchen, bringing in their own waitstaff, sommeliers, pastry, sous, and head chefs. Or they can hire a famous Michelin-star chef just for the evening. Some members will even do their own cooking. The whole idea was Noah's after he and Jackie returned from a trip to Provence and were invited inside Philippe Dubois's private food club. Or I should say, only Noah was invited inside, because membership was male only."

"Philippe, the star of the hit streaming series on television?" I asked. "The one where he goes to tiny nondescript villages in France and just about kidnaps the best home chef in the town, then goes to their homes and cooks with them?"

"One and the same. I'm surprised you watch cooking shows," she said, then yawned.

I laughed. "Just because I don't cook doesn't mean I can't enjoy watching others do it." My mind went to Patrick's eggs Benedict and my father's pot au vin. "I'm surprised Chef Patou wasn't invited tonight."

"He's in California accepting another award. He comes back on Tuesday. Chef Patou and Bella are considering becoming members at Privé, though they'll miss tomorrow's opening sign-up. First come, first served."

"Who's watching over Pondfare?"

"Bella. Chef's better half. She took over my slot as sous chef. It was about time she got credit for helping us when we got swamped in the kitchen. While Pierre's been out of town, I've been stopping in at Pondfare to lend a hand."

"Wow. You must be a great multitasker."

"I've learned from the best. But I do agree the timing isn't great because of tomorrow's membership drive." She smiled. "Chef Patou can't help it that he's such a great chef and keeps winning awards and competitions. He was hands down the favorite at last year's Taste of the Hamptons."

"And you're a great chef right along with him. After the meal I just had, maybe you will be this year's winner. Soon you'll have a cookbook just like his." I nodded my head to the ginormous cookbook on the stand in the middle of the counter.

"Maybe in thirty years. Now, you get home. I apologize for making you our server and dishwasher. But with Sasha . . . Well, you saw." Anger flooded her eyes once again.

"No problem. Well worth the meal. And if I hadn't been here, Lee Cutler wouldn't have given me the job of decorating the cottage out back."

"Be careful of him," Kelsie said, locking her eyes on mine. "He knows how to get what he wants. No matter what the cost. And if he doesn't get what he wants, he'll do everything in his power to destroy you."

Kelsie had just mirrored what Sasha said earlier. "Oh, great. You mean he could ruin my Hamptons Cottages by the Sea reputation?"

"That would be hard to do. But yes. Just be careful. Once, one of our meat suppliers gave Chef Patou Lee's side of beef meant for one of Lee's Cutler's Meat Wagons. You would have thought the supplier had stolen Lee's firstborn."

"Does he have kids?" I asked.

"Not that I know of," she said with a strange look on her face. "I guess it's possible."

"If he ever does," I said, "let's hope they're not girls."

"You have to admit, if Lee did have kids, they'd be gorgeous."

"And if he ever has boys, they'll probably be born chewing mystery-meat jerky and wearing cowboy boots with those metal toe taps."

"The same ones that scratched the pickled-white floorboards in the Bordeaux Suite," she added.

"That's what those marks were," I said. "I thought one of the furniture delivery guys did that. So, what did Lee do to that poor meat supplier?" I asked, thinking of what he could do to me and my reputation.

"He threatened to pull him from providing the meat for his entire fleet of New England food trucks and canceling all our upcoming orders for Privé. Lee put up such a stink that the supplier had to give him his next two shipments of meat at a deep discount." Kelsie got up and went to one of the refrigerated drawers and withdrew a bottle of water, French water, then yawned for the second time.

"I think you're right. Time to head home and get a good night's sleep." I didn't want to hear any more about the meatman and his reputation. "Can't wait for my head to hit the pillow." *And hopefully not have any dead llama nightmares.* "You coming?"

"No chance. Still have prep work to do for tomorrow. The same ten courses we had tonight. But like we just discussed, it won't be an everyday thing. Thanks again for helping. And I hope you're happy that the consensus was that you did a fabulous job on Privé's décor."

"I don't know if Jackie was that enthusiastic."

"At least she didn't complain about your cooking like she did mine," Kelsie said. "Jackie's not the gourmet, her husband is. Noah's father is a renowned chef and restaurateur."

"Oh, wow. I never put the two together. Noah is Parnell Fairchild's son? I love Chef Fairchild's Bar Frites restaurant in Manhattan—my favorite French bistro. Aren't there Bar Frites in every large city in the U.S.?"

"Yes. And in London and Quebec. Between you and me," Kelsie said, looking toward the door to make sure no one overheard, "Noah and his father had a big blowout on the phone the other day. Noah was asking for a loan. I think it had something to do with Jackie refusing to front him for his next movie project. When Jackie married Noah last year, husband number three, I'd bet she'd thought Noah was loaded based on his father's millions."

Now it was my turn to yawn. I could listen to gossip like the rest of them, but I was starting to worry I might nod off on the eighteenmile trip back to Montauk. However, that didn't keep me from asking one more question. "Aren't you worried about Sasha not showing up tomorrow? She's going to have a pretty wicked hangover."

"Hopefully, she'll be able to work. I suppose even ten percent of Sasha is better than no percent. She's a lost cause. And so damn obnoxious."

I avoided giving my opinion, and said instead, "Hope she doesn't have any bruises on her neck from Bethany. No one deserves that."

"I agree, Bethany was off the rails. But I could almost understand her fury."

She could? "What was that all about? Do you think Bethany took it out on Sasha because you told her Privé wouldn't serve Garnier Vineyards' wine? Seems like a pretty extreme reaction. I'm sorry about mentioning the possibility to her."

"How could you know Bethany would go off the deep end? She hasn't been the same since her husband died. But I think I know what pushed her over the edge. It was Sasha's comment about Bethany's Tom. Before he died there were rumors in the restaurant circuit that while Sasha was working at the winery, Sasha and Tom had a fling."

"Was Sasha the sous chef at Garnier Vineyards for their tapas plates?"

Kelsie laughed. "No. Maybe if she had been, she'd be a more seasoned chef. Sasha did the wine tastings in the main barn. Boy, could she sell wine."

"Do you believe the rumors?"

"Not for a second. I knew Tom. He was devoted to Bethany. Running a winery, along with two tasting venues on the North and South Fork of Long Island, took up all his time. But you've seen how gorgeous Sasha is. That is, until she opens her mouth. I don't blame Bethany. What woman wouldn't be jealous of a beautiful ex-model hanging around their man every day?"

Jealous enough to choke them? My mind flashed back to last May, when I first saw a photo of my on-again, off-again boyfriend Cole in a lip lock with his first mate. As far as I knew, the pair were still together, which hadn't bothered me because of Patrick. But I'd be lying if I said I hadn't thought of *figuratively* wringing Cole's neck after I'd found out his first mate, Billie, who I'd thought was a male, turned out to be a female. "Well, Bethany should feel lucky someone didn't call nine-one-one," I added.

"Are you kidding! Jackie Fairchild would never allow bad press. Remember, she's related to—"

"Jacqueline Kennedy Onassis's father, Black Jack Bouvier," I finished for her, and we both laughed.

I got up from my chair and said, "I'm going to head out. Unless you need me?"

"Sasha should be sobering up soon. I'm good."

"Don't let her drive home," I said, thinking of the tragic accident involving Patrick's wife and daughter.

"Of course not. I'll take her home if no one else volunteers. And, Meg, thanks once again. Hopefully, things will go smoothly tomorrow."

"They will," I said without much conviction. I knew when you had a bunch of pot stirrers like those at Privé, a recipe for disaster would soon follow. For some reason the picture of Sasha pushing Lee away after he'd gone to kiss her flashed in my mind. "Was it just me," I asked, pausing under the open archway, "or did Lee take his sweet time in rescuing Sasha from Bethany's chokehold?"

"Maybe he was just stunned by Bethany's aggressiveness. Sasha and Lee have always been lovey-dovey. It seems no longer the case. Nepotism at its best. Maybe now I can fire her. You saw her. Spoiled rotten. Maybe he forgot to buy her a piece of jewelry from London Jewelers in East Hampton and she's pouting?"

"What was all that business she told us about not coming here late at night."

"I have no clue. She's delusional. Nothing's going on. I would know."

I said goodbye to Kelsie. Then stopped by the Burgundy Suite. The place we'd just shared a meal and witnessed an attempted murder, wanting to make sure it was in design order. It was. Then I headed down the hallway toward the front exit. As I passed the Provence Suite, the door was slightly ajar, so I peeked inside.

Sasha was on her back, sprawled out on a Josephine chaise. She was so still it was hard to tell if she was breathing. I tiptoed across the room and looked down at her, noticing no discoloration on either side of her long neck. As I went to feel for a pulse, she jerked, flailed her arms and legs, and turned on her side, proving she was alive and kicking. *Thank God!*

I hurried out of the suite and into the hallway and thought about turning back and going to the kitchen to remind Kelsie that Sasha was in no shape to drive. Then I remembered Kelsie saying if no one took her home, she would.

Not my worry, I thought, opening the front door and hurrying down Privé's front steps.

Halfway to my car I paused on the flagstone walkway and looked up at the clear evening sky and saw a comet streak by. I took it as a good omen and felt my mother looking down at me. She'd be proud of what I'd accomplished inside the farmhouse.

When I reached my car, I glanced back at Privé with a smile on my face.

My smile soon turned to a frown.

There, visible in the tall well-lit window of the Provence Suite were two figures. One of them was Sasha. Her arms were raised, and she held a large ceramic blue-and-white French bulldog in her hands. The antique bulldog was part of a set of two that flanked the fireplace. It was heavy. And ridiculously expensive.

I trotted to the front of Privé, shimmied behind a hydrangea bush to the right of the window, and peeked in at the same moment Sasha chucked the bulldog at Noah's head. The dog grazed his temple and blood oozed down his cheek. I hadn't heard the crash of the bulldog against the blue-and-white porcelain tiles under the mantel, but I was able to read Noah's lips when he shouted, "You crazy witch!" I might have been wrong about the word *witch*; it was possible the word started with a *b*. I took a step away from the window. Things were getting too volatile at the old farmhouse.

Maybe I should forgo decorating the cottage. How could I do it in a week anyway? It would be prudent of me to walk away now before I found myself involved in another Hamptons murder. Then I remembered all the wonderful items I'd spied when removing the shutters in the stone cottage's loft space. Items I was told to get rid of—or as I interpreted—keep for myself or use in my clients' cottages. Plus, I'd be working at the rear of the property, nowhere near the farmhouse. I stepped away from the window and told myself the same thing I'd told Kelsie a few minutes ago, *get a good night's sleep and assess things in the morning.*

"What the hell are you doing in the bushes, Ms. Barrett!" a loud female voice shrieked.

I turned to see Jackie standing in front of the shrubbery with the flashlight from her phone aimed on me.

"Just checking that the right shutter is secure," I mumbled, waiting for one of her talking downs, but all I heard was silence.

I saw why.

Jackie's eyes were trained on the scene in the Provence Suite between her husband and Sasha.

I scurried past her, calling back over my shoulder, "Have a good night." Then I jumped in my car, trying not to burn rubber as I exited the grounds.

Things were getting dicey at Privé.

And I didn't mean that in a culinary way.

Chapter 6

The next morning, after meditating on the beach, showering, dressing, and washing down an untoasted Pop-Tart with a huge mug of French roast, I woke Jo. I had to carry all twenty-three pounds of her down to the kitchen, where I unceremoniously plopped her on the floor. Then I gave her a lecture about how she shouldn't pout because I was out of her favorite brand of cat food and eat what was in front of her. I was running late for meeting Elle and her trusty pickup to start clearing out Privé's cottage.

When I'd called Elle last night and told her about the ten-course dysfunctional dinner, she'd said, "Oh, no. I have a bad feeling about this . . ." How many times had Elle uttered those same words, and how many times had I ignored them—and always to my detriment. Knowing that Elle and Bethany were friends, I'd left out the part about Bethany choking Sasha. I also failed to mention the scene where Sasha threw a ceramic bulldog at Noah Fairchild's head, drawing blood. I only had a week to finish the interior of the cottage and I needed my trusty newlywed sidekick to help me.

"So, you get to keep everything in the cottage you didn't use in Privé?" Elle had asked. Her worry must have disappeared at the thought of rescuing vintage items from the cottage. I'd assured her that things would be fine, even though I knew the vibe at Privé wasn't too different from the past few, okay, five times that I'd been involved in a murder investigation.

"What do you think, Jo?" I asked after I filled her water bowl. "Don't you think this time the odds have to be in my favor, and I won't stumble upon a dead body?"

Jo ignored my question, stretched, then went to stand sphinxlike in front of her food bowl. I took a second to admire her silky Maine coon coat, noticing that the hair coming out of her ears was long enough to braid. I thought back to when Elle and her future husband, Detective Arthur Shoner, had forced me into adopting Jo in exchange for some inside information from the East Hampton Town Police Department's computer. Jo and I had had a rocky start, but I would never trade her for a well-behaved pet. She had a way of keeping our relationship fresh. You never knew what monkey business she might be up to at any given moment.

"Come on, Josephine. Give me a break. Eat what's been given you. I have people to meet and places to go. Next time don't sleep so late." Jo swiped her meaty paw in my direction. It was a good thing I was wearing jeans. She stared down at her food bowl, which was filled with dry kibble, then back up at me. It was clear she wasn't happy and thought she'd drawn the short straw of having me as her owner. I thought of it in the reverse. Jo owned me, not the other way around. In Jo's defense, between working at Privé and trying to squeeze in time with Patrick, I had been neglecting her. One more week and I would lavish all the attention my feline deserved. Elle had suggested that I rescue another cat to keep her company. No way. Especially after what happened to Mr. Whiskers when Georgia, the owner of The Old Man and the Sea Books in Montauk took care of Jo last February.

"Sorry, Jo. Mommy must go to work so she can afford that ridiculously expensive gourmet canned cat food you like. Too bad you couldn't have had Chef Kelsie's coquilles St. Jacques like I did last night. No doggie bags allowed at Privé, or in your case, kitty bags—too uncouth. It doesn't matter anyway because I ate every morsel put in front of me."

Jo looked again at the food in her bowl, then angrily meowed. The white patch of fur above her lip made her look like she'd just lapped a bowl of cream, reminding me of the time when I was a newbie cat owner and I'd given her half-and-half, not knowing felines were lactose intolerant. Lesson learned when she'd upchucked all over the antique wedding-ring quilt I'd just had professionally cleaned.

"Give me a break, Jo. Just this once."

Her one eye gazed at me in disdain, then she turned, shook her tail in irritation, and walked out of the kitchen with her head held high. It would be a cold day in Hades when Josephine Eater Barret would eat dry food.

Once I hit the road, instead of taking the fastest route to Sagaponack, I opted for Old Montauk Highway, the curving hilly road that followed the Atlantic shoreline. The morning was just too perfect for me not to indulge in the postcard views that made me feel grateful that I was able to wake up every morning in my cozy cottage by the sea.

When I reached the small hamlet of Amagansett, I slowed down, thinking about my job ahead. Decorating small cottages was my forte; however, recreating a masculine man cave wasn't really in my wheelhouse. *Maybe I'll hang a pair of antlers above the cottage's fireplace.* My mind traveled back to the memory of the animal hanging in the Privé's walk-in refrigerator—Meatman Lee Cutler's llama—and I shuddered. I'd bet Lee would want more than antlers above the mantel. He'd want the whole head.

Last evening when Lee had brought up the cottage at the dinner table, Jackie had reiterated her demand that women be allowed. "No boys' club at Privé. I won't forget how I wasn't allowed inside the Epicurean Society in Provence." She'd turned to Noah and said, "Thanks in part to my milquetoast husband, who didn't stand up for me." Then she'd elbowed her husband so hard that his pinot noir splashed onto the white Belgian lace tablecloth I'd purchased in a Madison Avenue antiques shop. Good thing the two hundred dollars I'd spent on the tablecloth hadn't come out of my pocket. I knew the recipe for getting wine stains out, but just like I had to let go of the items in my clients' cottages once the job was finished, I had to let go of my attachment to Privé's décor. That being said, I made a mental note to tell Kelsie how to get the stain out.

After passing Hook Windmill in East Hampton, I cranked up the radio to one of my favorite songs. It was a new day and there were treasures to be found. The elm-lined streets were quiet, probably because it was six thirty in the morning. If I came back in a few hours, the streets would be packed with the summer people wanting to make the best of their last Hamptons weekend. After Monday, the locals would reclaim the East End of Long Island, and Patrick and I would continue our journey of getting to know each other. I just needed to get him to open up and share with me when he was in emotional pain—talk things through together. Until he did, I had a feeling I'd keep comparing myself to his deceased wife.

I cruised through the center of East Hampton. Lining both sides of the main street were white clapboard New England shops selling luxury goods, art, antiques, and home goods. East Hampton had a healthy number of restaurants for fine and casual dining. Bridgehampton, the town closest to Privé, also had many top-tier restaurants, and I wondered if the exclusive dining club would survive the competition. The rich and famous might want to have a private place to dine, but how about the celebs who liked to be seen and heard—their photos and videos plastered all over social media and *Dave's Hamptons*.

On the outskirts of East Hampton, a sign advertised that the weeklong Hampton Classic horse show would be running through Labor Day. I'd attended last year's solo because Cole had bailed as usual. This year, Elle's hubby had used his Town of East Hampton Police clout to secure prime seats in the VIP tent for the final day of the competition. It would be the first time Patrick and I double-dated with Elle and Arthur, and I couldn't think of a better couple to do it with.

In Sagaponack I turned onto Albatross Lane. As I got closer to Privé's gates, a black SUV came barreling out from the driveway used for delivery trucks and staff at the rear of the farmhouse. I quickly pulled to the side of the dirt lane, slammed on the brakes, and held my breath as it zoomed by, leaving behind a cloud of dust that settled onto my windshield like dense fog.

Really?

I put on my wipers. Five squirts of washer fluid later, I was able to see through the windshield. Someone had been in a hurry. After taking a deep breath, I pulled back onto the lane and continued cautiously toward Privé's open gates. Once through, I parked in the lot between the farmhouse and the cottage. With shaky hands I turned off the ignition. Not a good start to the day, I thought, glancing out my side window, where I spied Kelsie and Elle chatting on the farmhouse's front porch. Both wore smiles—all sunshine and rainbows. I exhaled in relief, got out of the car, and hurried toward them.

"Kelsie," I said, out of breath, interrupting their conversation. "Was someone just here driving a black SUV?"

"There you are, you naughty girl," Elle chided. "Chef Kelsie just told me a few things you left out of our phone conversation last night."

I glanced at Kelsie, giving her a stern look.

She shrugged her shoulders. "How was I supposed to know you hadn't told her?" she said. "Thought you two were joined at the hip and shared everything."

"We are, and I usually do," I answered. "I just don't like to give it to her all at one time. Elle has a tendency to turn into my mother."

Elle grinned. The multitude of freckles on her pert nose told of her honeymoon in the sun, half of which was spent in the South of France, the other half on Italy's Amalfi Coast. Elle said, "I resemble that remark! From what I've heard, your mother was wonderful."

I laughed, but my mind was still on the car. I turned to Kelsie and repeated my question.

"No one was here that I know of."

"A black SUV exiting from the delivery entrance just about crashed into me."

Kelsie shook her head. "Sorry. I've been here since five in the morning and I haven't seen anyone."

"Elle, how about you? You see anything?" I asked.

"No." There was concern in her eyes. "Do you think Bethany came here to cause more trouble? Kelsie, you know her. It's so out of character for her to act like that."

"Yes. I am very concerned about her behavior," Kelsie said, worry lines creasing her brow. "Why don't you two come inside for a cup of coffee before you get started on the cottage? My coffee's been compared to rocket fuel."

"Just the way I like it," I said.

"Good. And I make a mean cappuccino, too." Kelsie took a step toward the door. "Let's not worry about Bethany. Things will work out. They always do."

Famous last words, I thought, thinking about Elle's friend's theatrics last night.

"Count me in," Elle said, "I need a jolt of caffeine after the sleepless night I had. And that was before I heard Bethany almost choked someone to death. I'm shocked. Bethany is the most laidback, down-to-earth person I know. She even teaches wine and yoga classes at Garnier Vineyards."

"Wine and yoga," Kelsie said, raising an eyebrow. "A person has to be pretty stressed to want to do both. I would think one or the other would do the trick."

Elle laughed. "Hang around Meg a little longer and you might want to sign up for one of Bethany's classes."

"Hardy-har-har, Elle. Remember, if it wasn't for me stumbling onto Caroline Spenser's bloody corpse, you wouldn't have met your future husband."

Kelsie laughed. "Enough talk about death and corpses. It looks like a perfect day for Privé's opening. Seems like summer came and went in a heartbeat. I'm sad to see it go."

"Oh, I love fall in the Hamptons. There's even a nip in the air," Elle said, sweeping her gaze over the view that featured a sculptured topiary garden that fronted the pond separating Privé from Garnier Winery. "Byron did a fabulous job."

On my recommendation, the partners had hired Hamptons premier landscape architect and my former love interest, Byron Hughes, to do Privé's outdoor spaces. As usual, no one was disappointed, including Jackie, who'd flirted with Byron every chance she got. I couldn't blame her. He was a handsome guy, but there'd been no spark to our connection. Nothing like the electricity I felt when even the tip of Patrick's pinky finger touched mine. Kelsie was right. Things always worked out for the best.

"Let's get crackin'," I said, grabbing Elle by the wrist and dragging her toward where Kelsie waited next to the huge double doors that I'd painted the same shade as Privé's shutters. I was dying to get to the treasures in the cottage but knew another cup of coffee wouldn't hurt.

Once inside Privé, Elle oohed and aahed as she passed by the suites named after different wine provinces in France. "Wow, Meg. You've done quite a job. I'm impressed."

"Thanks partly to you, my friend, and all the wonderful things I used from Mabel and Elle's." I patted her on the shoulder as she stopped in front of a country French *comtoise* grandfather clock. Even Jackie hadn't complained about the three-thousand-dollar clock I'd bought from Elle's Sag Harbor antiques and collectibles shop. The starring quality of the nineteenth-century clock was its pendulum and surround, which was embossed with a hand-painted decoration of sunflowers, a sheaf of wheat, a sickle, and clusters of grapes.

"I think that's one of my favorite pieces," Kelsie said, nodding her head in the direction of the grandfather clock. "Meg, I love all the furnishings and accessories you've chosen. The perfect blend of old and new."

"Thanks, Chef."

As we continued down the hallway, we passed the Provence Suite. I glanced inside to see if there'd been any other casualties from Sasha's tantrum with Noah. Everything seemed in order, with the exception that not only was the shattered bulldog missing, but also its mate.

We followed Kelsie into the kitchen and Elle and I each grabbed a bar stool at the counter. Kelsie went inside the butler's pantry and started working the levers on the espresso machine like a barista at Starbucks. She called out, "Meg, can you get me some milk from the fridge to the left of the ovens."

"No problem." Not only did Privé have a walk-in fridge-freezer, but it also had a huge combination refrigerator-freezer hidden behind custom-made panels of wainscoting that matched the rest of the kitchen's walls. I tapped the upper right corner and voilà! It opened. And like Kelsie, everything inside was organized—a little different than my own small fridge, which held mostly take-out leftovers. In my defense, I did write down the date and contents in sharpie on the top of the containers so I wouldn't get food poisoning.

"I don't see any milk," I said, "just heavy cream."

"Do you mind checking the walk-in? The glass case on the left," Kelsie asked from the pantry.

"Only if you promise there's no llama carcasses in there."

"Promise. Lee took it out last night."

Elle turned on her bar stool and gazed at me quizzically. "Llama carcass?"

Another thing I'd left out when talking to Elle last night. "I'll explain later." Not that it was a big deal, because we wouldn't be eating at Privé anytime soon, especially after Jackie had mentioned that Privé's yearly membership dues were in the three hundred thousand range.

Antsy to get to work on the cottage, I hurried to the walk-in's door. After stepping inside my hand automatically felt for the light switch on the right. But there was no reason to flip on the switch because the lights were already on. I shivered. Not from the cold, just the memory of Mr. llama, who I'd reasoned was a male—which was more palatable than if he'd been a female, like those on my favorite pjs featuring long-lashed prancing llamas adorned with pink bows on their ears.

I took a tentative step in the direction of the refrigerated showcase, trying to avoid the area where *he* had been hanging. Passing the spot, I couldn't help but glance down at the floor. *Was that a smear of blood?* I backed away and followed the perimeter of the small room. I opened the case and grabbed the glass bottle of milk, noticing it came from a local organic farm in Montauk, then I scooted toward the exit. When I was almost at the door, I stepped on something that pierced the sole of my Keds. "Son of a biscuit eater!" I put the bottle of milk on the empty metal cart. Then, holding on to the wall for support, I took off my sneaker and saw that the post from a gold and diamond stud earring had gone straight through to the bottom of my heel. The wound was tiny. Only a pinprick of blood had surfaced. I pried the post from the rubber sole and put my sneaker back on.

After grabbing the bottle of milk, I opened the door and stepped with relief into the warm kitchen, the scent of espresso filling the air.

"Didn't you guys just hear me yell?" I asked, then walked to the pantry and handed Kelsie the bottle of milk.

"Please don't tell me Lee hung something else in the fridge section. He promised to keep only butchered meat for Privé's use in the freezer section of the walk-in." She took the bottle from my outstretched trembling hand.

"No, he didn't. I stepped on this." I held the stud in the air. The stone was about the size of a small button, not huge, but big enough if it turned out to be the real thing. "Is it yours? Or your sous chef's?"

"No. I don't wear jewelry of any kind in the kitchen," Kelsie said. "And I don't allow Sasha to wear anything either. Once she lost a ring in the pastry dough and I made her eat the entire sheet of pastry until she found it."

I laughed, and Elle just looked clueless because she'd never met Sasha. However, she knew Kelsie from our many meals at Pondfare.

Kelsie handed me a frothy cup of cappuccino, then followed me out with Elle's.

"Aren't you having a cappuccino?" I asked her.

"No. I've had my quota for the day. I bet the earring belongs to Jackie," she said.

I took a seat and Kelsie placed Elle's cup in front of her. She said, "If you give the diamond stud to me, I'll make sure to give it to Jackie when I see her. Which I hope is pretty soon because Sasha is nowhere to be found." She reached for the earring. I gave it to her, and she stuck it in the pocket of her apron.

"I'm surprised Jackie Fairchild would go anywhere near the walk-in," I said. "I would think it's beneath her pay grade. I sure didn't see her come anywhere near the kitchen last night."

"She occasionally assists her husband when he's cooking," Kelsie said.

"Definitely beneath her," Elle said.

"You know Jackie?" Kelsie asked, surprised.

"Meg told me she was one of the partners," Elle answered. "Everyone in the Hamptons knows that Jackie Fairchild is a distant cousin of Jackie O's father—"

"Black Jack Bouvier," Kelsie and I responded at the same time, then we all laughed.

Elle slurped at the cappuccino, leaving her with a milk mustache that resembled my feline Jo's. "We once shared a table at a fashion retrospective for Halston at the arts center in Southampton," she told us. "I'd loaned out a few items from my closet, including a gold lamé floor-length dress that supermodel Lauren Hutton had worn in a seventies perfume ad."

I pointed to my own lip and Elle patted her mouth with a napkin. That's what friends were for. Giving a heads-up on spinach in the teeth or toilet paper stuck to the bottom of shoes.

"You must have quite a closet, Elle," Kelsie said.

I laughed. "That's an understatement. Half of her vintage clothing has been loaned out to the costume designer of *Mr. & Mrs. Winslow*."

Kelsie raised an eyebrow. "Mr. and Mrs. Winslow?"

Elle explained about the prime network miniseries set in the 1930s that was being filmed in Bridgehampton—the same series that Patrick was writing the screenplays for, and Elle and I were working on retainer as assistants to the set and costume designers.

"Currently," Elle said, "we're working on the second two-hour episode, where Lara gets kidnapped and Jack has to play nice with a group of thugs in order to get her back. Although, knowing the way

Patrick wrote the character of Lara Winslow, I'm sure Lara will find a way to make her own escape. She's one tough cookie. Academy Award winner Zoe Stockton plays Lara to a tee."

"Sounds similar to *The Thin Man* book and movies by Dashiell Hammett," Kelsie said. "Loved those movies. My grandma's favorites. And working on set design and wardrobe sounds like tons of fun. Let me know if they need a chef for craft services. Especially if the membership drive doesn't go well today," she added.

"Chef Kelsie, from what Meg *did* tell me about last night's dinner," Elle said, "you have nothing to worry about. And after that scone I just had, we could definitely use you on the set of *Mr. & Mrs. Winslow*. The food reminds me of my middle school's cafeteria lunches, and that's not a good thing. I think even Meg could do better. I bring a bagged lunch to set. Our producer is on the cheap side and probably took the lowest bid offered for our meal service. By the way, Meg, what was your favorite course from Chef Kelsie from last night?"

"Wow, that's a tough one. I would have to say the brioche bowls with the foie gras. No, wait, the baked stuffed striped bass."

"Chef Patou's *bar farci*," Kelsie said.

"Is it in his cookbook?" Elle asked. "I'd love to take a photo of the recipe to hold me over until I can get my mitts on a copy. The Old Man and the Sea Books sold out in one day. Mine's on back order.

Kelsie turned and went to the hidden refrigerator, opened it, and placed the half-empty bottle of milk inside. When she came back to the counter, she said with a grin, "I'm sure Meg can loan you her signed copy, seeing as she doesn't cook."

I glanced at the empty stand on the counter where Chef Patou's cookbook had been last night. Elle tipped her mug in my direction. "Yes, Meg. Please explain. Why do you have his cookbook if you don't cook? For cottage décor?"

"That's easy. Looking through his cookbook is like walking down memory lane. It's fun recalling all the great meals I've had at Pondfare. I've already picked out a few recipes for my father to make the next time he comes to visit."

Elle laughed. "What about Patrick? He sounds like a great cook. Have him prepare your heart's desire from Chef Patou's cookbook."

I smiled. "I just might." I'd told Elle last night about Patrick's wife being a chef and his reaction at Garnier Vineyards on Thursday. Elle had convinced me that I had nothing to worry about, telling me that the fact I couldn't cook a lick meant that Patrick wasn't looking for a carbon copy of his deceased wife. I prayed she was right.

Elle got up and rinsed her mug at the sink and put it in one of the two dishwashers, then asked, "Kelsie, can I take a photo of the recipe, even though I know it won't turn out the way you made it? Arthur has a new hobby, fishing. And striped bass is his fav. I'd love to surprise him."

"Oh, my," I said, "I can just picture you in the kitchen dressed in one of your vintage getups. A June Cleaver apron, perhaps?"

When I turned to Kelsie to ask her where the cookbook was, hoping to get things moving along, she was looking off into space with a frown on her face.

"Is everything okay, Chef?" I asked.

"Yes, sorry. I was just thinking about all the things I need to do before the partners arrive. You know the old saying, too many cooks will spoil the broth. I'd prefer to get everything ready before they come in and give me their opinionated two cents. And it looks like I'll have to do it without Sasha's help. Late as usual. Honestly, I'd rather do it myself."

"When I left last night, Sasha was passed out in the Provence Suite," I said. "But Noah must have woken her, because on my way to the car I saw her throw a ceramic French bulldog at Noah's head. And she didn't miss," I added. "And get this. Jackie also saw it."

"What a freak," Kelsie said, shaking her head.

"Say what?" Elle put her hands to her face like the figure in the famous *Scream* painting. "Projectile bulldogs, chokings. Meg, I say we leave Chef Kelsie to do her magic. No offense, Chef, but this girl" — she pointed at me — "is a trouble magnet. After we leave, you might need to burn some sage in her wake."

Kelsie laughed.

But I didn't.

Because Elle's statement was dead on.

Chapter 7

Four hours later, Elle said, "I don't know if the *radassier* will fit in the bed of the truck."

"The whaddy-sier?"

"The country French ladderback bench."

"Oh, I forgot, Ms. Warner, I mean Mrs. Shoner, that you worked for hoity-toity Sotheby's before coming to *American Home and Garden* magazine. You mean the three-seater, right?"

"It's gonna take a while until I get used to my new last name."

"You and me both," I said.

"You're next. Megan and Patrick sitting in a tree . . ."

"I don't know if marriage is in my future. I'm almost in the spinster category, and I do have a cat, thanks to you."

"Thirty-three does not a spinster make," Elle said. "So what should we do with this bench?"

"I haven't decided. A three-seater is a hard sale. It's why I didn't put it in Privé. My car's already packed and your truck has just enough room for one more box. I only have a few days to find furniture to fill the cottage. *Manly* furniture. Maybe after I unload my car, I'll drive over to Sag Harbor and see what's in your carriage house that we could use."

"Sure, but we should wait until Maurice is finished doing an inventory of your and my things. I'm sure you'll find things there that you forgot about. It'll be a piece of cake. Cottages are your forte, and from what I've seen, so are large French farmhouses. You lucked out that almost everything in the loft area of the old cottage was already in boxes. Even that large carton filled with paintings. I peeked inside at a few. Some are awful. But I spied one that looked promising. You're going to have fun going through them."

"It will be Christmas in August," I added. "And you will be by my side when I do."

"It will probably be September before we get a chance. It's only two days away."

"True," I said, finagling the last box into the bed of Elle's truck.

Elle stepped over to help. "You said the farmhouse was built in 1945, but the contents in the cottage look much older."

"I'm guessing the cottage was here way before the farmhouse. I suppose you could ask your pal Bethany about it. If you dare?"

"I do want to talk to her. I can't picture her being so riled up as to cause physical harm to someone. Maybe you can come with me?" She gave me her puppy dog look.

"I'm not one of her favorite people right now."

"I'll vouch for you."

I repeated what Kelsie had told me about the rumors that when Bethany's husband was alive he'd had an affair with Privé's sous chef. "Jealousy is a strong motive for violence. Per my father, the strongest."

"Now I know who Sasha is," Elle said. "She used to work in the wine barn. She is gorgeous, but I never saw anything untoward between her and Tom. All I ever witnessed was how much Tom adored Bethany. I'll wait a few days, then go over to the winery and have a chat with her. Bethany was the one who recommended the boutique hotel in Provence that we stayed in for our honeymoon. It was heaven on earth. Now back to the bench. We could tie it to the bed of the truck or onto the luggage rack on the top of your car. It wouldn't be the first time."

Elle had a smidgeon of dirt on top of her nose that I used a clean tissue from my pocket to wipe away. "Maybe I can use the bench in the cottage's mudroom. I've measured all the rooms. Tonight, I'll draw up the design plans to present to Lee Cutler at tomorrow's dinner."

"What does Patrick think of your planned dinner with Lee?" Elle asked

"Haven't had a chance to tell him. He's working on a new book. It's top secret."

"Is he one of those writers who closes themselves off for days, only coming out for food and sustenance?"

"He's just started the book, so I'm not sure. I'll find out. Plus, I've been so busy with Privé, I don't have room to complain. Let's secure your truck so we can get out of Dodge before Privé's elite future members start showing up."

I went to the other side of the truck's cargo area and Elle threw me a rope. She said, "The *radassier* might be fun to use in an upcoming episode of *Mr. & Mrs. Winslow*. I can picture Jack and Lara sitting on it, their pooch in the middle seat, both sleuthing out the clues for the third episode, 'The Lighthouse Caper.'"

"I love it. You should suggest it to our director."

"You mean our *new* director. We haven't even met him yet."

"Or you could take the bench and put it on Mabel and Elle's wraparound porch? I bet you'd sell it as soon as you put a price tag on it. And if you don't have room, you could just store it in the carriage house."

"I've been meaning to talk to you about that. I was going to wait until after we fill our carts with goodies at the Bridgehampton Arts and Antiques Show, and we go to the Candy Kitchen for lunch. Might as well tell you now. Maurice and his partner are going to be moving into the carriage house."

"What? What happened to their darling little Sag Harbor cottage?"

"It's a rental. But that's not why they're moving into the carriage house."

"Is it because Maurice, your trusty manager of Mabel and Elle's Curiosities, spends more time at the shop than with his partner . . ."

"No, it's because I made Maurice co-owner of Mabel and Elle's. Now that Arthur and I are married, we're looking to move. We'll still keep the main floor of the house as the shop and use the top floor for my private collection of vintage fashions and accessories."

I couldn't believe what I was hearing. Elle's house in Sag Harbor wasn't just any house. It was a late eighteen-hundreds Victorian, complete with a widow's walk and a view of the harbor. I was thrilled she wasn't selling it, but I couldn't picture her living anywhere else. "Please don't tell me you're moving to Manhattan. Arthur didn't get transferred back to the city, did he? Even Riverhead would be too far. Plus, you told me he'd turned down the position of Suffolk County Police Chief." I felt tears well.

"Megan Elizabeth Barrett, do you think I would ever leave you? Where we're moving to does start with an *M*, but not Manhattan. Montauk! We're meeting with one of Barb's new agents Wednesday. If we find anything promising, I'll video chat for your opinion. Unless you want to come along?"

I went and hugged her. "You bet, I'll come along. I'm surprised Arthur is giving up his modern condo in East Hampton. I know you only do vintage."

"Remember what you always say to your clients — *A modern home can meld perfectly with that little touch of vintage or antique.* Only in this case, a vintage or antique home can meld perfectly with a little touch of modern. Arthur knows when to pick his battles, and where we live isn't one of them, especially now that he's obsessed with going fishing in Montauk with Doc — the fishing capital of the world."

"Sounds perfect. Similar to our junking, flea marketing, and fixer-uppering, now Arthur has a hobby to keep him busy."

Elle laughed. "Fixer-uppering? Yes, we all need hobbies. Maybe it will help him relax a little now that his archnemesis, the disgraced Chief Pell, is serving time behind bars for corruption."

"Working off-season at the East Hampton Town PD should be stress-free," I said. "And if it isn't, fishing with Doc, the retired Detroit PD coroner, will come in handy when your hubby gets involved in his next murder case."

"Please! No more murders in the Hamptons. We've had too many, and coincidently there's been a definite uptick in the numbers since you've moved here."

I ignored her jab. "I've never driven anyone to murder, just happened to be in the wrong place at the right time to flush out a killer or two."

"Thanks for the glass-half-full explanation," Elle said, adding a tsk-tsk. "But I don't think of things the way you do, especially not now that I'm married to a homicide detective who at any second could get caught in the line of fire. But thanks for reminding me. I not only have to worry about you and your shenanigans, but also my husband's."

"This is the Hamptons, and it's almost the off-season. No worries, buddy. I'm not in the mood for another murder investigation either. That's why I want to get the hell out of here with the cottage goodies before something else strange happens. Hey, speaking of goodies, if Maurice is moving into your carriage house, what are you going to do with all our packed-to-the-rafters projects?"

"Don't you worry. I'll make sure that whatever home or cottage Arthur and I move into, we'll have a separate barn or outbuilding. Or Duke and Duke Jr. will construct one. Working together on our projects is what keeps me sane."

"Phew! Me too, soul sister. Half of my stuff is in the carriage house. I've always wanted to participate in a barn raising. We could go to upstate New York on a road trip. Look for an old red barn that's falling apart, then pile the boards on a semitruck and reconstruct it in Montauk."

"Whoa, slow down, partner. One step at a— Did you hear that?" Elle cupped her hand to her ear.

I strained to listen, then glanced toward the front of the farmhouse. Kelsie was half walking, half running in our direction, staggering like a zombie in the old black-and-white film *Night of the Living Dead.*

Elle grabbed my elbow. "Uh-oh. What now?"

We rushed toward Kelsie.

When she got close enough, Kelsie managed to choke out, "Come quick. I've already called nine-one-one. She's dead. I can't believe it. She's dead."

"Who? Who's dead?" I asked.

"She's in the freezer . . ."

Elle put her hands on Kelsie's shoulders and gently shook her. "Who is dead?"

Chapter 8

Kelsie stood behind us, holding open the door between the walk-in fridge and the freezer. She was sobbing, with lots of gulping and running of the nose, occasionally letting out gurgling sounds that formed into words, then eventually turned into phrases, and finally full sentences. "Insisted . . . she come . . . she was too . . . I shouldn't have left her alone last night."

Sasha lay on her back on the slab cement floor, her head slightly propped up by the leg of a steel cart bolted to the ground. There was a sickening sweet smell of liquor in the dense air. Her skin had turned white and frosty, and her eyes were closed. Out of habit, using Elle to block Kelsie's view, I shot off a couple of photos with my phone, then I quickly shoved the phone back in my jeans pocket, got down on my knees, and assessed the situation. The sous chef must have stumbled in her drunkenness and hit the leg of the metal cart on her way down. Not being an expert in forensics but having seen more than my share of murder victims, it appeared that Sasha's death was a tragic accident.

So why the photos of the scene? I asked myself. Then I answered myself. Because after what went down last night, things might not be as cut-and-dry as they seem.

"Is she dead?" Elle whispered into my right hearing aid. "She looks like Snow White."

Glancing at Sasha's frozen features, I doubted a prince, including her boyfriend Lee Cutler, would be able to kiss her awake. "Pretty sure," I answered. Then I remembered something that retired coroner Doc once told me about a case he'd read in a medical journal about a man who was found frozen in a snowbank and pronounced dead at the scene. After they wheeled him, body bag and all, into the emergency room, the ER doctor took over and preformed two hours of CPR until he regained consciousness. His only long-term injuries were the loss of his toes and pinky fingers. After telling the story, Doc, my father's best friend and my surrogate uncle, had said with misty eyes, "Wish I could say that I'd brought one of my patients back to life. Forty years on the job and not one resurrection. It takes a toll on a person." Then, for my benefit, he'd switched to sunnier topics.

"At least, I'm pretty sure she's dead," I whispered to Elle. Then, inspired by Doc's story, I took off my sweater, made it into a pillow, and gently pulled Sasha forward until her head rested on the folded sweater. With chattering teeth, I went to work alternating between chest compressions and mouth-to-frozen-mouth breaths.

"I can't watch," I heard Kelsie say from behind me, "I'll be in the kitchen."

Elle continued to hold the door open between the freezer and refrigerated sections of the walk-in. After a few minutes passed, she said, "Meg, honey. I think it's too late for her. You've done your best."

I didn't answer, just kept going.

Three minutes later, the door opened between the kitchen and the refrigerated section, and two paramedics came inside. One was male, the other female. The female paramedic stepped into the freezer, bent next to the Sasha, then roughly pushed me aside. I explained about the man who'd spent the night in the snowbank.

"Just let me do my job," the female paramedic said. Then she felt for a pulse in the carotid artery. Not finding one, she promptly declared Sasha dead. "How long has she been in here?"

I got up from the floor and looked at Elle. She shrugged her shoulders. I said, "My guess would be about twelve or thirteen hours."

"Well, I doubt the guy you just told me about was in the snowbank for that long. You two should leave now. There's nothing you can do for your friend. I'm sorry."

I glanced down at Sasha. It was all so heartbreaking. Even in death she was stunning. She had on the same low-cut violet dress she'd worn at dinner last night. I noticed one thing: there weren't any bruises or marks on her neck, telling me that Bethany hadn't come back to finish what she'd started.

Taking a few steps backward, I extended my hand toward Elle. She grabbed it like a lifeline. Her hand was as cold as mine but in seconds our palms warmed, making me think how depressing it was that Sasha hadn't had anyone to hold her hand before she'd slipped into icy oblivion.

The door from the kitchen opened again. "Don't move the body," I heard a loud, familiar male voice say, "I'll take over."

I turned to see Elle's hubby standing in the fridge section.

"Arthur!" Elle exclaimed, obviously happy to see him.

We moved toward him and I let Elle tell him what had happened.

After she finished, he squeezed her shoulder and asked, "You okay? Southampton PD told me to batten the hatches until they could get here. There was an incident at the Hampton Classic. A missing horse of all things."

"I'm fine," Elle said.

"Not so for Privé's sous chef," I added, nodding my head at the body on the freezer's floor.

"You said her name was Sasha. Can I get her last name?" he asked, taking out his small notebook.

Elle looked at me and I said, "I'm not sure about her last name. You'll have to ask Kelsie. I just met her last night for the first time."

"Ms. Barrett, are you saying you were here last night and this morning?"

"Yes, *Detective* Shoner." I explained my role at Privé. I knew Elle had told him about it but obviously he hadn't been listening.

"Okay, you two. No reverting back to using surnames," Elle said. "We're family, remember. Meg, just tell him quickly about last night's dinner so we can get out of here."

He took notes as I gave him a quick recap of the players involved at Privé, including Bethany and the choking incident. Elle hadn't looked happy that I'd mentioned her friend, but she also didn't interrupt or try to defend Bethany's actions. Maybe because they were indefensible.

"Has the body been moved?" he asked, addressing the pair of first responders.

"No. Not by us," the skinny male attendant said, directing his gaze at me.

"I'd think you would know better, Ms. Barrett. Meg. After all, your father is a retired homicide detective," Arthur said.

"Well . . ." I then explained why I'd moved the body.

He gave me a chastising look, one he'd used many times in the past. Just because Detective Arthur Shoner was my best friend's husband didn't mean he was willing to soften his demeanor when it came to me and my penchant for getting into trouble. And then there was also the fact that his new bride was usually by my side when I did. The way I looked at it, if I hadn't interfered in past police investigations, a killer or two might still be roaming the Hamptons posh, gold-paved streets. Also, if not for me, Elle and Detective Arthur Shoner would have never met.

"We'll wait for you in the kitchen," Elle said, her shoulders relaxing in the presence of her take-charge husband. "Come on, Meg."

We were still holding hands as she pulled me toward the door. I followed her out and into the warm fragrant room. Trays of food were scattered over every available space. I'd also noticed plastic-wrapped trays of food in the refrigerated area of the walk-in when we'd first charged in.

Kelsie stood at the farm sink with her phone to her ear. She whispered something, then hung up, then deftly stowed her phone in her chef coat's pocket. I hadn't been able to read her lips, but she had tears in her eyes.

"Not more bad news, I hope?" I asked.

"No. I just can't believe this is happening. What are the chances that I wouldn't step inside the freezer until now? I only went in for a bag of ice for the oysters. There was no reason to go inside earlier because everything was already prepped and ready to go." She gulped back a sob. "If I would have gone in first thing this morning, maybe I could've saved her."

"Why do you think Sasha went into the freezer after you left her last night?" I asked in a whisper. "Did she have any reason to?"

"Not that I can think of. Everything we needed for today had already been thawed. I feel like this is a bad dream. I can't go forward with the membership drive until I talk to Jackie, Noah, and Lee. Where the hell are they?"

I didn't have an answer for her. If I was a partner, which thank God I wasn't, I would postpone the membership drive until at least tomorrow. Then I remembered that it was Labor Day weekend, the last official weekend of the summer season. Come Tuesday, there would be a mass exodus due west of summer people, including some of Privé's potential members.

I looked at Elle and said, "Should we leave? Or wait for Arthur?" I was exhausted—physically from our work in the cottage and emotionally from the scene in the freezer. Had Sasha had any close family? Children? She'd been young. Kelsie had told me she was in her early twenties. Still, her having a child wasn't out of the question. A vision flashed in front of my eyes of Elle's friend Bethany with her hands around Sasha's neck. I quickly erased it. This had nothing to do with me. Not even Elle's husband. Because soon, Southampton PD would be taking over.

"Let's just wait," Elle answered, "I'm sure my husband will want to ask us a few more questions."

"That policeman is your husband?" Kelsie asked, her eyes opening wide.

"Detective Arthur Shoner from the East Hampton Town PD," Elle said proudly.

We sat at the counter on the same bar stools we'd chosen this morning when Kelsie had made us our cappuccinos. Twenty minutes passed. During that time numerous law enforcement came and went into the walk-in. The only ones missing were Privé's three partners.

Just as I was about to tell Elle that I was going to head home to my cozy cottage, Arthur stepped out. In his arms was an evidence bag holding my sweater. Through the clear plastic I saw a reddish brown stain. Blood from the back of Sasha's head. I shivered violently.

"That's mine," I said, pointing to the sweater.

"You can get it back after we determine cause of death," Arthur said.

"Keep it. I just thought I'd mention it."

Arthur advanced toward his wife and smiled reassuringly. "It looks like an accident. But just in case the coroner finds something untoward, Southampton PD has sent a CSI investigator to take photos and collect evidence."

"Untoward?" Kelsie asked, adding a deep gulp. A lone tear trailed down her right cheek.

Elle, who up until this point had been silent, said, "Arthur, this is Kelsie. She was Chef Patou's former sous chef at Pondfare."

He wasn't in the mood for civility. "You're the one who called it in, right? Can I have your last name."

"Stevens."

"And the deceased's last name?"

"Morgan," Kelsie answered, blinking away the tears. Then her gaze locked onto the sweater. "Do you know how she died?"

Kelsie had changed into full chef whites. Short brunette curls sprung in all directions under her toque, and her forehead was covered in beads of sweat. I was reminded of how differently Kelsie's chef coat fit compared to the one Sasha wore last night. Kelsie's looked as if it had shrunk in the dryer. It fit her fine in the shoulders but not around the midsection. She'd even popped a button. Not that I was criticizing her appearance or physique. I was sure if I was a gourmet chef and had to taste-test everything before serving it, my stomach would be double Kelsie's.

"Was it alcohol poisoning?" Kelsie asked, turning to Arthur. Mascara mixed with tears slid down her cheeks in sooty rivulets.

"We won't know that until the coroner looks at her," Arthur said. "How long had she been in there?"

Kelsie looked at me, then Elle.

"I saw her last night around eleven, right before I left," Kelsie said. "Sasha was awake and promised me that she had a ride home."

Arthur said, "Who else was here when you left?"

"To my knowledge, no one," she answered. "Both lots were empty."

"So, when you left at eleven, Ms. Morgan was here alone? You're sure?"

"As far as I could tell. We do have a surveillance camera but only at the front entrance, not in the two parking lots, rear door, or cottage. But if it was an accident, why are you asking all these questions?"

"Because in the death of someone so young, there will always be an autopsy. Maybe you should have waited until she had a ride home."

Kelsie narrowed her eyes at Arthur. "She actually seemed quite coherent when I left. Her roommate dropped her off last night. I knew she didn't have a car, so there wasn't any chance of her driving intoxicated. I don't appreciate the insinuation that I am the cause of her death."

"I never said that, Ms. Stevens."

It didn't seem fair to blame Kelsie for Sasha's choice to keep on drinking. Maybe Sasha was just trying to fill the hole for something that happened to her recently. Something involving Lee Cutler. I knew the toll alcohol could take on a person. My father was a prime example. In his early years, when working as a young officer on the Detroit PD, he'd spent way too many hours in the morgue, and shared way too many whiskeys with the rest of the guys and gals from his precinct. It had been my mother and her news of a bun in the oven, *me*, that caused my father to put away the bottle. Maybe Sasha's drunkenness was a one-time deal because something or someone was bothering her? Between seeing Sasha chuck the ceramic bulldog at Noah's head, her irritation with Lee, Bethany's obvious hatred of her, and Jackie mentioning at dinner about Sasha and her husband whispering together, it seemed Sasha had issues with everyone, even Kelsie, who'd raged against her and threatened to fire her.

With Arthur's assessment that Sasha's death looked to be an accident, the web forming in my imagination was manageable. But I knew from experience how easy it would be for me to get tangled in its sticky center while a fanged-tooth spider dripping venom looked on. A silly analogy that reiterated the fact that I was tired, my entire body still shaking from my time spent in the freezer. What had Sasha been doing in the freezer? Kelsie said more than once that there was no reason for her to be in there. And where were Noah, Jackie, and Lee? Wasn't their big membership drive only hours away? I'd spied two cars parked in the circular drive of the main entrance when we'd followed catatonic Kelsie to the kitchen—a white Bentley and a black Mercedes sedan. Neither of those was the SUV that had almost run me off the road this morning.

There were too many questions with too many possible answers that had nothing to do with me.

It was an accident.

Or so I told myself.

Chapter 9

When we'd finally received the go-ahead to leave the farmhouse, I'd followed Elle to Montauk, where we'd unloaded twenty-seven boxes from Elle's truck and my car, then carried them into my small guest room. Normally, the boxes would go into Elle's carriage house. But with the news that her shop assistant Maurice would soon be moving in, that idea was off the table.

After Elle left for Sag Harbor, I considered opening a few of the boxes for a quick peek but I was too drained from the long day to do much of anything but feed Jo and make a cup of chamomile tea that would hopefully settle my churning stomach.

With tea in hand, and Jo nipping at my heels because I'd neglected to score her the fancy canned food I'd promised, I went into the great room. I placed my cup and saucer on the fireplace mantel, then tapped a section of shiplap paneling to the left of the fireplace. A narrow door opened, revealing my secret room. It wasn't really a secret because all my friends and family knew of its existence, but the cocooned space still provided an insulated getaway from the outside world. Plus, secret rooms were fun, just ask Nancy Drew and her sidekicks Bess and George.

I placed my tea on top of the candlestand table next to my cushioned window seat. The seat's bowed window offered a stunning northeastern view of the Montauk Point Lighthouse and the Atlantic shoreline. The scene soothed my soul and helped erase the memory of another scene. Jo hopped onto the window seat, then nestled on top of the crazy quilt. Not only did she purposely leave no room for me to sit, but she'd plopped on top of an antique quilt that she knew was off-limits. Not because of the quilt's age but because the quilt's velvet patches acted like a magnet for Jo's fur. "Okay. If that's the way you want to play it, I'll just sit on top of you." I hovered over her. She didn't budge, just closed her eye. "You asked for it." I reached both arms under the quilt and turned my head in case she went to swat me with her razor-sharp claws. I had a theory that when I left Jo alone in the cottage, she somehow got into the kitchen cupboard that housed my father's whetstone knife sharpener and gave herself a daily manicure. I'd tried once to clip them and had come close to getting stiches. Even her kindly vet made sure Jo was wearing her Hannibal Lector–type muzzle before they did the deed.

Holding the quilt with Jo still on top, I slid twenty-three pounds of fat and fur (not necessarily in that order) onto the thick-pile area rug. Before Jo could react, I hopped onto the window seat. When she glanced up at me, I stuck out my tongue.

Pretending she didn't care, she went to the door, head-butted it open, then left with only fur flying in her wake. I knew as payback she'd do some kind of damage to the rest of the house, but it was well worth it just to be able to stretch out and soak in the view.

I pulled the quilt up to my shoulders, still feeling cold from my time spent in the freezer with a corpse. Taking a sip of hot tea, I searched the beach for a man and his dog, trying to wrap my head around what had just happened at Privé. But all I could do was cry. Cry for the young chef who lost her life. Cry for Patrick, who had lost his wife and child. I also cried a few self-pity tears for the loss of my mother, who'd died so young and never had a chance to see the woman I'd become. My father had done the best he could. But sometimes you just needed your mom.

After a few deep breaths, I glanced at the candlestand table next me. On top was a psychological thriller that I was in the middle of reading. I'd had enough thrills for one day. I got up and pulled a volume of Elizabeth Barrett Browning's poetry from a shelf. Three of the walls in the small space held floor-to-ceiling bookshelves. The longer of the three was packed with my collection of gilt-and-cloth nineteenth-century books and volumes of classical poetry that I'd been collecting since I was a teen, most of them swiped off the shelves of my mother's antiques and collectibles shop in Detroit called Past Perfect. The shorter of the three walls held contemporary fiction, mystery, thrillers (all of Patrick's), and reissued classics in new colorful bindings. The mystery genre was my favorite — historical and contemporary. The usual rule was that they were all cozy and light, with just a touch of romance. The perpetrator was always captured and locked up. And everyone lived happily ever after — except for the victim, of course.

Between the view and my books, I had everything I needed in my not-so-secret room. Plus, this was one space where I could take out my hearing aids and listen to the author's voice without static, the words from the page of my books bouncing up at me like old acquaintances.

Our assignment for our next Dead Poets Society Book Club meeting was to talk about Elizabeth's poem "The Autumn." I went back to the window seat, sat, leaned back against the down pillows and started to read the poem.

> Go, sit upon the lofty hill,
> And turn your eyes around,
> Where waving woods and waters wild
> Do hymn an autumn sound.
> The summer sun is faint on them,
> The summer flowers depart,
> Sit still, as all transform'd to stone,
> Except your musing heart . . .

I must have fallen asleep, because when I woke it was dark and the fat cat was purring, more like rattling and gently kneading my chest. Jo also knew how to reach my softer side by nuzzling my nose and allowing me to scratch her behind her ears. Too bad most of the time it was only before mealtime. But we had our moments. The reason I wouldn't trade her for any other pet.

I made us dinner, her a can of tuna, me Tuna Helper. At nine, debating about whether to go upstairs and call it a night, a light blinked above the door that led out to my deck.

When I opened the door, Patrick, accompanied by his greyhound Charlie, asked if I wanted to come out and play. I gave them a resounding "Yes!"

We strolled the beach toward the Montauk Point Lighthouse. The full moon highlighted gently rolling waves with threads of gold. The beach was deserted, and it was almost as if we owned the shoreline. We stopped at the point where the boulders were too large for Charlie to leap over. Then, just at the point where Patrick reached to take me into his arms, a group of rowdy twenty-somethings, smelling like they'd taken a dunk or two inside a keg of beer, charged by. They kicked up sand and waved sticks of driftwood like swords. Charlie growled as they passed, her front legs trembling. It was the only time I'd ever seen her agitated. By her reaction to the marauders, it was obvious that even though the scars on the outside of her body had healed from her time as an abused racetrack dog, the ones on the inside hadn't. Patrick immediately calmed her by talking in a soothing voice while stroking the fur on her flank. After she stopped shaking, he offered her a handful of his homemade holistic treats.

Our romantic moment had been lost forever, but I was confident that soon there would be others. After Labor Day, just three days away, Patrick, Charlie, and I would reclaim our little slice of seaside heaven.

As we walked back to my cottage, we talked about our upcoming Dead Poets Society Book Club meeting. I decided earlier not to tell Patrick about the tragic accident that had happened at Privé, wanting to keep things light for both of our sakes.

"It was your suggestion we feature Elizabeth Barrett Browning," he said, picking up a stick and tossing it into the surf for Charlie to fetch. "Is that because you share the same last name?"

"No. But it would be interesting to see if I'm somehow related to Elizabeth." Then I asked him why the nonfiction book he'd written about classic poets with tragic pasts, *Tales from a Dead Shore — A Biography of Tortured Poets*, hadn't included any female poets.

"Unfortunately, there weren't many published female poets during the time period I covered in my book," he answered.

A lock of hair fell in front of his eyes and I swiped it away, only for it to fall back again. "Based on the book I own of love letters written between Elizabeth and her poet husband Robert Browning, it seems their marriage was near perfect. Poetry was their bond. So, neither one would make your tragic poets book."

"Maybe Elizabeth kept Robert from spiraling into a depression," Patrick said. "Kind of like how I feel when I'm with you."

I didn't want to read into his comment but was feeling all warm and fuzzy. I grabbed his hand, then kissed his rough cheek. We continued walking and I said, "Virginia Woolf and Sylvia Plath are too contemporary, but of course they would have fit in nicely in your book." Then I remembered something. "There was a period of time that might give Elizabeth Barrett Browning a postscript in your book. Following her many miscarriages, she became addicted to the opium drug laudanum. But there's a happy ending to her tale. Once her healthy son was born, she stopped taking the drug so easily prescribed to Victorian women by male doctors as a magic cure-all for every female ailment."

"Not fair," Patrick said. "Back then, there were only male doctors."

"Well, her story ends well. She ended up living blissfully happy with her poet husband and miracle son."

When we reached the beach in front of my cottage, I found a stick of driftwood. While Patrick and Charlie looked on, Patrick waiting for what I would write, and Charlie eyeing the perfect stick to play fetch with, I penned one of Elizabeth Barrett Browning's verses in the wet sand. Not the well-known verse that starts with *How do I love thee*—it was too soon in our relationship for that one. Instead, I left: *Earth's crammed with heaven, but only he who sees takes off his shoes.*

"Good one," Patrick said before kissing me good night.

I waited until they were out of sight before climbing up to my deck. I left my sandy sneakers outside, then opened the French doors and walked inside. The light scent of lavender from the reed diffuser by the door made me smile. All was well, I thought. Even Jo's snarl at my return couldn't upset my calm. "Hello, to you, too," I said. Then I saw a blinking light on my landline phone that told me I had a message. Did I want to pick it up? No.

But I did anyway.

It was Elle, calling to remind me we had plans to go to an antiques show in the morning. My shoulders relaxed and my spirits soared. Now all I needed was a good night's sleep.

"Come on, Jo. Bedtime." I followed her up to my bedroom, washed my face, changed into my pj's—not the llama ones—and fell asleep as soon as my head hit the pillow.

The warm, cozy feeling from being with Patrick and thoughts of all the treasures I might find at the show lasted until about two in the morning. I jerked awake from a ghoulish vision of Sasha's waxlike features and inadvertently kicked Jo in her giggly belly. Jo retaliated by opening her large jaws and snapping down crocodile style on my ankle, which luckily was protected by a top sheet, blanket, and fluffy duvet. I had to give her an *E* for effort. No one was allowed to wake Josephine Eater Barrett without warning.

I couldn't fall back asleep. I got up, opened my laptop, and started working on the plans for the cottage at Privé. "A busy mind keeps the worries away," I whispered to a snoring Jo. I was pretty sure that Lee would be canceling our dinner date for tonight. But I figured if I got the plans out of the way I could concentrate on more uplifting things, like scouting out furniture and décor for *Mr. & Mrs. Winslow*'s fourth episode, which was scheduled to be shot on location on Block Island, a small island that was officially part of Rhode Island.

In June, Elle and I had coerced one of Doc's friends who had a fishing trawler to take us to the island to check out the old guest house where most of the filming would take place. It was love at first sight. The magnificent structure not only had wraparound porches, but also a wraparound widow's walk and was perched on a bluff close to one of Block Island's three, yes three, lighthouses. We'd only been able to view the property from the Block Island Sound. What we didn't know was the shape of the guest house's interior. If the inn was empty, the assignment would involve numerous boat trips back and forth filled with cargo. But if we were lucky, the grand old lady might be filled with antiques and vintage items — things we could salvage and repurpose to fit the late 1930s time line. Either way it was a win-win.

At three, happy with the plans for Privé's cottage, I turned off my laptop. My eyes felt dry and scratchy, like someone had kicked sand in them. Surely I would be asleep in seconds, dreaming of all the treasures to be found at tomorrow's, or should I say this morning's, Bridgehampton Art and Antiques Show.

After what Kelsie found in the freezer, I should've known that wouldn't be the case.

Chapter 10

I woke at seven Sunday morning and immediately padded over to my small Juliet balcony, threw open the French doors, then stepped out and watched the sun rise over the Atlantic. The temperature was in the upper seventies and there wasn't a cloud in the sky, giving me hope that it would be a perfect day for vintage pickin'. I could have used a few more hours of sleep, but all I needed was strong coffee and the thrill of the hunt to spur me on.

At seven thirty, I was out the door, coffee in hand, and on my way to meet Elle in Bridgehampton. Before closing the door, I called out, "'Bye, Jo, wherever you are. Love you tons."

Twenty minutes later, I pulled into the lot behind the Bridgehampton Community House. I spied Elle's pickup and parked next to it. Elle stood next to a sign that read *Third Annual Bridgehampton Outdoor Art & Antiques Show*. Thanks to Elle and her connections we'd scored a coveted pair of early-bird tickets. Last year, we'd had to wait in line with the minions as we observed a gaggle of celebs and socialites milling about the show with mimosas and Bloody Marys in hand as they casually strolled the aisles. And in my competitive mind, snatching up all the prime treasure.

This year would be different because Elle and I would be right along with them, rubbing elbows with the cream of the Hamptons crop. However, no matter what their station in life, I wasn't above wrestling one of them to the ground over a must-have item. It was a cutthroat business, especially in the Hamptons, but Elle and I were always up for the challenge.

I drained the last sip from my third mug of coffee. The show was just what the doctor ordered—the perfect salve to get my mind off yesterday's tragedy. I had two categories of items to search for: late 1930s garden furniture and décor for the set of *Mr. & Mrs. Winslow*, and rattan and bamboo Aesthetic-era furniture for the cottage at Privé. And, if I happened to find any aqua 1930s McCoy vases or jardinières that I didn't already own, they would be purchased for my viewing pleasure only, then placed alongside my collection in my glass folly/design studio located at the rear of my cottage.

Glancing out my windshield, I saw Elle waving frantically for me to hurry. I hopped out, retrieved my trusty expandable cart from the back of my Wagoneer, hit the lock button on my remote, and jogged toward her.

"Why are you dilly-dallying?" she asked. "Time's tickin'. You have no idea what I had to do to get these tickets. Hey, did you see Cutler's Meat Wagons in the parking lot?"

I let my nose follow the smell of bacon. Or what I hoped was bacon. "I'm not surprised. Kelsie told me he has a fleet of four hundred trucks."

We started to walk toward the entrance of the show, Elle toting her own empty cart. "I bet Arthur would love to gnaw on something from one of his food trucks," she said. "Maybe a huge turkey leg like they have at Renaissance fairs. Arthur thinks he's *all that* now that he's fishing. He's behaving like Ernest Hemingway on steroids. He doesn't even wear a pocket square to work anymore. And last week I caught him dressed in the same suit for two days in a row. He's even watching these macho shows on obscure channels. One of them is called *Meat Eaters*, where these survivalists hunt and eat their prey up close and personal for all of TV land to view. Too up close and personal for me. I told him to switch to HGTV, or else."

"Good call," I said. "I wonder if Lee Cutler ever goes hunting for his meat. From what Kelsie told me, he just buys it from a broker. And by the way, Lee doesn't stock his food trucks with anything but red meat and fries. So no hormone-charged turkey legs."

"After you told me about the llama in Privé's larder, I've been toying with the idea of not eating any animals that have eyelashes. Chicken, turkey, seafood, and plant protein is all I need."

We presented our tickets to a middle-aged woman sitting at a table outside the show's open gates. The woman glanced at them, then at us, making it obvious she thought they were counterfeit. It could have been because we weren't dressed the same as the rest of the early-bird Hamptons elite. We both had on our flea market/ garage sale uniforms: jeans, baggy T-shirts, large sunglasses, and baseball caps. Our vintage 1980s fanny packs held jewelers' loupes, penlights, magnifying glasses, tape measures, along with magnets so we could discern silver plate from sterling, a wad of cash, and our debit cards. We might look pedestrian, but then again, we weren't shopping for our leisure. Vintage was our livelihood. Although Elle, thanks to her Great-Aunt Mabel, had been left very wealthy. But that didn't stop her from bargaining when it came to something for Mabel and Elle's Curiosities or vintage clothing and jewelry for her own closets (plural).

"Go on through," the woman said. She had pinched features and pursed lips like she'd just been sucking on a bowl of lemons. "Make sure you don't trip anyone with those large carts of yours."

I grabbed the handle of my cart and followed behind Elle, who'd stopped abruptly and said, "Oh, look!" She pointed to a booth to our right that was set up with makeshift barnwood walls. "There's Rita. Wonder who's minding the shop?"

Rita's shop in East Hampton, Grimes House Antiques, was nestled between two designer clothing shops in East Hampton. Once an old apothecary shop, it was one of the few places that sold authentic eighteenth- and nineteenth-century Americana. As I'd learned the hard way, Rita's prices were astronomical. Never again would I try to negotiate with her like I did at other antique and vintage shops, estate sales, garage sales, and flea markets (not-for-profit thrift shops were my one exception). The one time I did try to bargain, Rita had snatched the item from my hand, hmphed loud enough for her other customers to hear, then while glaring at me, hid the item under the sales counter. The next time I visited Grimes House, I saw that Rita had upped the price on the item. Lesson learned. All that said, going into her shop was like stepping back in history or touring a museum. Plus, unlike me, most Hamptons residents, celebrity clientele, and visitors had no problem shelling out the big bucks for one of her antiques — probably the reason she'd been in business for forty-something years.

We advanced toward Rita's space. She greeted Elle, but only nodded at me. In tandem with the Hampton Classic horse show, Rita's booth displayed an assortment of antique equestrian items, including equine paintings and etchings, figurines, and horse head busts. There was even equestrian antique dishware, including a hand-painted pitcher displaying a foxhunt scene with hounds and horses. The small placard next to the pitcher said that it was Wedgwood and dated from 1850.

I stepped next to Elle, who was looking at a glass case filled with cutout circular pieces of brass. "Bottle openers?" I asked.

"No, they're antique horse brasses. I've never seen so many together in one place. Leave it to Rita."

"What are they for?"

"They're decorative pieces or charms that hang from the horse's facepiece or the leather straps on either side of the horse. Very coveted by collectors. Some are shaped into a family crest, or a symbol of the horse's place of origin, or just decorative. You could think of them as horse jewelry. Some earlier ones. See those" — Elle pointed to a brass in the shape of a three-leaf clover with two small snakes facing each other — "are supposed to ward off evil."

"Cool," I said, pointing to a brass peacock. "What do they sell for?"

Instead of answering me, Elle nudged me and whispered, "Isn't that what's-his-name from . . . ?"

The male star from a popular western TV mystery series was admiring a hand-tooled leather saddle that sat on top of a wooden sawhorse. "Yes. It sure is," I whispered.

"That saddle reminds me of something that I forgot to share with you. You wouldn't believe this coincidence."

"Try me," I said, picking up a sterling loving cup etched with the date 1898.

"Remember when Arthur showed up yesterday at Privé and said he was covering for the Southampton PD because they'd been busy with a horse-napping at the Hampton Classic?"

"Horse-napping? Thought he said *missing* horse."

"Guess whose horse was kidnapped?"

"Whose?" I didn't have time for guessing games, especially when I spied an antique brass spyglass like one I owned, the same one that Patrick always admired when he was at my cottage. If the price was right, I'd buy it for his birthday. Then I realized I didn't know when that was. Which in turn reminded me of how little I really knew about him.

"Hello, Earth to Meg. Don't you want to know?"

"Yes. The horse owner. Who is it?"

"Jackie Fairchild. And naturally the horse's name is Black Jack."

"Really?"

"Really. Arthur says the horse is insured for five million."

"What will she ride tomorrow at the Hampton Classic?"

"Oh, that's not the only five-million-dollar horse in her stable. But I believe it was her favorite."

"That's obvious by its name," I said.

"If they kidnapped her favorite horse, the same one she planned to ride tomorrow, I bet it was someone close to her."

I smiled. "Look at you, my little grasshopper, making Sherlockian deductions."

"I've learned from the best. My hubby."

I stuck out my lower lip in a pout.

"And you, of course," she added with a grin.

I slipped in a non sequitur, "Your husband share any news on Sasha Morgan's death?"

Elle shook her head. "You know he wouldn't tell me anything about one of his cases."

"Technically it's not one of his cases. It's Southampton's."

"Well, I did overhear him saying that the coroner's report would be coming in sometime this morning. Can we make a pact? Let's not talk about it. I had the worst night. That poor sous chef's face kept appearing in my dreams. I lit a candle in her memory, and just as I was getting in bed, the candle blew out. You think it was a sign that she didn't die peacefully?"

"Was your husband anywhere near the candle?"

"No, he was snoring away. Nowhere near it."

"Was there an air vent above the candle?"

"Well . . ."

"Mystery solved."

"I want to believe you. Tonight, I'll light another candle. Far away from the AC vent. We'll see."

"Well, it's great that Arthur is getting info on Sasha's cause of death. That means he's still in the loop."

Elle gave me a sideways look. Then tsk-tsked me. "Why do we care about the autopsy? It was obvious what happened to Sasha. Especially after you told me how drunk she was. The only way I want to be involved is if the authorities focus their attention on Bethany because of her out-of-character actions on Friday night. Bethany just doesn't have it in her. I promise you."

I remembered the other parts of Friday evening. "You might be right, the blown-out candle could be a sign."

Her eyes opened wide. "You just said it was air from the vent. Do you ever take anything seriously?"

I hadn't wanted to tell Elle that last night I'd had my own tears and nightmares about Sasha. "Of course I do. I take vintage shopping very seriously. Now, let's get buying." I took a step backward and felt warm breath on my neck. Booth owner Rita was standing behind me.

She leaned toward Elle and said in a hushed tone, "Did I hear you talking about Jackie Fairchild? Are you friends?"

"Jackie's an acquaintance," I said. "Why?"

Rita turned her head and gave me a dubious look, "Well, if you run into your *friend*, tell her she owes me for the Black Jack Bouvier papers she took home for authentication. It's been a month. Not that I believe she's related to Black Jack's daughter, Jacqueline Kennedy Onassis. Now there was a lady. True American royalty and a huge collector of Americana."

"You knew Jackie O?" Elle asked excitedly.

"Of course. I knew, or know, everyone in the Hamptons, my dear. She was a frequent visitor to my shop when it first opened."

Elle's cheeks pinked with excitement.

"You just missed it," Rita said. "I just sold a whole lot of memorabilia that I'd purchased from a sale at Grey Gardens shortly before Edith Bouvier Beale's death."

"Wow!" Elle said. "You knew the famous mother and daughter, the subject of that documentary on Grey Gardens, and even a movie and Broadway play."

"I started to watch that documentary," Rita said. "I felt it was an invasion of their privacy. I turned it off after the first five minutes. Edith's daughter, who they called Little Edie, had been kind enough to invite me to the house before the sale started because once I'd rescued one of her cats. I live in the same neighborhood."

And what a neighborhood it was. No wonder Rita didn't care how high her prices were. If she lived in the same East Hampton oceanfront enclave as Grey Gardens, she was probably born with a platinum spoon in her mouth.

"How was Edith, the mother, related to Jackie O?" I asked.

"Edith was Jacqueline's aunt. Little Edie was Jacqueline's first cousin. Edith's brother was John Bouvier III, Jacqueline's father."

"Black Jack!" I said.

Rita peered over the top of her glasses at me. "Yes, Ms. Barrett. John Bouvier's nickname was Black Jack. And for all intents and purposes, he was a scoundrel."

"Why did they call Jaqueline Bouvier Kennedy Onassis's father Black Jack?" Elle asked.

"Boy, that's a mouthful," I couldn't help saying.

Rita snorted dismissively, then continued, "It seems pretty obvious that his nickname had something to do with gambling. John Bouvier was a stockbroker and an equal opportunity drinker and philanderer, living a flamboyant summer lifestyle at his East Hampton home, Wildmoor. Some of the photos I got from the Grey Gardens sale showed weekend polo matches on Wildmoor's grounds, others showed teenage Jacqueline when she came to visit her father during summer vacations. I could tell by some of the photos that young Jackie Bouvier had a close relationship with her father. There is one shot of Jacqueline atop her favorite horse, Danseuse, proudly holding up two victory horse show ribbons from the dressage category. Her father, Black Jack, is standing next to her and Danseuse, grinning with pride."

"So, the former first lady actually shopped at Grimes House Antiques," Elle said. "That's amazing."

"Before her death in the 1990s, Jacqueline would often stop in when she was in the Hamptons. Interior design was a passion of hers. Especially Americana. As for the other Jackie, Mrs. Jackie Fairchild, I don't believe she's related to any of the Bouviers. I already did a search with the head historian at the East Hampton Library, and we couldn't find anything that said she's related to John Bouvier. I should have never let those papers out of my sight. They belong in the Smithsonian."

"Let me get this right," I said. "Jackie Fairchild swindled you out of the same papers you believe belong in a museum?"

Rita looked at me from behind her round tortoiseshell glasses that magnified her owllike mud-brown eyes. "Move along, Ms. Barrett. Unless you're buying."

Thinking about the money in my bank account from my design services at Privé, I snatched an antique brass horse-head walking stick from an umbrella stand and said, "I am buying."

Rita tried to hide the look of surprise on her face but didn't hesitate to grab my debit card for the transaction.

Two hundred and fifty dollars later we stepped out of her booth. Rita called after us, "Ms. Barrett, I think you'll find a little surprise when you unscrew the horse-head handle."

As we walked away, Elle said, "What did she mean by that?"

I stopped and grabbed the walking stick from the cart, then carefully gripped the handle and turned it counterclockwise.

"Wow!" we both said at the same time. A sharp dagger-type knife was soldered to the horse's neck. Something straight out of a James Bond movie.

"That walking stick would be great to use in *Mr. & Mrs. Winslow*," Elle said. "Remember the scene we read in Patrick's screenplay where Lara Winslow's old Uncle Charles fights off a couple of assassins with his cane? Using the walking stick might make better theater."

"Good idea. I only bought it to prove I was monetarily as worthy as Rita's other upper-crust customers."

"You don't have to prove anything to anyone. You're always worthy in my book," Elle said, giving my shoulder a squeeze.

"Thanks, pal. Now, let's do what we really came here for. Shop until we drop, or at least until they let the general public in."

"Okay. But you went to the left at the last show. It's my turn!"

To cover more ground, Elle and I usually split up at estate sales, collectibles shows, and flea markets. There was a method to our madness. After many years of research, I believed there was a herd mentality when it came to which direction a crowd would start their browsing. Most people went to the right; hence, the reason Elle was so excited to go to the left. The road less traveled. And we always had each other's backs when it came to what the other collected, or was searching for, and would send out a text with the coordinates of the item.

"Ready, set, go!" I said, and we took off.

Three rows later, I saw it. A mannequin wearing a sequined 1930s dress worn by Bette Davis in a film whose title I couldn't recall. The earrings, bracelet, and necklace matched the dress perfectly, but I knew the jewelry hadn't been worn in the same movie as the dress. But the evening gown and jewelry did have one important thing in common: they belonged to Elle and were meant to be used on the set of *Mr. & Mrs. Winslow* in a scene where actress Zoe Stockton, who plays Lara Winslow, attends her niece's debutante ball and finds her brother-in-law face-first in the champagne fountain—dead as a proverbial doornail.

Instead of texting Elle, I called her.

Two minutes later we were grilling the booth owner on how she'd come upon the dress and jewelry. She'd told us that a beautiful actress who had won an Academy Award for her supporting role in *Scoundrel* had sold the dress and jewelry to her for twenty dollars, adding, "I thought the dress would be cute if I hemmed it above the knee and resold it. My mom's the best seamstress."

"Twenty dollars! Cut the dress!" Elle screeched. "Well, these items didn't belong to her. She had no right to sell them. They're mine."

The young woman put her hand to her mouth. "Are you saying Zoe Stockton is a thief? Is she stealing to feed that drug habit I read about in the tabloids when I was in line at the supermarket? Wait until I tell my friends!"

Before things got out of hand, I interjected, "No, of course not. Ms. Stockton isn't a thief. Nor a drug addict. I'm sure there's some kind of mix-up. How much are you selling the dress and jewelry for?"

When the dealer named her price of sixty dollars, Elle said, "Sold!" Elle pulled three twenties from her fanny pack. "What if I told you I paid five thousand dollars for the dress alone," she said, handing her the cash.

The dealer opened her mouth to speak but nothing came out.

As we walked away, Elle pulled me aside. "I can't believe Zoe would do something like this. What do you think? And the price she sold them for was so low. She must be desperate for money. She knows the worth of the costumes and accessories that I've loaned out for use on the set." Elle put the dress in her cart and the jewelry in her fanny pack. "We need to find her. I want a word with Ms. Stockton. And it won't be pretty."

Elle was Zoe's biggest fan. And vice versa. I glanced down at the crumpled dress at the bottom of Elle's cart. "You're right. Zoe knows all about the dresses star-quality provenance. So does Felicity, the set director, and Martha, the wardrobe designer. There has to be some kind of explanation."

"What possible explanation could there be? Do you think Zoe really does have a drug habit?" Elle asked, furrowing her brow.

"I don't believe anything those rags say about celebrities." What I didn't want to say was no one knew what people did in their private lives. It was concerning, but Elle had her dress and jewelry, and we had a football field of vintage to discover before the masses entered the show. "We better get crackin'. Vintage treasure waits for no one. We'll deal with the Zoe issue another day."

"Okay, Scarlett O'Hara, but remember, it wasn't you who's been swindled. I thought Zoe and I were friends. Let's split up again. But keep your eyes open for Zoe. Don't approach her. I will."

I gave her a salute. "Yes, ma'am!"

A burly guy, dressed like a lumberjack, came up to us with his mammoth chest puffed out and his hands in fists. "If you two don't plan on buying anything, move along. You're blocking the front of my booth. All the moneyed crowd is passing me by. You have no idea how much I shelled out for this small space."

Not one to be bullied, I stood up straighter and said, "Fine with us. And here I was about to ask you the price of that bayonet over there." I had no plans to purchase the lethal-looking thing. Plus, I already had the horse-head dagger. One antique weapon was enough. Once again, I was trying to prove I was as good as the other affluent early birders. Something I would have to ponder the next time I meditated on my beach.

The man soon changed his tune at the thought of his first sale of the day. He scurried over to a burled wood smoking table where a long-barrel shotgun with a bayonet was leaning. "My apologies, ladies. You sure know an antique when you see one. It's from the Civil War. I have the papers to prove it. Belonged to Yankee Corporal William Powell. It's in pristine condition for its age." He wore a huge smile that exposed a gold incisor that reflected the sun, salivating at the thought of selling the rusty thing.

Only that wasn't about to happen.

Elle marched over to where he stood and said, "What? Are you crazy?" Her elflike face was twisted in anger. If she'd been a cartoon character, steam would have been billowing out of her ears. "There's no way that gun and bayonet are from the Civil War. My guess is it came from the Prussian War. Plus, someone married the bayonet to the shotgun. And did a shoddy job of it, at that. See the new hardware." She huffed, then pointed.

Having at one time worked at Sotheby's as an Americana expert, Elle knew her stuff. But I was beginning to get concerned that she might pop the guy in the kisser, either that or pop the bulging blood vessel on her temple. And even though the guy was wider than he was taller, his muscled biceps told of daily workouts at the gym.

I stepped between them. "Elle, honey. Time to move on. Don't waste your time with this charlatan." I grabbed her elbow to pull her out of harm's way, but she wouldn't budge.

"See, I was right about you two," the man said with a growl. "You don't have the capital to shop at such an exclusive show, so you've decided to make up lies and aspersions to my expertise and character. Leave. Before I call security."

Elle wouldn't back down. "Do that, and I'll tell that man sitting over at that table there." She pointed. "You know, the guy with the white beard who happens to be one of the main appraisers on the *Antiques Road Show*, that you've got a shill operation going on here. I suppose you're touting that wood dough bowl over there as an American primitive. Well, it's not! It's a European repro!" Elle raised her voice loud enough to turn heads. Her jaw was clenched, and her cheeks were pink under a constellation of freckles that made her look ten years younger than she was.

My best friend was angry, and I didn't think it had anything to do with the shotgun or the dough bowl. More to do with actress Zoe Stockton's theft. I could count on one hand the times I'd seen her this way. I grabbed her wrist. "Come on, tiger, we better get moving or we'll miss out on all the good *authentic* stuff."

Reluctantly, Elle grabbed a hold of her cart and followed behind me.

We stopped at the end of the aisle and I asked, "Are you okay?"

"Yes, or at least I will be as soon as I get my mitts on Zoe." She stuck out her chin, took off her baseball cap, then, shielding her eyes from the sun with her right hand, she searched the crowd.

I was afraid to leave her alone. "Hey, buddy. Let's do something different this time. Let's walk the show together. Remember, there's nothing either one of us could possibly need. And we both know what holes need to be filled for *Mr. & Mrs. Winslow*'s next scene."

She smiled. "You know that vintage shopping has nothing to do with need."

"I agree. But just a little reminder. We have all those boxes to go through from Privé. Twenty-seven to be exact."

"You're right," she said as we continued down the next aisle. "But if I see Zoe, you might need to restrain me. You don't want to know what I'll do if I catch the star from *Mr. & Mrs. Winslow* trying to pawn off some of my other items. Also, keep your eyes peeled for any furniture or smalls she might have swiped from the set."

"I've got your back. However, remember, innocent until proven guilty. Maybe Jeremy Prentice, our illustrious cheapskate producer, sent her out to raise some capital. You know what a tightwad he is."

"He'd never go that far. And if he did, he wouldn't use the star of his miniseries to be his middleman. Just think of the bad press."

I shrugged my shoulders and surveyed the booths. Instead of setting my sights on an antique treasure, they landed on Zoe Stockton's tall form. She stood at the end of the aisle, handing off a vase to a dealer who in exchange handed her back a pile of cash.

"Look!" I pointed in Zoe's direction. Before I could stop her, Elle was off.

I couldn't follow as fast as I wanted because Elle had left her cart behind. I grabbed both hers and mine, then called out as I parted the expensively perfumed crowd, "Coming through. Small emergency!"

When I reached the dealer who'd given Zoe the cash, I asked, "Did you see in which direction that tall woman just went?"

"What woman?" she asked with a smile. Even though her face and neck were covered in a subway map of wrinkles, her classic beauty shined through. Her white hair was pulled back in a French twist and the emerald ring that sparkled on her wedding finger was the same color as her eyes.

"The one who gave you that Rookwood Pottery vase." I pointed to where it stood behind her on a small table.

"I have no idea where she went, my dear. But isn't she a beauty?" She turned, reached for the vase, then turned back to me, swaddling it in her hands like it was a precious crown jewel. "An exquisite example of Edward Diers's scenic tree vellums."

"What are you asking for it?"

"If I did put a retail price on it, it would be around seventeen hundred dollars. But it's going straight into my personal collection."

I was in a quandary. I didn't want to involve the police, and I needed to track down Elle before she did something to Zoe that she might regret. I grabbed the woman's business card—luckily, she was local. Elle's cop husband could take care of the legal ramifications later. Before going in search of Elle and Zoe, I asked the woman one more question. "How much did you pay for the vase?"

Her eyes opened wide in surprise. "She only wanted twenty dollars. But my conscience wouldn't let me buy it for such a low price. I gave her two hundred. The young woman nearly collapsed on the ground. If you're interested in anything else, please let me know." She turned and went to assist a potential customer examining a pair of Staffordshire china dogs, reminding me of the bulldog figurine Sasha had thrown at Noah Fairchild last night. Not a scene I relished remembering.

I grabbed both carts and scurried off in search of Elle and Zoe.

As usual, things weren't going as planned . . .

Chapter 11

Thirty minutes later, I found Elle sitting at a table under a white tent with a Bloody Mary in her hand. "I lost her," she said, looking defeated.

"Well, she couldn't have gone far."

Elle stuck out her delicate chin. "We'll go to Windy Willows this instant and see if she's there."

"We aren't filming until next week. No one will be there."

"Our producer might."

"He'll never disclose what Hamptons estate Zoe's renting."

"I'm sure I can persuade *Mr. & Mrs. Winslow*'s producer to give us her address. Or I'll threaten legal action. Plus, who knows, Zoe might be there lurking around in the mansion's shadows. Pilfering more antiques and vintage."

"Lurking? Sorry, I have a hard time picturing beautiful, confident Zoe Stockton lurking."

"Maybe she got fired from the miniseries?"

"That's impossible; they're still working on the second episode. And she's a main character. We better tread lightly. We don't want to be the ones getting fired from our positions of helping Felicity with the set décor and assisting Martha with the costume design. We just got our union cards and we're making union wages. All thanks to Felicity."

"Ugh," Elle said.

"My sentiments exactly."

"What did that dealer tell you about the vase Zoe sold her?" Elle asked, her eyes pooling with moisture and defiant at the same time.

I filled her in as delicately as possible, then said, "Since when do you drink alcohol at . . ." I glanced at my watch. "Nine in the morning." I took Elle's plastic cup from her hand, nibbled at the stalk of celery, then took a sip of the Bloody Mary.

"It's a virgin," Elle said, laughing. "Though I did consider the other option. But I need my wits for when we find Zoe."

I handed her the cup. "So, what's the plan? Confront her without backup?"

"I'll have you for backup."

"What about your hubby?"

"He's got enough on his plate. Anyway, you never needed the police before to get you out of one of your predicaments. Why should this be different?"

"Not exactly true. East Hampton Town PD's Morgana Moss did come in handy last spring," I said.

"I'll say." Elle got up and threw her cup in a recycle bin. "There's no danger involved. We're talking stolen goods, not murder. It will be a nice change. Let's go catch a thief." She came next to me and grabbed the handle of her cart and I followed her down the center aisle, through the open gates leading out of the show, and into the parking lot.

While we were exiting, the general public was still waiting outside to be let in. They would be paying only a fraction of what Elle had paid for our early-bird tickets. As we passed by, Michelle Foster, a former Cottages by the Sea client, called out, "What's wrong, Meg? Nothing worth buying?"

I looked down at my cart, which only held the horse-head walking stick. She was right, I couldn't recall in recent memory ever leaving a show with only one item. Then I glanced at Elle's cart with the crumpled dress at the bottom.

"Is it worth going inside? Is it too pricey?" someone else called out.

"Definitely a great show," I said. "We had to leave something for you guys. Happy finds."

Because of Oscar winner Zoe Stockton's exploits, the tickets hadn't been worth the ink they'd been printed with.

We'd decided to leave Elle's pickup in the Community House's parking lot in case we wanted to come back for another go before the show closed at five. I'd forgotten to ask Rita about the price of the brass spyglass I wanted to buy for Patrick. I prayed it would still be there if we did return.

Shopping the last hours of an antiques and collectibles show was always a crap shoot. The best vintage would be taken, but seeing Elle and I loved refurbishing vintage castoffs almost as much as buying the cream of the crop, I'd found the end of the show was prime time to score bargains. Most dealers would take lowball offers, especially those with large pieces of furniture they didn't relish loading into their vans and carting back to their storage units. Glassware and china was another category where dealers were willing to negotiate prices. They didn't want the hassle of individually bubble wrapping each piece and packing them away for the next show on their circuit—praying they didn't break on the journey.

A couple minutes later, we peeled out of the Community House parking lot. I saw there was still a line of people, mostly men, *real* men, waiting in line to sample Cutler's Meat Wagons fare. I turned left on School Street, then took another quick left onto Bridgehampton's main street. Traffic was heavy as usual, with both sides of Main Street packed with throngs of tourists and summer people, most of them toting shopping bags. The quaint hamlet was set up much like its big sister East Hampton: tree-lined streets, New England architecture, and mostly white or natural cedar shake façades sporting white window boxes overflowing with late-summer flowers and foliage. The only difference between the two hamlets was that Bridgehampton had more art galleries and home décor shops than East Hampton. And East Hampton had more restaurants, clothing, and jewelry shops.

When we reached Windy Willows, the oceanfront estate the production team of *Mr. & Mrs. Winslow* had rented to film the miniseries, no one was there—not even Brian the caretaker. After stopping at a yard sale, where Elle found a vintage fifties rhinestone brooch to add to her collection of five or six hundred, I convinced her we needed a break, and we headed to the Bridgehampton Candy Kitchen. Nothing like a malted or a milkshake and grilled cheese, while sitting at the old soda jerk counter, to cheer a person up. Two well-done extra-cheesy grilled cheeses later, I wasn't sure the meal worked on Elle, but it had certainly worked for me.

As we left the Candy Kitchen's parking lot, Elle was still going on about Zoe Stockton's thievery. "Legally, that dealer with the Rookwood vase is in possession of stolen goods. Did you get her business card?"

"Yes."

"Everyone has their price," Elle mused. "Except for you, Megan Barrett. I still think you should reconsider selling Rita the apothecary cabinet I bought for your cottage's housewarming gift.

She needs a replacement for the one the governor's wife bought from her shop. She's willing to pay double what I paid for it. We could always find another."

"Are you kidding?" I stopped the car at the pedestrian crosswalk to let a group of lanky model types cross the street, then looked over at her. "That cabinet was my best gift ever! And it came from you. I wouldn't sell it to Rita for any price. Like you, the cabinet is priceless."

"Aww, shucks, you'll make me blush. Felicity is going to be heartbroken about that vase Zoe stole. You know the way they film their scenes out of sequence. It's important to keep *Mr. & Mrs. Winslow's* set the exact way it was staged in the first scene, all the way until the last one is in the can."

"In the can? Love the movie lingo you're picking up. But I'm not sure anyone watching the miniseries will notice a disappearing then reappearing vase."

"You would."

"True," I said. "Something about having a hearing loss keeps me more in tune to visual clues."

"Eagle-eye Barrett," Elle said.

"So, what do you want to do now?" I asked.

"We have plenty of time to go back to the show," Elle said. "But first, I have a favor to ask. Seeing that we are so close to Garnier Winery, I wouldn't mind stopping by to check on Bethany. I think after everything that happened yesterday I should be the one to tell her about Privé's sous chef."

"If she doesn't already know."

"Arthur said they weren't releasing anything. They're having a hard time finding her next of kin and still waiting for the autopsy report to be finalized."

"It's sad to think the police can't find Sasha's family. Wouldn't Lee Cutler know?"

Elle shrugged her shoulders. "I'll make it quick. Promise."

"I don't know her as well as you. But you didn't see her face as she was choking Sasha."

"Even more reason to check on her. I've known her for twenty-five years. During the summer when I stayed with Aunt Mabel, Bethany and I would go up on the widow's walk and have tea parties with a pair of antique bisque dolls we hijacked from Great-Aunt Mabel's shop."

"I didn't know you spent your childhood summers in Sag Harbor. Lucky you."

"Oh, yes. Some of the best of my life."

I thought back to my summers in Traverse City, Michigan, and felt the same way. "Okay, we'll stop by. But maybe I should wait in the car. You talk to her. I don't think I'm her favorite person at this point."

"Okay. I'll make it quick."

Five minutes later we pulled into the gravel driveway of the winery. I lucked out and got the last available spot. Shoppers were exiting the barn with bottles of wine in shopping bags, some holding cases. Business was booming. The main barn was where the wine tasting took place and next to the barn was a gift and wine shop. The retail side of the winery was located on the east side of Route 27. On the west side of the highway, there was row after row of Garnier Winery grapevines lush with fruit to be harvested. I knew from a wine tour I'd gone on with Elle when we were scouring the North Fork of Long Island for vintage and antiques that September was when the white grapes would be ripe, and usually October for the reds.

"I still can't understand why Bethany is so upset about Privé," I said as Elle opened the door to get out of the car. "Did she ever mention it to you?"

Elle stuck her head inside the car. "No. We haven't been in touch recently. You know: wedding, honeymoon, *Mr. & Mrs. Winslow.* But I plan to make up for it. I'll be right back."

I watched her walk away, thinking how lucky I was, and for that matter Bethany was, to have a friend like Elle.

While I waited, I killed ten minutes searching online marketplaces for items to go into the cottage at Privé. I knew there were more than a few pieces of furniture in Elle's carriage house that we'd scored on a trip to the Adirondacks that would be perfect for the rustic vibe Lee Cutler was going for. I was also cognizant of the fact he might be even more picky with my choices than Jackie had been—if that was possible.

Ten minutes passed, so I moved on to searching my phone's

browser for any kind of news release about Sasha Morgan's death. Nothing. Then I switched gears and went to my friend Barb's website, SandandSunRealtyMontauk.com. I smiled thinking about the good news that Elle and her hubby were going to look for a place to live nearby. But before the page could load, there was a loud rapping at my driver's-side window.

Startled, my phone flew up in the air. I caught it, then rolled down the window to see Elle's flushed face. "Come quick!" Then without saying anything more, she ran toward the barn.

I grabbed my handbag, jumped out of the car, and sped after her. *Now what?*

When I entered the wine-tasting barn, I saw that it was packed. Elle stood next to a door on the far side of the room, beyond the high-top bench-type tables. I hurried toward her, then, bending at the knees and out of breath, I wheezed, "What's wrong?"

"Arthur just called. They're going to bring Bethany in for questioning about a murder."

"Murder!" I repeated. Then I stupidly asked, "Whose?"

"Sasha's."

"Holy cow!"

"There wasn't time to ask Arthur any details," Elle said. "But I did tell Bethany that she needed to call a lawyer. She doesn't have them on speed dial like you do. Trust me, Bethany's not a killer. Southampton PD should be arriving in about a half hour to take her in for questioning. I need you to call your friend and attorney Justin Marguilles. Ask him to represent Bethany. He's the best in the Hamptons."

"If they're only taking her in for questioning, why does she need a lawyer?"

"Arthur said it's better to be safe than sorry."

"How was Sasha murdered?"

"I don't know any details, and Arthur made it very clear that we can't tell anyone that he'd warned us about Bethany being taken in."

"She told us Friday night before she went for Sasha's neck that she had a lawyer and was starting a lawsuit against Privé."

"Not a criminal lawyer. She's a wreck. You've been in similar circumstances. Maybe after you call Mr. Marguilles, you can calm her down."

I was about to protest about getting involved but Elle was right, I'd had my share of being questioned by the police. But usually as a witness, not a suspect. Then I remembered that I'd also been at Privé the night Sasha died. Or, I should say, was murdered. Depending on the details of the autopsy, I might need my own lawyer. "Okay, I'll call."

Relief swept across Elle's face.

I placed the call and got through to Justin, who happened to be out of the country and not planning on coming back to the Hamptons until after the winter holidays. He gave me the number of someone he said was a good friend. Then he'd chuckled and said, "He's the *second-best* lawyer in the Hamptons." I thanked Justin and placed a call to Howard Rudolph, who'd immediately answered and reassured me that he would be at the winery in ten minutes. He was just down the road at the Bridgehampton Art and Antiques Show.

What were the chances?

It looked like it was Bethany's lucky day.

Well, maybe not.

Chapter 12

When we entered the stockroom of the wine-tasting barn, Bethany was sitting in a swivel desk chair with her back to us, looking out a window that had a view of the pond.

There wasn't time to waste before Howard Rudolf arrived, so I blurted out, "Bethany, why do you think the police want to question you?"

She wheeled around and I saw that she'd been gnawing on her bottom lip. She licked away the pinpricks of blood and said defiantly, "I've no clue. I had nothing to do with Sasha's death. They can't blame me for that mild choking I gave her."

Mild choking? It was true that when I'd seen Sasha on the Josephine chaise in the Provence Suite there'd been no marks on her neck, and she'd been very much alive when she chucked the china bulldog at Noah's head.

"I saw security cameras when I used my key to get in Friday night," Bethany said. "They'll see exactly when I came in and when I went out. Elle just told me Sasha was found in the walk-in freezer. I wouldn't even know where the freezer was. I never set foot in Maison Garnier's, I mean, pretentious Privé's new kitchen."

So, there it was. Even with Sasha's death, which obviously wasn't accidental, Bethany was still upset about the ownership of Privé.

"Then why do you think they want to take you in?" I repeated. Elle gave me a piercing look, but I held my ground. We were minutes away from Bethany's new attorney arriving.

Instead of answering, Bethany looked at me and said, "I wonder who told them I was there Friday night?"

I shook my head in the negative.

"Meg would never do that," Elle assured her.

Bethany glanced at Elle, then back at me, not quite meeting my gaze. "What will happen to Chardonnay if I'm arrested? She's all I have after Tom passed." Bethany began to cry, and Elle went over to comfort her.

"Chardonnay?" I asked.

"Her malti-poo," Elle said. "Bethany got her from Officer Morgana

Moss a couple years ago when Morgana was breeding Maltese poodles before joining Montauk's East Hampton Town PD.

"Oh," I said, thinking it was too bad pets can't offer alibis.

"Don't you worry about Char," Elle said, "Meg or I will take care of her."

Now it was my turn to give Elle a dirty look.

Bethany wheeled herself back to the multipaned window that looked out to the pond separating the winery from Privé. Without turning around, she said, "By the way, Meg, you did a terrific job on the interior of Maison Garnier. If only Gramps could have seen it. The blue room used to be his study. Many a Sunday afternoon . . ."

I didn't buy into her saccharin-sweet change of heart about my decorating prowess. Sasha Morgan had been murdered, and like the police, I still believed Bethany should be at the top of the suspect list. But then I glanced over at Elle. Bethany was her friend. Not just any friend, but a childhood friend. I had to give her the benefit of the doubt. And Bethany wasn't the only one who had issues with Sasha. Starting with her boyfriend, Lee. Why hadn't he driven Sasha home Friday evening? Maybe he'd come by and they'd gotten into an argument. Noah and Jackie each had their own issues with Sasha. Jackie was upset about something concerning Sasha and Noah. And the gash on Noah's temple from the china bulldog was proof he had a motive to kill her. And finally, there was Kelsie. It seemed doubtful Kelsie would murder Sasha because she was a substandard sous chef. But the way Kelsie screamed, bullied, and carried on in the kitchen Friday night seemed out of character for the Kelsie I'd thought I'd known. If there was one thing I'd learned from my father, when it came to murder, motive was as individual as fingerprints. It would be a process of elimination. But, until we knew Sasha's cause of death—oops, I used the word *we*—until the *police* disclosed why they were bringing Bethany in, her lawyer would have to take over the job of protecting her.

I was willing to stay out it. But was Elle?

"You know, a lot of weird stuff has been going on over there," Bethany said, getting up from the chair and peeking into the wine-tasting room. She turned back to us and said in a whisper that had me reading her lips, "At least once a week. Lights on at all hours. Cars in the parking lot after midnight. I even saw a limo parked there a couple days ago. I'm not just talking three or four cars. I'm talking ten or more."

"You can see the two parking lots from here?" Elle asked.

"No, I took my kayak over there. I couldn't get close enough to peek inside because of a pair of huge snarling dogs that were chained to a lamppost by the front door. That's the only door that I have a key to."

There was that handy key again. If I was one of the partners, I would change the locks. I knew they'd been pretty picky about who had a key when I'd been working at the farmhouse. Neither I nor Duke of Duke Jr. Construction could keep the key overnight. It had been in a lock box at the rear of the farmhouse with a code that changed every day. Sasha had also delivered a strange warning Friday night about something going on after hours.

"You wouldn't happen to have an extra key you could loan me?" Elle asked Bethany. "Meg and I can do our own late-night investigating."

Just when I'd decided to stay out of it, Elle decided to dive in headfirst.

"Sure. I have extra copies." Bethany walked over to an open antique rolltop desk, pulled out the drawer, then retrieved a set of labeled keys. I outstretched my right hand to take them but instead of putting the keys in my hands, she handed them to Elle, then gave me a triumphant glare. I still wasn't to be trusted.

Two could play this game. "Is that how you got to Privé Friday night?" I asked. "You took a kayak across the pond?"

"No. I took my Tesla. Why does that matter?"

I was slightly relieved. The black car I saw tearing out of Privé yesterday morning was definitely an SUV.

Elle slipped the key chain into her handbag and asked, "Bethany, how long has this nighttime activity been going on?"

"About a month."

I was floored that things were going on at Privé after I'd left for the day. That explained a few things that'd had me puzzled. I'd thought Jackie had been rearranging some of the décor because she hadn't liked my staging. Were the partners holding their own private membership drive?

"Bethany, I think we should go outside and wait for your

lawyer," Elle said gently. "We don't want any of your patrons or staff observing what is obviously a miscarriage of justice. I'm sorry. I know if this case was in my husband's jurisdiction, he'd simply ask you to come down to the station on your own accord."

"Please thank him for the heads-up and for getting me the best lawyer."

"That wasn't Arthur. Meg is the one who got Mr. Rudolph."

I waited for my thank-you, but nothing came. Was Bethany still harboring resentments about my part in the remodel and décor of her old family farmhouse?

When we reached the parking lot, Elle asked Bethany, "Why did you sell the property if you have such an attachment to it? Are you having financial problems? I'm not prying, but it might help to know why you're so upset about the sale."

Bethany didn't respond, just broke into heartbreaking sobs. Finally, she managed, "I'm not having financial problems. If I could have had the farmhouse zoned commercial, like those thieves at Privé did, I would have built the best farm-to-table and vine-to-table eating establishment on the East End of Long Island. It had always been Tom's dream. Now it's my dream. I tried every avenue possible to get the farmhouse zoned commercial, but was told no at every turn. There was no sense sinking money into the farmhouse and making it my residence when I already have a beautiful oceanfront home. A home I shared with Tom 'til his last dying breath. He was happy there. So, I decided to sell the farmhouse and use the profits to build the restaurant we dreamed of on our property across the road."

"One last thing," I said. I'd debated on even asking but knew if she was arrested for Sasha's murder it might be the last time we got a chance to talk to her. "Did you find out your husband had been having an affair with Sasha Morgan when she worked here at the winery?"

"Who told you that!" Bethany screeched, turning the heads of shoppers coming out of the winery's gift shop. "Tom would never cheat on me," she said through gritted teeth. "We found out Sasha had been stealing unlabeled wine and reselling it online with her own label, *Sasha's Private Stash.*"

"Then how did she get a job as a sous chef at Privé?" Elle asked.

"I'm sure she didn't give Garnier Vineyards as a reference." Elle took out a tissue from her handbag and handed it to Bethany. "Was Sasha prosecuted?"

"No. She wasn't prosecuted. Tom wouldn't let me. He got her to pay us back every penny she made from the wine she pilfered. Plus, we couldn't call the police because she sort of blackmailed us."

Sort of? "What kind of blackmail?" I asked as the plot coagulated.

"Sasha knew we'd sold unlabeled bottles of wine to a local winery who'd had a bad harvest. She said she would contact *Dave's Hamptons* and have them do an expose on Garnier Winery and East End Winery. East End Winery did the same for us one year when we had a poor crop. It was nothing punishable under law because the fine print on the labels would have either their or our name and address and the original origin of the grapes. But if it ever got out, it would hurt both of our reputations."

"Oh, Bethany, that's terrible," Elle said.

I reiterated the first half of Elle's question. "Then how did she get the job at Privé?"

"How do you think? The same person who ponied up the cash to pay for the wine she'd stolen and sold online must have had something to do with getting her hired."

"Who do you think that was?" I asked, betting on Lee Cutler.

Bethany opened her mouth to answer just as a man walked toward us. By the way he was dressed and his confident nature, I assumed he was the lawyer that Justin Marguilles had recommended.

I took a step toward him. "Mr. Rudolph?"

"Yes."

"I'm Meg Barrett. I'm the one who called and asked you to represent Bethany Garnier. Thanks for coming so quickly."

Howard Rudolph was of the same ilk as Justin Marguilles. He made an impressive figure in his hand-tailored suit, which I guessed was Ralph Lauren. His white dress shirt had monogrammed French cuffs with platinum cufflinks in the shape of a Labrador retriever, and when a gust of wind blew up his tie, I could see the name Hermès printed below the logo of a horse pulling a cart. His tie coordinated with the expertly folded Hermès pocket square in his suit coat pocket. He wore Gucci loafers, no socks, adding a small degree of casual to his look.

Bethany's new lawyer handed each of us his business card. *Howard M. Rudolph* was embossed in raised gold letters. As he pulled his hand away, a ray of sunlight reflected off the gleaming platinum of his Rolex. He caught me looking at his wrist and said with a winning smile, "That's why my wife Julie and I were at the antiques show. I collect vintage watches and she collects estate jewelry."

A couple after my own heart, I thought.

"Now, let's get down to business," he said, his clear green eyes focusing on Bethany. "Why am I here?" Even though he dressed like he was one of the social elite, his smile and down-to-earth manner made me immediately like and trust him.

Both Bethany and Elle remained mute. It wasn't my tale to tell, but I did anyway. I left out the part where Bethany said she'd toyed with returning to Privé later Friday night to break into their wine cellar and bust up their stock of French wine and champagne.

As I was talking, a Southampton patrol car pulled into the winery's parking lot. Howard quickly asked Bethany, "Where were you between midnight and three yesterday morning?"

Boy, he was on top of things. Obviously, he'd already talked to Southampton PD. Or it was possible the case had already gone to Suffolk County Homicide. Either way, Bethany should be reassured that she was in good hands.

"I was uh, alone," Bethany mumbled, nervously rubbing her palms together like they needed warming. "I did talk to my sister on video chat sometime after midnight. She has a way of grounding me. That's good, isn't it? She would be on my call log. I know we talked for a couple of hours. As I was just telling Elle and Meg, you have no idea what's been going on over at Privé."

Howard raised his eyebrows. "Privé?"

I explained about the dining club but didn't mention my part in the interior design. Why complicate things?

Bethany continued, "Late-night meetings, lights on till all hours. If I didn't know better, I would say pretentious Privé was haunted. Maybe Grandpa's ghost is causing a ruckus," she said, adding a weak laugh.

Howard looked confused at the mention of *Grandpa*.

"I'm not going to be arrested, am I?" Bethany sniffled.

Before Howard could answer, two male officers got out of a squad car and walked toward us.

Howard nodded his head at the taller of the two. "Josh, how's the baby? I owe you a cigar."

Officer Josh grinned. "He's amazing."

Howard put his hand on Bethany's shoulder. "Josh, Ms. Garnier has hired me to represent her." He turned to Bethany and gave her a reassuring smile. "Everything will be fine, Ms. Garnier. Just don't say anything until I get there."

Relief showed on Bethany's face. "I won't. I promise. Thank you, Mr. Rudolph."

"Howard," he said.

"Howard," she repeated.

We watched Bethany get in the back of the squad car. She seemed in much better shape than before her attorney had arrived.

Howard started toward his car, then turned back, and said, "I suggest that going forward you two don't discuss anything about Ms. Sasha Morgan's death until I have a chat with my client and the powers that be."

"We won't," Elle promised. "And thank you."

"My pleasure. Your friend is in good hands." Then he strode away toward a navy SUV.

"Wow!" I said, adding a whistle. "Bethany's attorney sure has nice wheels. A GMC Yukon XL Denali."

"How do you know all that?" Elle asked.

"Really, you're asking a born and bred Detroiter that question? Plus, I looked into getting one before I got my custom-made Woody. But even with my father's Motor City connections the Denali was too pricey." Thinking about Howard's SUV, I realized something. If Sasha's time of death was between one and three in the morning, the person tearing out of the parking lot yesterday morning couldn't have been the killer. Unless they'd picked a suite in the farmhouse, curled up on one of the sofas, and dozed off.

As the Denali pulled away, Elle said, "That must be his wife, Julie. Wow, she's stunning."

Through the open passenger window, I glimpsed a gorgeous

woman with long, glossy black hair and a perfect profile. I said, "How cool is it that they like to go vintage shopping together. Now that's a marriage made in heaven."

"Speaking of shopping. We still have a couple hours before the antiques show closes."

"I thought you'd want to follow Bethany to the police station," I said as we started toward my car.

"Arthur would be furious if I did. Come on, it'll be a good distraction."

I didn't argue, even though I knew Elle's true motive for returning to the show was to see if Zoe Stockton was selling more things from the set of *Mr. & Mrs. Winslow*. "I'll go. But you have to promise you won't attack Zoe and end up having me or Arthur bail you out of jail."

"I have no idea what you're talking about," Elle said with a sly grin. "We have to find things to go into the cottage at Privé, right?"

"Yeah, right."

Chapter 13

Thankfully, we didn't run into Zoe Stockton or come across any other items swiped from the set of *Mr. & Mrs. Winslow* at the antiques show. On our way to the parking lot with our carts filled with loot, Elle got a call from Bethany saying that thanks to Howard Rudolph she was back at the winery, and so far no charges were being filed. Elle's last words to Bethany were, "You're innocent. Don't you worry. Meg and I are on the case. Just listen to your lawyer and everything will be fine."

Like a proverbial dog to its bone, Elle was committed to keeping Bethany out of jail. I prayed this time I would be the one riding shotgun, ready to throw out pearls of wisdom from my experience with local Hampton homicides, while at the same time savvy enough to stay out of the line of fire.

Who was I kidding?

I left Bridgehampton with Elle following me in her pickup. At my cottage, she helped me unload a late 1800s French country cabinet with layers and layers of chippy robin's-egg blue paint from the back of her pickup and onto a furniture dolly. As I watched her pull away, I realized I could've used her help steadying the cabinet over the rutted trail leading to my folly/design studio.

"You can do this!" I said to myself as I maneuvered the cabinet through the wooded area behind my walled cottage garden. Of course, because my hands were full, I felt my phone vibrate, telling me I had a text message. I knew it wasn't Elle because she never texted while driving. She planned to go to Sagaponack and check on Bethany, twenty miles away. I smiled, thinking it might be Patrick and felt an adrenaline rush.

After a little, no, a lot of blood, sweat, and yes, a few tears, I managed to get the cabinet inside the folly.

Technically, I'd moved into the folly before my cottage. A couple years ago, when my lease was up on my rental cottage and I was in the market for a new home, my friend and realtor Barb Moss sent me out to see the old Eberhardt property. As soon as I stepped foot on the undisturbed oceanfront property with its ramshackle cottage and walled garden, I knew I had to buy it. The white wrought iron and glass Queen Anne folly, hidden behind a copse of trees, was the property's icing on the cake. Come hell or high water, I'd been determined to buy it. Hell had come first with the seemingly impossible task of getting permits from the East Hampton Town Zoning Board. But there was a happy ending to my story because now I was the proud owner of my own little cozy slice of paradise. And I would be grateful 'til my dying day.

The interior of the folly was filled with mostly salvaged items. I'd created a makeshift table/potting bench by setting an aqua carriage house door that was worn and faded from years of salt air and sun on top of two wooden electrical spools. Both the door and the spools had been found abandoned on the side of the Long Island Rail Road tracks. At the rear of the folly was a wrought iron settee with a Colfax and Fowler fabric cushion. I'd added a pair of Colfax and Fowler pillows in a contrasting pattern, knowing it was a design no-no to play matchy-matchy with your cushions and pillows.

I scanned the space and realized the only possible place for the French cabinet was next to the settee. I wheeled it over, keeping the cabinet secured to the trolley until I could get assistance to take it off. It was a two-man job. More like a one-woman and one-man job, and that man would be Patrick Seaton. Which would give me a reason to see his handsome face while playing damsel in distress — a ploy he'd never fall for.

At the antiques show, I'd purchased the brass spyglass I'd seen earlier in Rita's booth. Its prohibitive price was probably the sole reason no one else had snatched it up. I'd had to bite my tongue not to ask Rita for a better deal but knew Patrick would love it. One thing about Rita, she knew her antiques and usually the provenance behind them. I was confident that as the price tag read, the spyglass was from the early nineteenth century. A couple years ago I'd purchased a brass spyglass at a Brooklyn flea market and found out the hard way that spyglasses were one of the most faked antiques in the twentieth century. However, just because an item was a reproduction, that didn't mean it wouldn't make a nice display piece. The repro spyglass eventually found its way onto one of my clients' mantels, next to a nineteenth-century oil seascape.

My pocket vibrated again, reminding me of my unanswered text. I sat at my rescued-from-a-Dumpster drafting table that I used as a desk, pulled out my phone, and read: *Meet me at Sarabeth's on the Bay. 8. Bring plans. L. Cutler.*

Holy smokes! Even after finding out about his girlfriend's death, Lee still planned on meeting me. Was it possible that the police didn't know the dynamics between Sasha and the partners at Privé? They obviously knew about Bethany choking Sasha, and I was sure they'd eventually call me in for questioning. In the meantime, there was only one thing to do, call Detective Arthur Shoner of the East Hampton Town PD.

Arthur didn't pick up. I left a lengthy message about what had gone down on Friday night, ending with, "Do you believe Lee Cutler still wants to meet with me? If I do meet him, am I in danger? And please share why the police think it was murder." I hung up, then called back and left another message. "I'm meeting him at eight, at a restaurant called Sarabeth's on the Bay in Watermill." Then I added, "See, I'm being responsible by letting you know." I hung up for the second time, refusing to analyze if I was more excited about getting info on Lee and Sasha or relieved that I still had the job of decorating the cottage despite the murder at Privé. I was pretty sure it was the first. I would take one for the team, especially knowing that the reviews for Sarabeth's were five stars across the board. The restaurant was at the top of my list to take my gourmet home chef foodie father the next time he came to town.

When I punched the restaurant's address into my GPS, I saw that it was a twenty-three-mile trip from Montauk to Watermill via Highway 27. Translated into time, especially with all the traffic during the last weekend of the summer season, I'd be lucky to get there in an hour.

It was close to sunset. A soft light filtered through the folly's rippled panes of glass. I opened my laptop, tweaked the plans for the cottage at Privé, then printed them out. Before putting the pages into my leather portfolio, I glanced at them. I was happy with the new interior design software I'd recently purchased and *fairly* confident that Lee wouldn't have a problem with them. If he did, I would listen. My client's aesthetic overruled mine. If I didn't think I could deliver what he wanted, I would recommend someone else who could, then walk away with my head held high.

I looked at my watch and realized I had a lot to do before it was time to *meet* the *meat*man. I was in the midst of shutting down my laptop when there came a rapping on the folly's glass door. Startled, I ratcheted my head to the right and breathed a sigh of relief when I saw my next-door neighbor Claire standing in the twilight. Claire lived in a cottage we'd nicknamed Little Grey. Little Grey had been built by James Greenleaf Thorpe, the same architect who'd built the famous, more like infamous, Grey Gardens in East Hampton. Thinking about the Beales, I wondered if Jackie Fairchild's claims were true that she was a distant cousin to the long-deceased mother-daughter pair. Which in turn made me think of Jackie F, not Jackie O, as being a murder suspect.

"Come on in," I called out.

She stepped inside and said, "So glad I caught you." Claire's dark green eyes met mine. Like Patrick, she was also a member of the Dead Poets Society Book Club. I knew Claire thought she was the reason that I'd joined the small group, but Patrick had been the bigger reason. Long before the club existed, Patrick and I had been playing pen pals in the sand—volleying dead poets' quotes back and forth like two pros.

Claire pranced over to the French cabinet, her long skirt swishing as she passed. "Wow, what a beauty," she said, running her hands over the smooth wood. "I see you did well at the show. Did you score any cloth-and-gilt antique books for your collection?"

"As a matter of fact, I did. One by William Cullen Bryant. Pristine condition. Only thirty bucks."

"Good for you. No Elizabeth Barrett Brownings, our next dead poet?"

"Sadly, no. But I do have a few of hers on the shelf in my secret room. Feel free to borrow, any time."

"Thanks. That's the reason I'm here, I wanted to let you know where the next Dead Poets Society Book Club will be meeting. Boris wants to have it."

"Our new male member," I said. "Hey, isn't it my turn in the rotation?"

"Well, yes—" Claire rubbed her hands nervously over her long gauzy cotton skirt. In her twenties Claire had danced with the San Francisco Ballet Company until she got in a motorcycle accident that left her right leg scarred. Which was the reason, forty-something years later, that no matter what the weather Claire only wore floor-length skirts. The accident was the impetus for her turning into an introspective award-winning poet. Her bound poetry collections, including her first book, *Tiger by the Tail*, had been reprinted and translated worldwide, even earning her the title of Poet Laureate. I'd lucked out having her as my neighbor. Sitting at her kitchen table, not only did she provide me cup after cup of herbal tea, but also cups of wisdom.

"Boris wants to make some of his famous borsht. Plus," she added with a grin, "I think we're still recovering from the last meal you served us."

"Ha, ha. Funny. Patrick helped me. It came out fine."

She laughed and a lock of long dark wavy hair streaked with strands of gray fell in front of her eyes. "I'm just teasing. I thought having Boris hosting might take the pressure off until you're finished with the restaurant." When Claire talked, she always used her arms and hands in big sweeping gestures, her hands cupped ballerina style.

"I am relieved. And it's not really a restaurant, more of a high-end gourmet club."

"I heard Kelsie left Pondfare to become the chef de cuisine. I hope it's not too much for her."

"Why do you say that?"

Claire hesitated.

Claire had also met Kelsie at knitting class. She wasn't one for gossip, but I hoped after I told her about Sasha's murder, she'd share everything she knew about Privé's chef. Kelsie was a friend, but she was also a murder suspect.

I filled her in on what had happened, wiping away my tears at the part where I told her how I'd tried to resuscitate Sasha and about the blood left on my sweater when I used it as a pillow for Sasha's head. I finished with the startling news that the coroner had deemed Sasha a victim of foul play.

"Oh my God, that's awful!" Claire said. "I think you're brave for doing what you did, trying to save her. But who could have killed her?"

"The billion-dollar question," I said, then grabbed a tissue and blew my nose.

Claire had listened the way she always did, giving me her full attention, not interrupting until I was finished talking. "I can't picture Kelsie murdering anyone. And I don't know any of the other people except one of them by reputation."

"Who is that?"

I wasn't surprised when she'd told me it was Lee. "Cutler's Meat Wagons were banned when I lived in California. There was some kind of scandal about one of the cuts of meat he was using. You know us vegetarian, animal-loving, laidback Californians. I'll ask my daughter; she might remember what it was about."

Then I told her about how volatile Kelsie had been with Sasha on Friday night. "Not the woman we know from knitting class," I added.

"I have seen a change. Not that she ever got angry with me, but her behavior has been so erratic. Up one minute, down the next. And . . ." I could tell by the expression on Claire's face that she was conflicted about sharing something. After a few minutes, she said, "Kelsie and I go to the same therapist. I recommended Joan to her because of a conversation we had at the Blue Agave Tea Room. Kelsie's emotions were all over the place, especially when she talked about her ex and trying to conceive. Between you and me, I was worried she might harm herself because of her losses. Joan has helped to heal my internal scars from the motorcycle accident and my husband's passing; I was hoping she could help Kelsie. So far, she's only made it to one appointment."

"I'm a believer that therapy helps," I said, motioning for Claire to take a seat on the settee. "I went to a therapist in New York after I found my fiancé, Michael, in a compromising position with his ex-wife. It helped me to make the decision to leave Manhattan and never look back. Which I haven't."

Claire nodded her head. "I've even noticed an improvement in my poetry since I've been in therapy."

I smiled. "Hard to improve on that, Ms. Poet Laureate 1996."

"You'd be surprised by how a calm inner body makes for a calm, and yet very fulfilling, outer life. Joan's also an acupuncturist and believer in the healing of Indigenous American medicines. You would love some of her remedies. She uses a lot of the herbs like the ones you're growing in your kitchen garden."

"Is she the reason Patrick collects seaweed for your leg?"

"Yes, ma'am."

"I'm glad Kelsie might be getting help," I said.

"With everything you just told me, I'll try to get her to come over for tea. What does Patrick think of all this?"

I looked away and cleared my throat.

Claire gave me a knowing look, got up, and went to stand next to the dry-erase board.

An hour ago, my left hand had taken on a life of its own. I'd grabbed an eraser, cleared the board that had been used to plot my last client's interior design, and started a murder board. I'd put Sasha Morgan's name in the center, enclosing it in a bubble, like the center of a wheel. Then I'd drawn five spokes coming out, each representing a suspect in Sasha's murder: winery owner Bethany Garnier; horse stable owner and Privé partner Jackie Fairchild; movie producer and partner Noah Fairchild; owner of Cutler's Meat Wagons and Privé partner Lee Cutler; and a bit reluctantly, I'd added angry chef de cuisine Kelsie Stevens, who'd told me Friday that in a year's time she would get a percentage of Privé's gross profits.

I cleared my throat. "I, uhm, haven't had a chance to speak to him yet. I'll tell him tomorrow on the way to the Hampton Classic horse show."

"So, he doesn't even know about your dinner date tonight with one of your suspects on this board? Didn't you say Lee Cutler was dating the murdered sous chef?"

"Yes . . . I promise to tell Patrick everything tomorrow. I did let Arthur know." My intent was to invite Patrick to the folly in the morning so we could go over my version of a murder board and add any particulars as they came along. We had done a similar exercise last May, and it had helped solve a crime and catch a killer.

At the thought of Patrick, I glanced over at Claire and mumbled, "Has Patrick ever brought up his wife, Catherine, to you? Did you know that she used to be a chef?" I held my breath.

"Patrick only mentioned her once," she said, looking out through the panes of glass to the wisteria vines overhanging the rear of my walled garden. "It was when I'd confided in him about the accident with my leg, and he told me about his wife and daughter. If I share something with you, do you promise not to mention it? Seeing how close the two of you have become, I think you should know."

"Of course," I said, holding my breath.

"He feels responsible for the accident."

"I thought it was a drunk driver?"

"It was. But a few days before she died, Patrick had gotten into an argument with his wife. The guilt almost destroyed him."

I thought about when I'd first moved to Montauk and I would watch him from my deck, shrouded in darkness and melancholy as he paced up and down the beach in front of my rental cottage. "Do you know what they argued about?"

"His career as a suspense-thriller writer was at its peak, and he'd been asked to write the screenplay for his latest blockbuster. Only it involved going to California to do it. His wife didn't want him to go. You see, while he was at home writing his bestsellers, he was also a stay-at-home dad to his daughter. His wife had a full-time job."

"As a chef?"

"Patrick never told me what her job was or her name. Only that they'd argued. He'd gone to California to write the screenplay. He was there when the accident happened. His wife was coming home late at night after picking her daughter up from her sister's."

"And a drunk driver."

"Yes."

We were both silent for a moment, our eyes moist with tears. My heart breaking for what he'd gone through.

"Now, let's not get all gloomy. Fortunately, time does heal most wounds, or at least allows the good memories to outshine the bad," Claire said, coming over to me and swiping a tear from my cheek. "We can't change the past, but we can change our today. And I would say Patrick Seaton's days have been looking pretty rosy since you came into the picture."

"Thanks, friend. I better get going if I'm going to meet Lee Cutler."

"Be careful."

"Promise."

"Don't go anywhere private with him."

"Yes, Mother." I realized I would be proud to call Claire my mother. She was around the same age my mother would have been if she were alive. They were both free spirits, nature lovers, and shared the same philosophy that you can do anything you desire in life.

After Claire left, I went inside, fed Fat Cat her dinner, showered, wanded a few layers of black mascara onto my fair eyelashes, added a touch of blush to my cheeks and tinted peach gloss to my lips. I subscribed to a no-nonsense approach to getting ready and captured my unruly blonde hair that had been bleached by the summer sun into a loose chignon, letting the curls spring where they may. I made a point of not positioning each curl in front of my hearing aids, like I'd done in my teens when they'd been a source of embarrassment. Those days were gone. And when I felt insecure, my mother's words would creep in: *Never argue for your limitations. You're perfect as God made you.*

Jo looked on from the bed as I rooted through my closet for something to wear. I wasn't out to impress Lee Cutler. But I did want to go for a more upscale professional look than the one he was used to seeing when I'd worked at Privé. My go-to summer uniform had been jean capris, sneakers, and solid cotton T-shirts.

"I don't know, Josephine. What's the best way to dress when interrogating a possible killer, the same man who is also your new boss?"

Jo answered by gagging a few times like she was about to unload a juicy furball onto my white matelassé duvet.

"Don't be so dramatic."

She gave one last wretch, swallowed, then closed her eye.

"False alarm?" I asked. "You might be right. I should keep it simple. Don't overthink things.

I chose a sleeveless summer dress in a pale turquoise and put on a pair of flat sandals. Opening my jewelry box, I removed my mother's single pearl on a delicate gold chain necklace and matching pearl stud earrings. At the thought of studs, my mind flashed to the diamond stud I'd stepped on Saturday morning in the walk-in fridge at Privé. It was hard to fathom that the entire time I was in the refrigerated section that Sasha's frozen corpse had been lying behind door number two. Kelsie had said the earring belonged to Jackie. If instead the stud really belonged to Sasha, that meant she might have been murdered in the refrigerator section of the walk-in, not the freezer, making the crime even more disturbing.

I went over to my bedside table, where I'd been charging my phone. The table was littered with nighttime props, positioned to seduce me into cozy slumber—a green-tea-scented candle, a schooner in a glass bottle, my parents' wedding photograph in an antique sterling silver frame, and my grandmother Barrett's music box that played Debussy's "Clair de lune." After taking my phone off its charger, I opened my photo app to search for the shots I'd taken of Sasha's corpse. They weren't as gory as the fictitious crime scene photos shown on television cop shows, making them even more eerie. These photos were real. I enlarged the last photo of Sasha, focusing on her face. There it was. The twin diamond stud to the one I'd stepped on yesterday morning. I played back the scene of going into the walk-in fridge for milk for our cappuccinos. Not only had I stepped on the stud, but I also remembered the small puddle of blood under where the llama carcass had been hanging the night before. Could that have been human blood?

Lee Cutler had access to the walk-in, it's where he hung his disgusting meat. I made a mental note to fill in Elle's husband about the earring and the blood. For now, I'd leave out the fact that I took postmortem photos. I was still determined to do my sleuthing from as many degrees of separation as possible. If only Elle would do the same.

"I'd better leave before I change my mind," I told Jo. Even though the room was warm, I shivered and reached for the white cotton sweater on top of the trunk at the end of my bed. I threw it over my arm and said farewell to my comatose feline.

Instead of leaving my cottage via the kitchen door, I grabbed my portfolio and went out the French doors to my deck that overlooked the beach and a calm Atlantic. I stood there for a moment, searching the twilight for a man and his greyhound. Couples strolled the shoreline arm in arm, squeezing in their last romantic moments before heading homeward from their summer vacations. The sky to the west still had a touch of peachy pink, forecasting that tomorrow there would be fair weather for the Hampton Classic horse show. But I knew from a weather alert I'd received earlier on my phone that a tropical depression was brewing in the Caribbean and might be on track to cause havoc as it tracked its way north.

Just what we needed.

Chapter 14

I was running a few minutes late, and as predicted, the Labor Day traffic in Amagansett, East Hampton, Wainscott, Sagaponack, and Bridgehampton was moving at a snail's pace. No, a snail would move faster. On the drive, I'd tried to puzzle out the pieces in Sasha's murder but couldn't even come up with a corner piece. I had no attachment to any of the suspects like Elle did, making it easier to look at things objectively. Of them all, Kelsie was the one I was unable to picture as a killer. Based on experience, that should put her in the number-one slot as the murderess. Both she and Bethany had anger-management issues. Admittedly, Kelsie's temper with Sasha Friday night was on the aggressive side. But to go as far as killing Sasha seemed inconceivable.

The closer I got to Sarabeth's on the Bay — the bay being Mecox Bay — the more anxious I became. Watermill was a small hamlet that was still considered part of the Hamptons — more like a Hamptons stepsister. Not an ugly stepsister like in *Cinderella*. My realtor buddy Barb had told me that Watermill was ranked one of the wealthiest areas in the United States. Every year, Elle and I would go to Watermill Museum for its yearly quilt show. I hadn't missed one since moving to Montauk. We would always make a day of it by visiting the Milk Pail Market and U-pick Farm, and our favorite stop, Mecox Bay Dairy for their selection of gourmet cheeses. I tended to be a cheese-aholic, preferring cheese and warm-from-the-oven bread with slabs of melting butter, over a sweet dessert, any day. The only dessert that trumped my love of bread, butter, and cheese was Patrick's dark chocolate molten lava cake with its gooey center. Patrick always finished off the cake with fresh raspberries and a dusting of powdered sugar.

I passed Watermill Prime Meats and my thoughts naturally went to my upcoming dinner date. Was it a date? No. Though I'd learned after googling Lee and viewing him in a myriad of A-list party photos that he was considered one of the Hamptons' top wealthy bachelors. In a few recent party pics, Sasha had been at his side. The pair made a stunning couple in the looks department, but what happened behind the scenes was something that I planned to find out tonight.

Once on Bay Avenue, I followed the road east until it snaked its way south. Up ahead I saw welcoming light spilling from the windows of a white shacklike structure perched next to a boardwalk overlooking the bay. The lot was full, and I had to wait for a tiny Miata to leave before I could park. After turning off the ignition, I pulled down the lighted visor mirror and said to my reflection, "Meg Barrett, you can do this." My reflection didn't look so sure, reminding me that today was the first day in the past couple of weeks that I hadn't touched base with Patrick. I felt my confidence wane even more.

Oh, no. I'd forgotten that Patrick and I had made plans to meet this afternoon at three to pick a stain color for a bench he'd made from reclaimed barnwood for my small oceanfront deck. I was sure he would understand once I told him about Sasha's murder and helping Bethany get a lawyer. Was I fooling myself? Had I subconsciously blown him off? Knowing he wouldn't be happy I was meeting a potential cold-blooded killer for dinner. Patrick wasn't my father, I thought stubbornly.

Then I smiled because I knew my father would tell me to go ahead with my sleuthing. But only if I had backup. I reasoned that my message earlier to Arthur could be considered backup. Plus, the feeling I had for Patrick was the farthest thing from daughterly you could get. And Claire. Claire knew where I was going.

The parking spot I pulled into was so cramped that the only way I could get out of the car was to climb over the gearshift and exit via the passenger door. Even then, I had a hard time squeezing out. And, just as I reached my hand inside to grab my portfolio, a gust of wind blew the car door closed, catching all four fingers on my right hand. I shouted a few choice curses up to the universe, shocking a couple in the parking lot who were holding doggie bags. They grabbed hands and scurried to their car. I called after them, "I'm okay. No need for concern."

But I wasn't okay. My fingers pulsed with their own individual heartbeats, and when I passed under a streetlight, I could see a red line where the door had left its mark. Good thing I didn't play the piano. It could have been worse. I just hoped this wasn't a foreshadowing of my appointment with Lee, or payback from when I was coming out of the walk-in Friday night and had bashed him in the kisser with the door. The same kisser Sasha hadn't wanted to kiss Friday night.

Karmic payback? A warning? Whatever it was, the pain was almost unbearable. I opened the car door again. Then, using my shoulder to keep the door open, I grabbed the portfolio with my left hand, and moving out of the way, I let Mr. Wind close it.

As I walked toward Sarabeth's, laughter, music, and the aroma of delicious food filtered out from the open windows and lifted my spirits. But after I climbed the porch and reached for the door handle, a current of excruciating pain radiated up from my fingers to my wrist. Tears stung my eyes and I looked up at the star-studded sky and said for the second time, albeit a tad less convincingly, "You can do this."

The host led me over to Lee. He was seated at a cozy table for two next to an open window overlooking the bay. I sat across from him, put my napkin in my lap, then said, "Sure smells good. I've read some great reviews about this place."

He informed me that he'd already ordered our meal. Even the wine. Ironically enough, the only wine Sarabeth's offered was from Garnier Vineyards. Lee had chosen a pinot noir. A pet peeve of mine was when my date ordered for me. But in this case, I wasn't going to complain, wanting to stay in Lee's good graces as long as possible and hopefully glean some intel about his girlfriend's murder. Plus, he wasn't a date.

Lee picked up his half-full glass of wine and took a sip, then appraised me like I was a prime cut of meat that he was thinking of grilling. I waited for him to pour me a glass of wine. But he didn't. So, I poured my own. I took a sip and smiled at the smooth taste. So far, the only difference I could see between Garnier Vineyards' pinot noir and the French pinot noir served Friday night was the price.

The meal went fine. There were a few awkward pauses on my part, but the food was extraordinary — or should I say every blood-red or black-and-blue barely cooked meat item on the menu Lee had ordered had been extraordinary.

When I asked him why he'd chosen Sarabeth's, he told me it was because he was thinking of changing meat distributors for his New York food trucks and wanted to check out Sarabeth's supplier.

"You don't want to try any of their seafood items?" I asked. "I read in Zagat that their oyster stew is out of this world." Every time a waitperson holding a seafood dish passed our table, I would lean over and inhale its intoxicating scent.

"Haven't you read the side of my food trucks? Real men," he said then nodded toward me, "and real women only eat red meat. Not seafood. Red meat's good for your blood and has plenty of protein."

"How about pork? The other white meat."

"Ha!" he said. "That's an advertising gimmick to get all those health-kick wusses to eat pork. Pork is officially considered red meat."

"Hmmm, never knew that." So far, every topic of conversation had something to do with meat.

After our entrées were finished, I asked what he'd thought of Sarabeth's. Big mistake.

"I don't know what all the hype's about. The servings are small and there's way too many vegetables and sauces. They don't offer one bone-in rib eye for a man to sink his teeth into."

I disagreed and quickly changed the subject by handing him the folder with the plans for the cottage. He scanned my design renderings and said, "Looks okay. Just don't listen to Jackie and add any froufrou girly stuff to junk it up. We're talking high-caliber movers and shakers who want to get away from their wives and girlfriends."

"Thought you agreed that women would be allowed inside the cottage," I couldn't help saying.

He winked a long-lashed green eye at me and chuckled. "I know from experience—women don't like the smell of *stinky* cigars. Jackie will see."

Not true, I thought. Morgana Moss from the East Hampton Town PD loved an occasional cigar. So far, I hadn't found a good segue from talking about my plans for the cottage to his girlfriend's murder. But I'd had enough of his macho b.s. and dove in. "Did Sasha like cigars?"

Instead of answering, Lee threw his napkin on the table and made a gesture to a passing server that he wanted the check.

"No dessert?" I asked.

"We'll just do coffee."

While we waited for our coffee, I watched him poke the space between his two front teeth with the tip of a toothpick. When he was finished digging around, he examined the sliver of meat he'd extracted, then tossed the toothpick onto the white linen tablecloth. I almost gagged at the sight. Apparently, real men meat-eaters also lacked table manners.

"So, were you happy with the quality of the meat?" I asked, looking around at the cozy coastal décor. Wishing I was sitting at a table with Patrick, not Lee.

"I'm not impressed. Their meat's okay, about equal in quality to what I'm using now."

I'd thought the short ribs and filet had been fantastic. But I wasn't an expert on cuts of red meat. I was a huge fan of the way Sarabeth's chef de cuisine had prepared each course; the vegetable side dishes had almost out-wowed the main protein. Lee hadn't touched his veggies, and I had to wonder if his deep Hamptons summer tan was masking jaundice caused by a bad case of scurvy. I would definitely bring my father and Patrick back to Sarabeth's and order a few of their beautiful, aromatic *seafood* dishes.

"How many food trucks do you have?"

"I've stopped counting. Somewhere in the four hundreds. In every state but California. Their restrictions are over the top regarding the cuts of meat that my trucks can carry. Until I find someone better, I'll stick to my current supplier. But if he pulls something like he did last month, he's gone. Too bad my overseas' shipment of meat hasn't cleared New York's Port Authority. In my opinion, they're too thorough checking overseas shipping containers. What do they think they'll find? Human cargo munching on Wagyu beef from Japan? Terrorists hiding inside a kangaroo carcass?"

Kangaroo! Ew!

"What's that look on your face? Kangaroo is very lean and tasty."

"Is it legal to import?"

"Of course. I get my Australian kangaroo from a meat distributor in New Jersey, they ship it UPS two-day air. If you like, I can order some for you?"

"I think I'll pass. But thanks." All I could think of was a little joey hanging in place of the llama meat I saw in Privé's walk-in.

"Those namby-pamby PETA idiots from California have banned Kangaroo meat. I didn't even know about it until one of my trucks got fined. And in Massachusetts, only my food trucks on Martha's Vineyard can serve Kangaroo. You squeamish types eat cows and veal. Do you know what they do to baby anemic cows before they slaughter them?"

I remembered what Claire had said about Cutler's Meat Wagons being banned from California. Now I knew why. "Can we change the subject?"

He did as I asked and went on to tell me about one of his trips hunting in the Yukon, but I lost him at the word *skinned*, and I didn't tune in until he started talking about the impressive roster of rich-and-famous foodie members the partners had snared to join Privé.

"I thought your membership drive would be canceled yesterday?"

"Yes, it was," he said, looking disappointed. So far not one mention of Sasha. "But this morning we were able to set up tables outdoors."

Not about to give up on my mission to get him to talk about his dead girlfriend, I said, "I'm surprised you don't like dessert. Especially knowing your girlfriend, Sasha, was a pastry chef." I put my hand to my mouth, like I'd regretted what had just come out— which I hadn't. "I'm so sorry, I should have offered my condolences as soon as I sat down." I reached over and patted his hand. He pulled it away like I had cooties. Then he turned his gorgeous eyes on me. Clear eyes, without a drop of moisture in them, and shrugged his shoulders. "Thanks. Tragic accident."

So, he didn't know that Sasha had been murdered. If I hit Lee with the element of surprise, it might just help Bethany's case. Or I could let it go, decorate the cottage, and get my intel by working next to Privé.

Before chickening out, I asked, "Have the police talked to you? They've talked to me." *Not technically*, but he didn't need to know that. Plus, I had talked to Arthur, if only via voice message. That must count as something.

The waiter approached us with a pot of coffee. When he reached the table, he turned over our cups, then filled them. I kept my eyes trained on Lee's face for a reaction to my previous statement.

Lee waited until the server walked away and said, "Yes, they've talked to me. Naturally." He raised a dark eyebrow. "But why would they talk to you?"

"I was there minutes after Kelsie found Sasha in the freezer. I can't believe the police are saying it's a suspicious death. Do you know anyone who might have wanted to harm Sasha?" I'd purposely used the word *suspicious*.

"Who told you that? I thought it was an accident. You were there Friday night. That crazy winery wench probably finished what she started." He glanced at the bottle in the wine bucket with the Garnier Vineyards' label glaring at us. A little more calmly, he asked, "What do you know?"

I ignored him and kept going, "How come you didn't take Sasha home Friday night? Did you know that she'd been there all night and that Kelsie didn't find her until Saturday afternoon? Weren't you worried about her? Sasha told Kelsie and me that you two were dating." My last statement was a lie, a white lie, the way I looked at it. Plus, who would refute it? Sadly, not Sasha.

"I'm out of here!" he screeched. "Where's my damn check?"

Even though the din in the restaurant was almost deafening, especially for someone wearing hearing aids, the room quieted. Sarabeth's patrons turned their heads to watch us. Lee clenched his jaw so tight that his bottom teeth covered his top, reminding me of a piranha's. There was so much vehemence in his red-faced scowl that just in case he decided to reach over and punch me, I pushed my chair back from the table.

"Stick to working on the cottage, Ms. Barrett," he growled, not looking half as attractive as I'd thought when I'd first entered the restaurant. "Just a warning. Take care and butt out of anything having to do with Sasha Morgan."

A skinny busboy stepped cautiously toward our table. With a tremble in his squeaky voice, he said, "I'll tell Todd you're ready for your check, sir."

"You do that!" Lee said, not worried he was the center of attention. Obviously, real men were used to it. I wasn't.

"I'm sorry, I didn't mean to pry." I wasn't sorry. White lie number two.

"For your information," he said, "Sasha told me her roommate was picking her up. Also, Sasha and I aren't, I mean weren't, boyfriend and girlfriend like in some rom-com you gals like to watch. We had an agreement. No strings. As if my social life is any of your business." He raised an eyebrow. "Maybe I should find another interior decorator to do the cottage?"

My eyes met his. I almost got up to leave, but my mother had taught me good table manners. I took my napkin off my lap and placed it on the table. I was embarrassed by his behavior during the meal and felt like I'd sold my soul to the devil just to decorate the cottage and collect my 50K fee. If he could threaten me, then I could threaten something of my own. "Again, I'm sorry if I've upset you. It's just that Sasha told me about the spat you two had." White lie number three. "If you want me to give you back the agreement we just signed, I'm more than willing to recommend someone else."

It was like someone flipped a switch. "That's not necessary," he said. "I apologize. I've been under so much pressure since this all happened. That explains the text I just received from Noah that said Privé will be closed until at least Wednesday."

He seemed disappointed that her death had interfered with Privé's membership drive. "It would have been nice if Noah had mentioned why Privé is off-limits so we can get ahead of any bad press."

"Yes, sometimes things like a little ol' murder can put a kibosh on our best laid plans."

He didn't even notice my sarcasm and said, "It will ruin Privé before we even open the doors. As an employee, I hope I can count on your discretion, and you'll promise not to mention this sorted affair to anyone."

"Of course not," I said, smiling Splenda-sweetly. White lie number four. Did four white lies constitute a whopper? I just hoped they didn't come back to haunt me.

By his lack of emotion about murdered Sasha, I almost believed him when he'd said they hadn't been in a close relationship. Why else would he meet the day after her body was found to discuss the cottage? Where was the raw emotion? Any emotion?

Lee stood as our waiter approached the table with his hand outstretched. "Your check, sir."

He grabbed it from the young man's shaky hand and looked

down at it. In a loud voice that once again quieted everyone around us, he said, "About time. Tell your head chef they need to try some of the meat from one of my Cutler's Meat Wagons and learn a thing or two about dry rubs." He extracted two hundred-dollar bills and a business card from his wallet and tossed them onto the table. "More than you deserve," he added snobbily.

Embarrassed, I glanced around the packed room. Thank God there wasn't one familiar face.

Then, like something from a Bram Stoker novel, my last statement proved false.

A familiar-looking woman came flying out from the kitchen's swinging doors and made a beeline toward us.

I stood up from the table.

It was Catherine. Patrick's dead wife.

I'd never fainted in my life.

But there was always a first time.

Chapter 15

My eyes seemed glued shut and my mouth felt like it had been stuffed with quilt batting. Had I been shanghaied? Slipped a Mickey like in the current episode of *Mr. & Mrs. Winslow* that we'd just filmed? If that was the case, then why hadn't Jack or Lara Winslow come to my rescue?

Muffled noise droned in the background. I must have lost the hearing aid in my right ear because I wasn't able to make out what the person next to me was saying. I rubbed my eyes. When I opened them, I found myself lying on my left side on a cot in a crowded office that was stacked with cartons. I turned onto my back. Pain radiated from the back of my head. I reached my hand behind my head and felt a lump about the size of a goose egg. Okay, it was more like a robin's egg.

Things started to take focus. My head felt like it weighed a ton and the air in the small room smelled yeasty, with a hint of garlic. I realized that I must be in a back office at Sarabeth's on the Bay. I felt my ears for my hearing aids. Sure enough, the right one was missing. Glancing to my right, I saw a cute auburn-haired child wearing pigtails and braces sitting next to me.

With a lot of effort, I pulled myself up onto my elbows. Then, once I was in a sitting position, I turned and looked at the girl.

When her blue eyes met mine, they turned to glee. She shouted, "She's awake. She's awake!" Then she shot up from her chair and ran out of the room. The same room that started to spin around me. I laid back onto the cot. Through the fog, I remembered having dinner with Lee. All of a sudden, like the aftershock of diving into frigid early June waves at Ditch Plains Beach, I recalled the last thing I'd seen before losing consciousness.

Patrick Seaton's dead wife.

Only she was alive and kicking.

I closed my eyes. But Catherine's face remained in view. Every inch of her face had been etched on my memory from the time I saw a photo on Patrick's mantel of his supposedly dead wife Catherine and their daughter Lucy.

Though, one thing didn't make sense: the girl I just saw wasn't Lucy. I clenched my eyes tighter, hoping that when I opened them

112

I'd be up in my bedroom snuggled under my down comforter. "What happened?" I mused out loud, keeping my eyes closed. "Did Lee punch me? Or drug my coffee? Causing me to hallucinate?"

A familiar male voice said, "Who's Lee? Your dinner date?"

I opened my eyes to see Patrick looking down at me. Both anger and worry clouded his face. "Sophia, why don't you run out and get a bag of ice for Ms. Barrett. She has a big bump on the back of her head from hitting the table leg."

"Should I get Mommy?"

Patrick answered in a cold voice, "No. She's too busy. Ms. Barrett will be just fine."

Ms. Barrett? After the girl exited the office and I heard the door shut, I pulled myself into a sitting position, swung my legs around until my feet hit the tile, and said through gritted teeth, "Where's my handbag? I'm outta here."

"Not so fast," Patrick said. "Do I need to go after your date? Did he drug you?"

"Ugh, no. And he's not my date." Tears welled and I held back a sob.

The door opened and Sophia came in. Following behind her was Patrick's wife.

"Uncle Patrick . . ."

My mouth opened and Patrick said, "Meg, I'd like you to meet my sister-in-law, Sarabeth."

Chapter 16

As soon as I'd walked inside my cottage, I took off my left hearing aid and immediately put a call in to Elle. My right hearing aid was crushed and worthless, stored inside a baggie supplied by Sarabeth—a casualty of my sissyish fainting spell.

I explained to Elle about how I'd thought I'd been visited by a beautiful ghost who smelled like cinnamon and almond extract. Elle's reaction flashed across the screen of my landline Caption Call phone: **Identical twin sister! What are the chances!**

Then I went on to tell her how I'd ended up clearing the air with Patrick about why I was having dinner with handsome Lee Cutler, and that Patrick had followed me to Montauk after I'd felt well enough to drive. "He wasn't too pleased about the danger part of my Mata Hari exploits," I said into the phone.

Can't blame him. Why didn't you tell me you were meeting him? Both things sound dangerous. Meeting with Lee Cutler and driving with a possible concussion. Patrick should have taken you to the ER.

"He wanted to. I told him I was fine. Which I am. Except for my wounded pride."

Did you tell him the reason you fainted was because you thought you saw a ghost?

"Of course not," I said. "I told him that when I'd gotten up from the table after being so incensed by Lee's poor table manners that I'd tripped over my own feet, fell backward, and hit my head on the chair leg." *White lie number five,* I thought.

Did he buy it?

"I don't think so."

Speaking about falling and hitting the back of your head. Guess what? Arthur told me that Southampton PD is holding a news conference in the morning about the murder. And he also told me what Sasha Morgan's cause of death was.

"Injuries from Bethany's choking?"

No. I told you, Bethany is innocent. Arthur's being all hush-hush. But he did say she died from a bludgeoning to the back of her head and that the body had been moved to the freezer. You might have to see if Doc can get any info from the coroner.

114

They've asked Arthur to help in an auxiliary compacity. Don't you think this news rules Bethany out of the equation?

"Maybe. But you know how these things go. Everyone is a suspect until they aren't." I didn't want to tell Elle that Bethany wasn't out of the woods yet. Especially after she'd told us she had keys to the farmhouse.

Back to tonight. Two things. Why didn't you tell me that you were going to meet carnivore Lee? And two, did Patrick confront Lee at the restaurant?

"Thankfully, Lee slithered away after they carried me into Sarabeth's office."

So, are you and Patrick good now? He doesn't think you were stepping out on him, does he? And he doesn't suspect that you thought he was lying about his wife being dead?

"All good," I said without much conviction.

When Patrick had walked me to my cottage door, he'd given me a small peck on the cheek, then said, "Better go check on Charlie. See you tomorrow." I'd almost forgotten with everything that was going on that tomorrow was our double date to the Hampton Classic horse show with Elle and Arthur. And even though I'd told Patrick before we'd left Sarabeth's on the Bay about Sasha's murder and the reason I was dining with her possible killer, the scowl on his face had never softened. I didn't pass on to Elle that judging by his hasty retreat a few minutes ago, there were still a few gaps in our fence that needed major repair. I was the most culpable because I'd kept Patrick out of the loop regarding Sasha's murder. Not to mention that I'd ridiculously believed that Patrick would lie about his wife's death. On the other hand, if he would open up more, I would have known that Catherine had a twin, and wouldn't have made a fool of myself.

So, how did it end up that Patrick was at Sarabeth's?

"It was a coincidence," I said into the phone. "Unless . . ."

Unless what?

"Claire was the only one I told. Oh wait, I also left a message with your hubby. Does he even have Patrick's phone number?"

Not that I know of.

"So, it must have been Claire or just a coincidence. He's been so closed off about anything relating to the tragedy of his wife and daughter, but you'd think he would have mentioned that his deceased wife's identical twin sister owned a nearby restaurant. By the way, his niece is adorable."

Maybe he doesn't see them often because they remind him of his wife and daughter. It's gotta be hard.

"That's an understatement." After Patrick's and my first kiss three months ago, I'd done what any other red-blooded infatuated female would do. I researched anything I could find on author and screenwriter Patrick Seaton. I'd drawn the line on pulling up any newspaper articles or photos of the car accident that had happened over three years ago. I wasn't given to flights of fancy, so how could I have ever believed he, or for that matter the news media, had lied about the tragedy? I would chock it up to being burned in the past by Cole and my ex-fiancé, Michael, and never admit to Patrick that I'd fainted because of his deceased wife's doppelgänger.

I've gotta run, but did you happen to see *Newsday*? Jackie supposedly paid the ransom for Black Jack, but never got him back. The ransom money was never picked up. Arthur said the Fairchilds contacted the police after they went to the designated pickup spot in Eastport. When they got there, no horse.

"I hope the horse isn't harmed."

You and me both.

"That is strange. But let's not worry about horses or the Fairchilds. Instead, let's get a good night's sleep and have fun at the horse show. I think we deserve a little fun.

Sweet dreams. Love you.

"Love you back." Then I hung up the phone, thinking that after what I'd been through today, it was doubtful I would have sweet dreams.

I told Jo that it was time to call it a night. I turned off the lights in the kitchen and saw that my phone on the counter was blinking, telling me I had a voicemail. I picked it up and looked down. It was from Lee.

All he'd said when I'd looked at the transcription was: *Hope you will keep to yourself any conversations we had about poor high-strung Sasha. I've thought about your plans for the cottage and I'm still on the fence. I'm sure we'll work it out. Just do your part and help us keep a low profile about what happened at Privé. I mean, you wouldn't want to lose a chance of getting fifty thou for a week's work, would you? Or worse. L.*

Or worse? Was that a threat?

I looked down at the phone and thought about calling Patrick. Something told me it was a little late to be asking for his help. It would wait until morning. Maybe by then, Sasha's killer would be arrested. I picked up Jo and gave her a big kiss on the nose. She was so surprised, she didn't even struggle. "Come on, kitty. Time for bed." She wasn't Patrick, but she was comforting all the same.

Chapter 17

I woke Monday morning with a regret hangover. Regret that I'd ghosted Patrick yesterday and blew off our plans to work on the bench. Regret that I hadn't told him about my planned meeting with Lee. And finally, regret that I'd made such a fool of myself by fainting. Oh, and regret that I'd lied to Lee and told him I knew what he and Sasha had been fighting about. If Lee did kill Sasha, how far would he go to shut me up if he thought Sasha had confided in me? Lee's "Or worse," at the end of his voice message, still resonated as I considered my next steps with Patrick.

I'd heard that the best way to get over a hangover was to have a little hair of the dog. I bit the bullet and put a call in to Patrick. Thankfully, he picked up, and I didn't have to leave an awkward message. I asked him to please come and meet me in the folly so we could talk. Plus, I wanted to fill him in on any details I'd forgotten to tell him last night in my hurried explanation of why I was dining with Lee Cutler.

"I don't like the way we left things last night," I said right before hanging up the phone.

"Same," he answered.

Patrick arrived at my folly's door toting Charlie and a picnic-basket brunch. My glee at the sight of him, and the picnic basket, plus the kiss he gave me after he stepped inside erased my angst about last night's twin-sister restaurant debacle. Me, mad at the fact he'd thought I'd been on a date; and him, upset that I hadn't told him about meeting Lee at Sarabeth's or that Sasha had been murdered.

"How's the bump on your head?" he asked, placing the picnic basket on the small farm table in the center of the folly. "Did you sleep okay? I was worried you might have a concussion." His immediate concern over the now-deflated bump on the back of my head told me volumes on how much he cared.

"Completely gone. See." I took his hand and placed it on the back of my head. He felt around and visibly sighed with relief. I said, "The only thing remaining is my embarrassment at fainting and causing a scene."

"From what Sarabeth tells me, that Lee Cutler jerk was the instigator. By the way, he's banned from Sarabeth's."

"Good for her."

"Does that mean you're not going to work on the cottage?"

I avoided his gaze, went next to him, and opened the picnic basket. The smell nearly had me fainting again. Only this time it would be more of a pleasurable swoon.

"What happened to your hand? Did he do that?"

"No, I shut my hand in the car door. Good thing I'm a lefty. Oh-la-la! What do we have here, Mr. Seaton?"

"Good try at avoiding my question. You're a grown woman. But you must be aware of how dangerous it would be to work at Privé. At least wait until they arrest someone."

"Let's just take it one day at a time. I'm sure Lee and the partners will have to postpone everything until Sasha's killer is found." Charlie came over to us and stuck her nose in the basket, sniffed, then looked up with pleading eyes. "You sure know how to spoil a girl," I chirped. "Or should I say girls. Right, Charlie?"

She licked her lips in agreement.

After we'd finished our waffles topped with fried chicken, grilled brown-sugar-crusted bacon, and warmed pure maple syrup, we lifted our plastic wineglasses filled with Patrick's homemade mean green antioxidant juice and toasted to each other's health. Then we laughed over the hypocrisy of consuming fried chicken and bacon, then washing it down with a health drink.

"I see you haven't filled in much," Patrick said, glancing over at the suspect storyboard that I'd started yesterday. "Do you want me to write as you dictate?"

"Yes, please." He was cognizant of the fact that it was hard to hear when my back was turned, and there was also the little matter of my right hearing aid being crushed last night. I'd called my audiologist first thing this morning but had to leave a message because they were closed on Labor Day. I'd have to wait until tomorrow.

I went over to the potting sink, washed my sticky hands, dried them, then came back to the table. "I remember last May when we worked together on a similar project. Go team."

Patrick laughed.

Twenty minutes later, the large dry-erase board had been transformed into a death-by-design board:

Sasha Morgan – Deceased. Bludgeoned. Weapon unknown. Privé's sous chef. Formally worked at Garnier Vineyards. Was fired after she stole cases of wine, then put her own private label on the bottles and sold them on the internet. Not prosecuted and someone paid off the losses she'd caused. Lee Cutler's girlfriend? Chef Kelsie threatened to fire Sasha more than once. Threw porcelain dog at Noah's head. Warned about coming to Privé at night and threatened to expose the partners with something if they didn't treat her right.

Bethany Garnier - Owner of Garnier Vineyards. Former owner of farmhouse and land bought by three partners who magically had the residential property deemed commercial. Rumors are that Bethany's late husband had an affair with Sasha. Choked Sasha at dinner on Friday. Was questioned by Southampton PD and released. Has known Elle since childhood. Has key to Privé.

Lee Cutler – One of Privé's Partners. Owner of Cutler's Meat Wagons conglomerate. Sasha's boyfriend? Claims he and Sasha had an open relationship. Eats Kangaroo! (I made Patrick add that.) A real narcissist (Patrick raised an eyebrow).

Jackie Fairchild – One of Privé's partners. Equestrian. Own's ritzy Hamptons horse stables. Her favorite horse, Black Jack, was kidnapped, ransom not taken, horse not returned. Jealous of something with Sasha and her husband, Noah. Supposed cousin of Hamptons royalty Black Jack Bouvier (Jackie Kennedy Onassis's father).

Noah Fairchild – One of Privé's Owners. Per his wife, Jackie, is a movie producer of flops. Son of Parnell Fairchild, the famous restaurateur and billionaire. Per Kelsie, Noah and Parnell are estranged. Seems that his wife holds the purse strings.

Kelsie Stevens – gets a small stake in the business. Was pretty brutal on Sasha in the kitchen Friday night. Didn't check the walk-in freezer until Saturday afternoon. Erratic behavior directed at Sasha, not like the Kelsie who was usually even-tempered when working at Pondfare.

When Patrick got to the bottom of the board he scrawled, **Meg Barrett** – At the dinner Friday night.

Then he turned with a mischievous grin on his gorgeous face.

"What the heck!" I walked over, grabbed the marker from his hand, and put in all caps: NO TIES TO THE VICTIM.

For obvious reasons, Patrick was leaning toward Lee Cutler and promised to do a little digging where he was concerned. Then he threw out a quote by Robert Browning, *"Our interest's on the dangerous edge of things. The honest thief, the tender murderer, the superstitious atheist.* But it's still too early to nominate anyone for the top slot," he added.

I agreed and recited a line from Robert Browning's wife, *"The devil's most devilish when respectable.* I'm just not sure who the devil is, respectable or not."

"Did they find Sasha's phone?" he asked, looking at the board. "Find out who her last calls were to, or from?"

"See, I'm glad you're here. You reminded me that I forgot to tell you that her phone was found next to her, the screen shattered. Something I'm sure forensics can fix. I'll add it under Sasha's name and try to remember to ask Elle to do some recon work."

"Sure you want to open that can of worms?" he asked.

"You're right. I'll ask Arthur. Better yet, you ask him at the Hampton Classic, once you two become best buds."

Patrick laughed. "You can't force friendships."

"Right again. And I don't want to drag you into this. I'm sure if Elle wasn't so hell-bent on protecting Bethany, I would bow out."

He raised an eyebrow. "I don't know, girl," he said, turning to Charlie, "what do you think? Is that last statement Meg made true?"

Charlie yipped in agreement, but of course she would. Patrick was her master and made her homemade meals. I would yip too if he moved into my cottage and did all the cooking.

He smiled and glanced at me before turning his attention back to the dry-erase board. "I know you. Even if Bethany Garnier wasn't Elle's friend you wouldn't let this go."

Of course he was right.

"Even so, it doesn't mean you have to get tangled in another of my messes. I just thought about how we brainstormed last May after what happened at Enderly Hall."

"I'm flattered. But you must admit that you have a lot of other people close to you that have more experience with these things.

There's homicide detective Arthur from the East Hampton Town Police, then there's your surrogate uncle Doc who is a retired coroner, and lastly, your father, a retired Detroit homicide cop who is only a video chat away."

"I'd rather have you," I said, smiling demurely and blowing him a kiss. "But you're right, we need to use all our assets. I was about to say, two heads are better than one, but I'll rephrase it: five heads are better than one."

His blue-green eyes sparked. "I'm all for catching a killer, if only to keep you out of harm's way."

My heart melted.

"Even if I know you don't like to be . . . uhm . . . what's a word you would use?"

"Coddled," we said at the same time and Charlie joined in with a very feminine bark.

My phone buzzed. I took it out of my pocket and glanced down at a text. After reading it, I said to Patrick, "It's Elle. She's all excited because she just overheard her hubby say that Sasha had a roommate named Allie and they lived in Montauk—or in Sasha's case, *had* lived in Montauk. Do you see what I mean? Elle's not letting this go until Bethany's name is cleared, and there's no way she'll let me bow out until that happens."

I went to my drafting table and opened my laptop.

As Patrick looked over my shoulder, I surfed around until I saw a slew of photos on social media sites that showed Sasha Morgan and her roommate, Allie Hines. Most of the shots were taken in front of the Surf Shed Bar and Grill in Montauk. The small hot spot was within walking distance of Patrick's cottage. "Let's make a pact that after the Hampton Classic, we go check out the Surf Shed. Maybe we'll run into Sasha's roommate, or at least find someone who knows where Sasha's roommate lives."

"Hmmm . . . We'll see. Why not, this time, you let Elle do the investigating? She's the one married to a top cop. I'm just a writer."

"Oh, you're more than a writer, Mr. Seaton. Anyway, Arthur would never let her investigate on her own. She needs us."

I was about to turn off my laptop when I saw a caption under a photo of Sasha and Allie standing in front of the Bay Street Theater in Sag Harbor. The caption tagged Allie as an actress in a modern-day version of John Steinbeck's *The Winter of Our Discontent.* "Look," I said to Patrick. "It's meant to be. Neither Elle, Arthur, nor the Southampton PD could get Allie to open up about her murdered roommate like you could, Mr. Screenwriter. She'll fall under your allure, hook, line and sinker. Just like I did when I first met you."

Patrick laughed. "I can tell I'm not going to win this one." Then he patted me on the head like I was his niece's age.

I wasn't deterred. "You could reel her in with the suggestion of a possible role in *Mr. & Mrs. Winslow.*"

"You know I don't have that kind of clout."

"That's why I said *possible* role." I didn't have to ask him to turn up the charm with Sasha's thespian roommate — he had it in spades.

"Okay, on one condition."

I closed the laptop and looked up at him. "What's that?"

"We do nothing illegal."

"Promise." In the back of my mind, I knew we had the East Hampton Town PD's Morgana Moss nearby at the Montauk station.

"Do you believe her, Charlie?" The greyhound tilted her head and glanced at him, then at me, and back again. Patrick laughed. "Let's pack up, Charlie. It's time to show Meg her surprise."

A few minutes later, after thanking Patrick profusely for the beautiful handmade bench that he'd bolted to the top of the landing leading down to my beach, then watching him and Charlie stroll down the shoreline and out of sight, I sat down and looked out at the calm ocean. All I felt was peace and contentment, along with anticipation of our double date with Elle and Arthur at the Hampton Classic. I was a lucky girl, I thought, watching a young couple walking hand in hand on the beach. *See, Meg. Scenes like that used to make you sad, even when you were still dating Cole because he was never around.*

As the couple disappeared from view, I got up from the bench and turned to go inside.

It was then that I saw it. Carved into the wood at the back of the bench was an inscription: *For Meg who loves the sea.*

And here I'd thought Patrick had been dozing when we were watching the rom-com movie *Notting Hill* and I'd pointed out my favorite scene at the end of the movie, where Julia Roberts's character is lying on a garden bench that has a dedication that reads

For June who loved this garden, from Joseph who always sat beside her.
Patrick hadn't added, *from Patrick who always sat beside her.*
But he'd left plenty of room to add it later.
I felt my heart swell.

Chapter 18

After planning weeks in advance, and in true Elle Warner-Shoner style, Elle and Maurice provided me with what I was to wear for Grand Prix day of the Hampton Classic. For every special occasion in Elle's life there was a vintage outfit to go with it. I'd never attended half as many charity events or gallery openings as Elle, mostly because I'd rather stay home with a good book or munch on a tub of popcorn in front of the tube watching a PBS Masterpiece Mystery, any character-driven detective series, or HGTV and the like. But it was good to know that I always had my duo of fashionistas on speed dial to help me navigate the Hamptons social scene.

I put on the 1960s sleeveless dress with a full skirt that Elle had chosen and glanced at my reflection in the gigantic gilt-framed mirror that I'd originally purchased for the interior of Privé. Naysayer Jackie hadn't liked the way it looked in the Burgundy Suite, and had said, more like demanded, "It needs to be hung on the wall and we don't have the time or the manpower for that. We're opening in days." I'd disagreed. And frankly, at that point, I'd had enough of her postulating when it came to my design aesthetic. But I'd kept my mouth shut, which had been a good thing because Jackie had said, "Take it home. It's yours." I'd immediately put in a call to my construction guys in case Jackie changed her mind. They arrived at Privé within the hour and transported the Louis XVI–style monstrosity to my cottage, then up the narrow stairway to my attic-style bedroom. I was now the proud owner of a thousand-dollar mirror (and that was the dealer's price). Instead of cluttering up my small bedroom, the mirror made it appear larger.

"Jo, can't you just picture me in an ensemble worthy of this mirror — all ruffled and coiffed in a powdered Marie Antoinette beehive wig?" Jo looked at me through a slitted eye, pretending she wasn't interested in my dressing diatribe. I did a bow and a twirl, then turned and walked toward her, pretending to hold out a plate in my outstretched arms. "Josephine, would you care for a piece of cake?" The *Let them eat cake* reference was lost on her, but she did know the word *cake*, and both of her hairy ears twitched at the thought of anything edible.

"What do you think, Jo? Am I Hamptons-worthy?" The teal color of the dress made my blue eyes appear bluer, which I was sure was no mistake on Elle's part. I was excited about Patrick's and my double date with Elle and Arthur and had spent more than my usual time on my makeup, even adding charcoal eyeliner. I'd corralled my wavy blonde hair into a loose French braid and had put on jewelry that had once belonged to my mother. "Honestly, Jo. What do you think?"

I might have imagined it, but I thought I heard her snort. Then again, I wasn't wearing my hearing aids. I put the left one in and glanced back at Jo. She had a mischievous air about her, like as soon as I left the cottage she was planning a retaliatory combat mission. Her exploits were so legendary that I'd thought of cataloging them, then writing a comical yet disturbing Edward Gorey–type children's book. Or better yet, submitting them to the Guinness Book of World Records for Nastiest Cat Hijinks Ever. To appease her, I said, "If I don't leave the house, missy, how can I pick up your kitty pâté?" I was getting good at the white lies. I knew there wouldn't be time to stop at East Hampton's Petpourri after the Hampton Classic. But Jo didn't have to know that.

After shooing her down the stairs, I grabbed a pair of high-heeled sandals from the bench at the end of my bed, also on loan from Elle's room-sized closet. I shut the bedroom door, then hurried down to wait for Patrick. We were rendezvousing with Elle and Arthur in the parking lot of the East Hampton movie theater, then we would all go together in Arthur's Lexus to the Hampton Classic.

I sat on the sofa in my great room and attempted to put on Elle's loaned Louis Vuitton sandals. The straps crisscrossed front and back in a complicated Rubik's Cube combination. It took me a good ten minutes before I got it right. Even though Elle was petite and four inches shorter than me, we were lucky to share the same shoe size.

Or maybe not so lucky, I thought, trying to stand up.

I took a teetering step, then another, worrying that I might leave heel marks on my recently buffed wood floors and made my way over to the island that separated the kitchen from my great room. I grabbed the Norma Desmond–style hat that Elle had provided from her arsenal of vintage accessories from the counter. "Everyone wears hats at these things," Elle had said a few weeks ago. "Think Queen

Elizabeth." I'd told her she was thinking more of the Kentucky Derby or one of Prince Charles's polo matches, but Elle insisted I wear it.

The doorbell rang and the light over the kitchen doorway flashed. I put on the hat and started toward the door. Halfway there, I realized I could barely see two inches in front of me because the hat's brim was so large and droopy. I flipped up the brim. It flipped down again. So, when I felt for the doorknob and opened the door, I not only opened it to Patrick but also his uproarious laughter.

"Are you really going to wear that thing?" he asked.

I took it off, ushered him inside. "Too much?"

"Way."

I Frisbeed the hat across the room, where it crash-landed on top of Jo, who was lounging by the fireplace on my cozy reading chair. Jo shot up like she'd been electrocuted, then flew to the floor with the hat still covering most of her chubby body. Her jerky dance across the rug reminded me of the magic kit my father had given me as a child that had included jumping beans. Once, I'd stuffed a couple of the jumping beans inside a decapitated Barbie doll head, then watched my young cousin scream in terror as the head scooted across the floor. Later, when my father explained the reason why the jumping beans jumped, the joke turned out to be on me. He'd told me that there was live moth larva inside. I had nightmares for weeks and refused to eat franks and beans just in case one of the jumping variety ever made its way onto my plate.

"Aren't you going to help Jo out?" Patrick asked.

I took a step toward her at the same time she rid herself of the hat. Jo scowled up at me, then very sweetly came over to Patrick and wound herself in and out of his legs, sending up a cloud of cat fur that caused him to sneeze.

"Bless you," I said. "Don't fall for her act. She just wants you to feed her. She'll turn on you if you don't deliver the goods. I have the literal scars to prove it."

Patrick glanced toward the kitchen and Jo's bowl that read *Cat from Hell*. "If that dry stuff is what you've been giving her, I don't blame her. I make Charlie's from scratch."

"Of course you do," I said, smiling. "As you know, that's a little out of my wheelhouse."

"I'll see what I can do to make a feline-friendly batch that's gluten-free."

"Knowing Jo, maybe you should also try to make it *glutton*-free."

We both laughed. Jo didn't. I went and picked up the hat and put it on the table at my kitchen banquette. Its ostentatiousness would be better suited for the set of *Mr. & Mrs. Winslow*, reminding me that I'd forgotten to fill Patrick in on Zoe Stockton's thievery and her subsequent reselling of stolen goods at the Bridgehampton antiques show.

After I explained, he said, "That doesn't sound like her. Are you sure?"

The way he spoke, it was almost as if he knew her well. *Too well?* For a moment I wondered if *Mr. & Mrs. Winslow*'s screenwriter and Ms. Stockton, the gorgeous Academy Award–winning star, had some kind of past.

"I saw it with my own eyes," I answered.

"You weren't wearing that hat, were you?" He nodded at the Norma Desmond hat.

"Funny."

"Well, I'm sure there's an explanation. Zoe told me she didn't plan on coming to town until filming begins next week, *after the hordes vacate the Hamptons* was how she put it." He leaned down and scratched Jo behind her ears. She sniffed his fingers. Then, realizing that he didn't plan on feeding her, she turned and walked away.

Patrick stood and said, "We'd better leave if we're meeting your friends in East Hampton at three."

I glanced at the clock on my mantel. "Yikes. You're right."

He grinned. "You're the only person I know who says 'Yikes.'"

That makes me one of a kind, I thought. Maybe it was a good thing that I looked nothing like Patrick's dead wife and her twin sister. I wouldn't have to worry that I was a carbon copy replacement like the new Mrs. de Winter in the Gothic classic *Rebecca*. I knew one thing from briefly meeting Sarabeth, she was no Mrs. Danvers. In fact, I hoped that one day Sarabeth and I would become friends.

"Have you ever been to the Hampton Classic before?" I asked.

"Yes, many times. I used to go every year but haven't gone in the past three or four."

His statement hung in the air for a minute. His wife's and child's deaths had been the obvious reason there'd been a break in his social calendar. I thought back to when I'd first moved to Montauk and would watch him from my cottage window as his downtrodden, solitary figure walked the shoreline. Soon after, I'd discovered his melancholy prose in the sand. Eventually, I'd gotten up the courage to add my own dead poets' quotes below his. Then our dance began. A strange way to start a relationship, yet at the same time prophetic of where we now stood.

"I sat in the grandstand last year," I said in an upbeat voice, wanting to keep things light. "But this will be my first time in the VIP tent. Hopefully, I'll get a chance to introduce you to star equestrian Jackie Fairchild. She'll be performing in the Grand Prix."

"And one of our suspects, the owner of the kidnapped horse, who's also a cousin of Jackie O's father Black Jack Bouvier, right?" he said with a grin.

I really admired a man with a sense of humor, especially if it matched mine. "One and the same."

I hobbled over to the whitewashed oak hall tree by the kitchen door, grabbed my tried-and-true straw hat off the hook, and put it on. Then I grabbed the Louis Vuitton handbag that Elle had talked me into buying when we'd gone back to the antiques show because it matched my sandals. I'd spent way more than I usually would on a handbag. I'd bought it for its utilitarian purpose, not its pedigree, because I knew it would be roomy enough to hold a pair of Keds in case the sandals gave me problems. Which they were doing at this very moment.

Once outside my cottage, Patrick and I were assailed with the aroma of mint, rosemary, and lavender from my kitchen garden. I stopped and took a deep cleansing breath. "If I could bottle the air, I would wear it instead of perfume," I said, watching Patrick put the key that I'd given him last week into the doorknob, then jiggling the handle to make sure it was secure.

As of yet, he hadn't offered me a key to his cottage—something I planned to ponder at another time. For now, I was determined to have a fun day. Not a glum day like the past few had been. I wasn't going anywhere, and hopefully, neither was he.

"You really should have a security system," he said, turning around. "Especially with what happened with that jerk at dinner last night. And his threat."

I had debated when we'd met this morning about not telling Patrick about Lee's threatening voicemail but had told him anyway. Even letting him listen to Lee's tone of voice. I was trying for more transparency where Patrick was concerned. Maybe if I didn't keep anything from him, he would be more open with me.

I put my hands on my hips and said in mock sternness, "I live in the small hamlet of Montauk. I refuse to get an alarm system. I might as well have stayed in Manhattan."

"Well, at least a video doorbell."

I nodded my head yes. "That, I will buy. But it would have to be light-activated."

"No problem, I could figure out something."

He came up to me and I put my arm through his as we stepped onto the bluestone path leading to the driveway. "You sure are handy."

"Coming from the woman whose toolbox is bigger than mine," he said with a grin.

"True. But I've never done woodworking or electrical stuff. I usually leave that to Duke and Duke Jr."

"Oh, by the way," Patrick said, scanning me from head to high-heeled toe, "you look amazing."

"I could say the same for you." I gave him a quick kiss on the cheek, inhaling the clean scent of his aftershave. He wore a white cotton button-down shirt that showed off his summer tan, a navy blazer, and dark jeans. His layered sandy brown hair curled around his ears. The perfect length and texture for a woman to run her hands through. Luckily, I was that woman.

"You're almost as tall as me in those shoes," he said.

"Not quite as tall as you. But it makes it less of a chore for you to bend down to kiss me," I said, adding a coquettish grin.

"Kissing you is never a chore, Ms. Barrett," he said in a husky voice, then gave me a kiss that was deeper and longer than the one I'd given him.

I felt my cheeks heat. I grabbed his elbow, and he helped me maneuver the narrow path lined with hydrangeas. Earlier in the summer, the nodding flower heads were a dazzling French blue, but now they'd turned a dark reddish purple. As a somewhat capable gardener, I knew I could have prolonged the flowers' vibrant blue by making the soil more acidic, but I preferred to see the change of color, another sign that fall was just around the corner. A harbinger that the summer people would soon be gone.

When we reached Patrick's Explorer, he opened the passenger door and I slipped inside. Before closing it he said, "I almost forgot. I talked to Sarabeth a little while ago. I'll tell you about it after we hit the road."

I squeaked out, "Great."

Patrick got inside, started the engine, then pulled onto the two-lane highway, and we headed west toward East Hampton.

After we passed through Montauk's main street, he said, "I called Sarabeth after meeting with you in the folly. I told her what happened to the sous chef at Privé, and when I mentioned the names of the owners, Sarabeth told me that she recalled some kind of scandal having to do with Noah Fairchild that was related to his famous restaurateur father. She was sure it would come to her, and in the meantime, she said she'd ask around the restaurant circuit for any gossip."

"I heard his father disowned him," I said. "And I do know that Noah's wife, Jackie, is always complaining about the fact that she's the one shelling out all the money for Privé. Maybe we could ask Jeremy, *Mr. & Mrs. Winslow*'s producer, if he knows anything about Noah Fairchild. Let me rephrase that. Maybe you could ask. Now that we have our union cards, I don't think cheapskate Jeremy is too fond of Elle and me."

"Okay. I'll ask. Sarabeth said she didn't want to get our hopes up, and that it might turn out to be nothing. She also wanted to know how you were feeling."

"Not even a slight bump on the noggin," I said.

"Is that another word Michiganders use?" he asked, putting his foot on the brake at a crosswalk in Amagansett as we waited for a troupe of surfboard-carrying teens to cross the road. "Well, I'm glad you're okay. You sure had me scared."

"I never asked you," I said cautiously. "Was it just a coincidence you showed up at Sarabeth's? Or did Claire send you to look after me?"

He put his foot on the gas, and a few minutes later we left the tiny hamlet of Amagansett. "Strictly a coincidence. It was my niece's birthday last week and I was dropping off her gift. I wasn't stalking you. If that's what you think?"

"Of course not," I said, not liking the direction the conversation was heading.

"Maybe if Claire had told me the reason you *were* with that creep," he said, "I wouldn't have gotten so jealous." He took his eyes off the road and they searched my face.

"No reason to be jealous, ever," I mumbled.

"But after you stood me up yesterday afternoon and I find out you're having dinner at a table for two with some crazy guy, a possible murderer, the same jerk who caused you to faint. You can't blame a guy for being jealous."

"You didn't know he might be a murderer at that point, so I'll take your jealousy as a compliment," I said, cracking a weak smile.

"It is," he answered. "To be honest, I'm not the jealous type. If there is such a thing. But you've bewitched me."

"Are you waxing poetic, Mr. Seaton? I really am sorry about standing you up. The whole Bethany thing happened. Then I had to hurry to meet Lee Cutler." I'd omitted the part where Elle and I had returned to the antiques show when I saw him clench his jaw at the mention of Lee. "I did call Arthur and leave a voicemail about where I was going. If that helps my case."

"Not really. You also found time to tell Claire. I'm not your father or Doc, but I wouldn't mind a heads-up next time something like this occurs. Which, knowing you, might happen sooner than later." He smiled but it didn't reach his eyes.

I could tell he was keeping his emotions in check, and I tried to plead my side of things. "This murder is Elle's baby," I said, rolling down my window for some much-needed fresh salt air. "She wants to prove her buddy Bethany is innocent. This time, I'm just her sidekick."

"Sidekicks get murdered all the time in my thrillers."

"That's fiction," I said.

"Based on fact. I should show you some of the NYPD files I have access to. And what about that threat you got from Cutler. I think that brings you right into the middle of the fray."

I turned and looked at him. "You have access to NYPD files? How come I don't know about that?"

He laughed. "I rest my case. Sidekick, my . . ."

I decided to take the plunge and ask about Catherine. She was there between us, whether he realized it or not. And even though I loved being with him, he still had his moments of being closed off and inaccessible. Not that I blamed him. But I had to be selfish, because at this point in my life, I suddenly realized I was ready for a long-term commitment. "Your niece is adorable. It must be comforting to have family so close by, especially after your loss. Wish my dad lived closer. Was Catherine a chef partner with Sarabeth?"

It was then that I realized that he'd never mentioned Catherine's name to me.

"No. She had her own restaurant."

And that was the last thing he said until we reached East Hampton.

So much for opening up.

Chapter 19

"OMG. Is that another one of *his* meat trucks?" Elle asked as we walked in pairs over the white wood-railinged bridge leading to the entrance of the VIP tent. I guessed the bridge was the Hampton Classic's version of the red carpet.

"Looks like it," I said. Beyond the warm-up ring with equestrians practicing their jumps, I saw a Cutler's Meat Wagons food truck in the parking lot. Grudgingly, I had to admit that his cuisine must be exceptional, because just like at the Bridgehampton antiques show, there was a huge line snaking its way in and out of the parked cars.

I glanced over at Patrick, and even though he wore a smile on his handsome face, his jaw was clenched in reaction to Elle's comment. He immediately released my hand and made a fist. I stumbled without his support. He deftly grabbed my elbow and steadied me.

"Sorry, Elle," I said to her back, "these shoes have to go. I'm putting on my sneakers as soon as we're seated." Elle didn't hear me because she was too busy looking ahead at all the celebrities who were showing their tickets at the entrance of the hospitality tent. I wondered if in the past when Patrick had attended the Hampton Classic if he sat in the grandstands like I had or the VIP tent. I knew he walked the red carpet at the Hamptons International Film Festival, so it would make sense that he would garner a seat in the hospitality tent. Although to his credit, Patrick never came off as a snob or name-dropped his *New York Times* bestselling author or award-winning screenwriter status. He was as humble as they came. Ashley, Patrick's publicist, would say *too* humble.

"Hey, where's the hat I loaned you?" Elle asked while we waited to show our tickets.

Patrick glanced at me and we shared a smile. "I was afraid it might fly away in the breeze. I knew you would be heartbroken if it got trampled under some horse's hooves, seeing that it was featured in that movie with Joan Crawford."

"Bette Davis," Elle replied.

"Plus, it was a little on the large side. I have a small head." Boy, I was getting good at the white lies.

"Bummer," she said. "But the one you're wearing looks fine. Only it's not vintage."

Of course, Elle was dressed head to toe in vintage. She wore a silk minidress that tied at the neck. You would think the huge neon flowers in the print would overwhelm her short stature. Instead, she looked stunning.

I'd been with her in her room-sized closet when she'd chosen what to wear to the Classic. The dress, shoes, handbag, and even bucket hat she'd chosen had all been vintage Gucci and I'd gotten a lesson on sixties and seventies Gucci fashion designer George Kenneth Scott. She'd said, "Ken Scott was known as the Fashion Gardener because of his large-scale vivid floral prints and expertise in merging romanticism and pop culture. The dress cost me a pretty penny at two thousand dollars, but it's already been loaned out to two charity event fashion shows, so I figure it was well worth it." It was one of the things I loved about Elle; she always gave back to the community. Next, Elle had showed me a section of her closet that featured more Ken Scott designs. If I had to guess, her closet's inventory might be worth more than her Sag Harbor captain's house with a widow's walk and a view of the bay.

Once we entered the VIP hospitality tent, I was blown away by the décor. White linen tablecloths topped each rectangular table. And in the middle of each table was a centerpiece consisting of a whitewashed wood window box filled with live flowering plants and greenery. The edges of the window boxes dripped lacy teardrop ferns and other green foliage, resembling a tablescape from the pages of a glossy home décor magazine.

"Wow," I said, after we were seated, and I glanced down at my place setting.

"Double wow," Elle said, taking a seat across from me. Arthur sat across from Patrick and they were already talking football instead of equestrian jumping.

We'd arrived early, but immediately a white-coated waitperson came to our table and filled our crystal flutes with bubbling champagne. Each of us had a gold-foiled charger on top of which was a white gold-rimmed porcelain dinner plate and matching salad plate. Topping the salad plate was a gold-foiled napkin ring that held a rolled white linen napkin and a sprig of fresh rosemary. To the right of the place setting was a water goblet, wineglass, and the aforementioned champagne flute. The porcelain bread plate to the left of each place setting also had a gold rim but centered in the middle of the plate was a depiction of a sepia-toned horse and rider. I glanced at the other three bread plates and saw that the horse and riders were being schooled in different disciplines. I quickly turned my plate over, and as expected, it was signed Rouard Limoges, France. My plate was titled "Leaping."

Elle followed my lead and turned her plate over. She said, "Mine says trot." She turned her husband's over and called out, "Halt."

I elbowed Patrick and he gave me a blank look. I showed him the script written on the back of my bread plate. "What does yours say?"

He turned his over and I thought he said, "Roar riding."

"Do you mind if we switch places."

"You want to swap plates?" he asked. "You can have it."

Patrick caught on after I pointed to my right ear, which didn't have a hearing aid. He immediately got up and we changed seats. I flipped over the bread plate. "Road riding." That made a little more sense.

Elle took advantage of Arthur and Patrick's break in conversation and asked her husband, "How long will Privé be closed for business?"

"Forensics is back there today. I really have no idea." Arthur appeared frustrated with his bride, and rightly so.

In East Hampton, right before I'd gotten into the backseat of Arthur's Lexus, Elle had come up to me and whispered into my left ear, "I got more info from Arthur's laptop." I'd rolled my eyes, then she'd shrugged her shoulders and said, "Hey, it was open for all the world to see. I'll tell you later."

The only topic of conversation on the ride to the horse show, East Hampton to Bridgehampton, had been Sasha Morgan's murder. I'd told Elle and Arthur about the storyboard Patrick and I had gone over this morning. I'd also filled Arthur in on the stud earring that I'd given to Kelsie. I hadn't told Detective Arthur Shoner that I knew the diamond stud belonged to Sasha. I would let the police do their job. Plus, I didn't want him to know that I'd taken postmortem photos of the body.

Elle had been overly excited about the storyboard, and I'd promised to send her a photo of it. Then I'd asked Arthur if he wanted one, too. He'd responded, "Sure, why not?" I could tell by the smirk on his face that he'd thought we were a bunch of amateurs. I'd wanted to defend myself, but I kept my mouth shut because I knew he blamed me for Elle's plunge into supersleuth, caped crusader and defender of Bethany Garnier.

The one thing that Elle hadn't mentioned in front of her cop husband was the info about Sasha having a roommate, obviously not wanting him to know that she'd been eavesdropping on his phone conversation with Southampton PD.

It was a short drive and nothing new was learned from tightlipped Arthur. The only thing he'd added when we pulled into the lot at the Hampton Classic was that the authorities didn't have enough evidence to convict Bethany Garnier, but added that at least in Southampton PD's mind, Bethany Garnier was *guilty* until proven innocent. I'd also asked if they were able to recover anything from Sasha's smashed phone. All Arthur had done was look at me through the rearview mirror and raise a furry eyebrow.

• • •

I took a sip of my champagne, realizing I hadn't eaten since brunch. I set the glass down, promising myself I wouldn't have any more until I had food in my belly. I had enough butterflies worrying that Patrick and Arthur wouldn't get along. They were as different as two men could be. Arthur with his designer suits, pocket squares, and in-your-face, what-you-see-is-what-you-get personality and Patrick with his quiet, introspective, and humble personality. But there'd been no reason to worry because Arthur and Patrick had moved on from talking about football and were now talking about fishing for sea bass off Montauk Harbor. I hadn't known that Patrick liked to fish. It wasn't my favorite sport. Especially the bait part and taking the fish off the hook, but I sure loved to eat Patrick's pan-braised sea bass.

Elle and I chatted about her and Arthur's upcoming move to Montauk. She had a big bucket list. "I'm confident Barb at Sand and Sun Realty will find us our perfect nest. I've postponed looking at houses until I'm sure Bethany is in the clear with all this business at Privé. Arthur has his hands full anyway, now that he's assisting Southampton PD and proving Bethany's innocence."

I saw Arthur give her a sideways glance, which I know she saw but ignored. Elle took a sip of champagne, then directed her flute in the direction of the huge video screen displayed on the far side of the Classic's Grand Prix course. "That's Jackie Fairchild, isn't it?"

I turned and looked at the muted video screen. The live feed showed the warm-up ring with a man standing in the center who was directing horses and riders with their practice jumps. His arms were outstretched, his hands tracing the air like he was conducting a symphony.

"How can you tell it's Jackie?" I asked. "Everyone looks the same in their equestrian outfits. I can't even tell the males from the females."

"Because Jackie's not wearing a helmet."

Elle was right. Behind the white rail fence at the back of the practice ring, I spotted Jackie dressed in full equestrian gear, but in her case, she held her black velvet helmet in her hand. Her blonde hair reflected the sunlight. But not all was sunshine and rainbows with Ms. Fairchild because surprise, surprise, she looked to be in an argument with her husband, Noah.

Noah was dressed in a white linen shirt, tan linen pants, and a straw panama hat. A fat cigar hung from his downturned lips, and his forearms were raised as if waiting for his wife to throw a punch. Thinking about Sasha and Noah's volatile spat in the Provence Suite on Friday, it seemed Noah sure had a lot of angry women after him.

"Looks like trouble in paradise," Elle said. "I assume that's Jackie's husband, the movie producer." She reached over and placed three fingers on her husband's chin, then forced him to turn his head toward the screen. "Look at the upper right part of the screen. There are two suspects who I bet are on Meg's suspect board," she said. "Jackie and Noah Fairchild. Maybe you should have a chat with them."

"Not the time or place. Plus, I told you, darling, I am a liaison, not an interrogator," he replied stoically.

I turned back to the screen. Because it was so large, I was able to zero in on Jackie's lips. I thought she said, "Sasha was your pear. If you had anything to do with her death, I'll turn you in myself." Then she pushed Noah away, but not before stomping hard with the heel of her tall black riding boot on Noah's foot. Noah's cigar dropped from his lips and he limped off. Jackie put on her helmet, then disappeared inside the stables that housed the show horses.

"Hope that scene isn't more exciting than the competition," Arthur said with a sigh. The screen changed to show a roster of horses and riders along with their standings for the Grand Prix finale.

"I just read Jackie's lips," I said. "She was asking Noah if he had anything to do with Sasha's murder. They must all have been questioned by now. Right, Detective? Lee Cutler hadn't known until last night when I told him."

At the mention of Lee's name, I saw Patrick stiffen and sit straighter in his seat.

I was saved by Arthur, who ignored my question and changed subjects. "This is my first Hampton Classic. I always thought it was a horse race, or at least a competitive polo match. Something more exciting and athletic than a bunch of leaping equines."

"And fishing for hours with Doc, with nary a sea bass to show for it, is edge-of-your-seat excitement?" Elle asked, laughing.

Arthur scowled. "You weren't complaining the other day when I brought home my catch."

Elle grinned. "Next time, make sure you don't leave the receipt to Gleeson's Market in the bag."

Arthur's cheeks reddened, and he looked down at the opened program each of us received when we'd entered the VIP tent. "Is it true, like it says here, that the Grand Prix course takes just eighty-nine seconds? The food better be good."

"I'm sure it will be," Elle said. "Can't you smell it?"

We all sniffed the air, then Patrick said, "The Grand Prix jumper class course may only be eighty-nine seconds, but there are usually thirty-five to forty horses in the final competition. The Grand Prix trophy comes with a three-hundred-thousand-dollar purse."

"Nothing to sneeze about," I said.

"And like in all professional sports," Patrick said, "there's money from advertisers and promises of paid endorsements, and even money for stud fees. Many of these horses and jockeys have been in the Olympics. The best of the best. Wait until you see how truly fluid horse and rider are."

"Poetry in motion," I added.

"Exactly," Patrick said.

Elle looked toward the Grand Prix ring. "I can see by the banners around the ring and even the names printed on each jump in the circuit that the sponsors are top-notch: Hermès, Longines, Hamptons Stables & Equestrian Center . . ."

"That's the name of Jackie Fairchild's business." I pointed. "And look. Under the clock. A Garnier Vineyards banner."

"Bethany said she'd be here," Elle said. "I'm meeting her at the open bar during the break between the Grand Prix and the finale, where the top three with the lowest score compete for the whole enchilada. You coming with me?" She looked to me, then her husband. "Meg?"

"Sure," I said.

Arthur narrowed his eyes at me. "I'll accompany you, wife. I'm sure Meg would rather stay with Patrick. Right, Meg?"

Patrick squeezed my hand under the table. "Right," I said.

Then it was Elle's turn to shoot me a disappointed look. "Husband, anything new on Jackie's kidnapped horse? How much was the ransom that they didn't take?"

"Good try, wife."

"Answer my question, husband," Elle said, grinning.

"I can't disclose that."

"What if the kidnapping is related to Sasha Morgan's death?"

"I don't see how," he said. "It doesn't matter. Not my rodeo. Leave it up to Southampton PD."

"I will. But you promised if Bethany gets charged, you'll do everything in your power to exonerate her," Elle said petulantly.

"Yes, yes," Arthur said, patting her hand. "A promise is a promise. Speaking of Southampton PD. Meg, I held them off as long as I could. Told them that you would come by tomorrow morning and give them a signed statement."

"How come I don't have to make a statement?" Elle asked. "I was with Meg when Kelsie brought us to the freezer. Plus, I want to put it on the record that Bethany is innocent."

While Arthur explained his reasoning for not involving Elle, I took off my sandals and switched them out for my sneakers. Afterward, I jumped up and said, "Need to powder my nose."

Patrick jumped up too. "So do I."

"You have to powder your nose?" Elle said, winking one of her large brown eyes at him. "Your nose doesn't look that shiny, Patrick. And it's only an hour and a half until the Grand Prix event. Hurry back or you'll miss the food."

I answered by blowing her a kiss.

Chapter 20

I was a hundred yards ahead when Patrick finally caught up to me. "Oh, no, you don't. I know you're going to confront that couple on the screen. Not a good idea."

"I'm not going to do anything dangerous. In fact, join me. Don't you want to meet two of our suspects?"

He didn't answer, so I took it for a yes. I noticed as we walked through the tent that men and women were glancing admiringly at us. It looked like Elle and Maurice had made the right choice for my wardrobe. And Patrick—well, Patrick was gorgeous all the time, even when dressed only in board shorts after a day surfing. I grabbed his hand. "We'll pass as a Hamptons power couple, holding hands, and displaying our all-access VIP badges as we stroll over to the perimeter of the warm-up ring where we saw Jackie and Noah arguing."

"You're incorrigible."

"Thank you. Now, we have to move fast."

As we pushed through the crowd near the bar, Patrick said, "I just saw Jeremy Prentice."

"Our esteemed producer?" I said. "Wonder if Zoe Stockton is here? If she is, you better not tell Elle. She'll have Arthur arrest Zoe for stealing props from the set, then reselling them at the antiques show. I would rather that we talk to her."

"We?" he asked. "I don't think the Hampton Classic is the right place for that."

We paused at a bottleneck at the bridge. Fashionably late VIPs were still streaming in. "I don't think there's any right place to confront Zoe. Better us than Elle or Arthur," I said as we stepped onto the bridge. It was like going down the wrong way of a one-way highway. The bridge was so narrow that we had to turn sideways to let a new line of perfumed couples, the women all wearing hats, squeeze by. I guess Elle had been right about wearing a hat. Although, when I came last year and sat in the bleachers, the only hat I wore was a Detroit Tigers baseball cap.

I smiled at a few faces from TV and screen that looked familiar. Amazingly, they smiled back. Confident of our couple appeal, I said,

"I think we could pass as five-million-dollar horse owners. That's what Jackie's kidnapped horse is worth."

"Maybe not," Patrick said, glancing down at my Keds.

"Don't be a snob, Patrick Seaton. Hey, what's your middle name? I should know that by now."

"You should?"

I jerked my head to look at him.

Thank God he was smiling. "James."

"Okay, Patrick James Seaton, let's go meet the Fairchilds."

A few minutes later I said, "I don't see them. Do you?" There was no Jackie and no Noah. "This has to be the same place that we saw them on the big screen. I recognize the advertising banner on the fence."

"Come on, Nancy Drew. You tried."

"One sec. There, look, Noah's cigar." I ran to the spot and Patrick followed. Before bending down, I made sure that the huge screen wasn't focused on us like it had been on Noah and Jackie. Instead, it was replaying last year's Hampton Classic Grand Prix three-horse jump-off for the big prize.

I crouched and asked, "You have a tissue?"

"No," Patrick answered.

I reached for the cigar, picked it up from its unlit tip, and blew off the loose dirt from the end that'd been between Noah's grimacing lips. "DNA," I said, standing up.

"Okay, Madame Curie."

"Thought I was Nancy Drew?" I handed him the cigar to put in his jacket pocket.

He did, then said, "Oh, you're a bunch of famous women rolled into one curious bundle."

"Hmmm, good try. You have to admit, having Noah's DNA couldn't hurt seeing he's one of four suspects."

"You mean five. You forgot Bethany Garnier."

"Right. Bethany. Elle's confidence that she is innocent is starting to wear off on me."

"And don't you think that forensics might already have his DNA as part of their investigation? Or do you have a lab in the back of your folly?"

"No, it will be backup. Maybe they haven't talked to him yet.

What if Noah skips town before they have a chance?"

"What's that orange thing?" Patrick pointed to the ground near where I'd found the cigar. I bent again and brushed away the soil with my fingertips to reveal a square orange plastic key fob with a small key attached. "Looks like a locker key," I said after standing.

From behind Patrick's back, I saw Noah Fairchild approaching us. "Hurry," I whispered. "Put it in your pocket."

Patrick looked confused but did as I said.

"Meg. What a surprise." He looked to the ground at the spot where I'd picked up his cigar and the key. Then he took his right loafer and brushed it across the soil in an attempt to find either the cigar or the key.

I was betting on the key. "Did you lose something?" I asked.

He looked at me, "Uh-h-h, yes. My wife." He laughed. "You haven't seen her, perchance?"

Yes. We and the rest of the Hampton Classic spectators saw the pair of you arguing. "No, sorry," I said. "Mr. Fairchild, I'd like you to meet Patrick Seaton." Then I turned to Patrick and said, "Mr. Fairchild is one of Privé's owners."

Patrick extended his hand. "A pleasure to meet you, Mr. Fairchild."

"Please, call me Noah. You wouldn't happen to be *the* Patrick Seaton, screenwriter and author, would you?"

"He sure is," I said with a little too much enthusiasm as I watched Patrick's cheeks go pink. "Mr. Fairchild, I mean Noah, is a movie producer."

Patrick feigned recognition. I'd already asked him if he'd ever heard of Noah Fairchild and he'd said he hadn't. But he had heard of Noah's famous restaurateur father, Parnell.

They shook hands and Noah said, "Boy, would I love to have a chat with you sometime, Mr. Seaton."

"Patrick."

"Patrick," Noah said with a grin. "Maybe we could talk about bringing your last novel to the screen?"

"Sounds good," Patrick answered.

I was glad Patrick was playing along. I knew that his latest novel, which hit the bookshelves last May, was already optioned for the screen.

Noah reached in his pants pocket and took out a gold money clip with a stack of bills and business cards. He withdrew a card and handed it to Patrick. "I'm available any time. That's my private number. I live local. Call day or night. Hey, Patrick, you don't happen to be a foodie by any chance? If so, why don't you consider becoming a club member at Privé?"

Patrick took out his wallet and stuck the card inside, then returned it to his pocket.

"You'll be surrounded by the best gourmands in not just New York but also in the world. Our roster is getting close to full, so don't take too long to decide. Meg, here, will tell you all about it. Won't you, sweetie?"

Of the three owners, I'd always liked Noah the best. But I prickled at being called sweetie.

Noah hit the palm of his hand against his forehead like he'd just realized something he'd forgotten. "Patrick, I just recalled that your wife, the famous Catherine Harris, was a top chef. My father worked with her at Feed the Hungry benefits at the Met. She wowed him, and that's hard to do. Believe me, I know from experience. Your best is never good enough with dear ole Dad," he added sourly. He put his hand on Patrick's shoulder. "By the way," he said sincerely, "I'm very sorry for your loss."

"Thank you," Patrick answered. I tried to read his face but couldn't. Now I realized why Patrick had stayed out of the public eye for so long. Everywhere he went in the Hamptons, he was reminded of Catherine and Lucy.

"Will Privé be open soon?" I asked Noah. "We heard Sasha's death wasn't accidental. It was ruled a murder."

Noah didn't answer, just took a step toward the stables. "I better find Jackie," he mumbled. "I know how she gets before the big jumper-class finale."

I couldn't just let him go. "I'm sure Sasha's murder and Jackie's horse getting kidnapped would take a toll on a person's nerves before an event like this. It would mine. Especially if they're about to compete in an event as renowned as the Grand Prix. Please send Jackie my best. We'll be rooting for her in the hospitality tent. Won't we, Patrick?" I asked, slipping my arm through his. As soon as it came out of my mouth, I regretted name-dropping that we were seated with the rest of the Hamptons elite. And it certainly wasn't like me to latch on to someone else's coattails, namely Patrick's, just to feel part of the in-crowd. I was reminded of a quote by Mark Twain, aka Samuel Clemens: *It may be called the Master Passion, the hunger for self-approval.* In my case, I wrote it off as just a momentary lapse in self-worth at the mention of Patrick's Catherine.

Would I ever become Patrick's Meg?

"I sure will tell her," Noah mumbled.

As he walked toward the stables, I whispered to Patrick, "So, what do you think? Did you see what a good job Noah did of covering the gash on his forehead with makeup? I almost mentioned that I witnessed the charming scene between him and Sasha but worried it might keep him from confiding in us down the line."

"Us? I think, when we get back to the table, you hand over the cigar and key to Arthur. And my other advice would be not to do it in front of his wife."

"I'll tell you what. I'll think of a reason to get Elle away. When I do, you give Arthur the cigar and key. He won't laugh at you about the cigar like he would me. My father always told me never to underestimate the small things, saying, *You know my method. It is founded upon the observation of trifles.*"

"Your father said that?" he asked. "It sounds familiar."

"Well, he was quoting Doyle's Sherlock. After tonight, I promise to relinquish you from all future duties. And you'll be happy to hear that I've decided not to work on the cottage at Privé. No one blackmails me and gets away with it."

"A very wise, although surprising, decision, Megan Elizabeth Barrett."

"Thank you, Patrick James Seaton."

"Wonder what Lee will have me do with the stuff we took out of the cottage? Maybe he'll tell me to keep it."

"See, there's a silver lining to doing the right thing."

"Anyway, it'll be fun going to the Surf Shed to try to ferret out Sasha's roommate. We'll be like new age Mr. & Mrs. Winslows."

I was used to Elle rolling her eyes at me, but this was the first time Patrick had.

At least when he did it, he had a smile on his face.

Chapter 21

My appetizer and main course from the buffet had lived up to its description on the menus we were presented with at our table. There'd been so many choices that I'd had a hard time narrowing it down to mesquite-grilled jumbo shrimp with siracha dipping sauce, tricolor beets with goat cheese, and orange-glazed cedar wood plank salmon. I'd avoided the red meat options because last night at Sarabeth's I'd had enough of eating like a carnivore and sitting across from one. At that thought, I recalled the nightmare I'd had before waking this morning. Something to do with Lee dripping blood from his vampire-sized incisors onto the sweater I'd used under Sasha's head, then laughing and telling me it was only wine. A French cabernet. Elle always liked to repeat her dreams to me, then look them up in one of her books for interpretation. In my case, no interpretation was needed.

As Patrick and I carried our desserts back to our table, I said, "Seeing that you scored the last piece of piecaken, I hope you plan on sharing. Do you even know what all the layers are?"

"I think the placard said lemon cake, strawberry swirl cheesecake"—he dipped his pinky in the frosting—"with lemon frosting, and on top . . ."

"Strawberry pie," I finished for him.

"Nope. Rhubarb pie. My favorite. But if you ask nicely, I might consider splitting it with you."

"Oh, pretty please with rhubarb on top. If you do, I'll give you a *sliver* of my almond cake topped with poached pears and crème fraîche. Hope it's as good as a similar dessert I got at Topping Rose House in Bridgehampton when I went with my father. He raved about Jean-Georges's cuisine the whole ride home."

"Only a sliver? Hardly seems fair."

"If you ask nicely," I mimicked.

"How come I wasn't invited with you and Jeff to Topping Rose House?" Patrick asked.

I thought back. "Because we weren't a thing back then."

"Oh, are we a thing now?"

I stopped halfway to our table and looked up at him. "We certainly are."

Patrick grinned from ear to ear.

We started walking, both balancing our generous dessert plates with both hands. I slammed on my brakes when I looked to my left and saw a couple sitting two feet in front of me. It was Jeremy Prentice and actress and thief Zoe Stockton.

"Look!" I elbowed Patrick. His plate went flying, acting more like a turducken than a piecaken as it landed upside down on a passing waiter's tray.

"Good catch," Patrick said to the poor guy. Then he turned to me and said, "What the heck!"

I ignored him and moved next to Jeremy's chair.

Zoe had on a large-brimmed hat like the Norma Desmond one I'd left at home. She was facing away from us, her head turned toward the Grand Prix course. Nothing was going on. Even the huge screen was turned off. Had Zoe seen Elle or me at the antiques show and was purposely avoiding me?

Patrick stepped closer to me. "Ms. Stockton, I'm so glad you're back in town," I said in an overly loud voice. "Patrick didn't think you were coming back until filming begins next week. Right, Patrick?"

He mumbled something I couldn't hear because he was standing next to the ear without my hearing aid.

Zoe didn't answer, just kept her head turned away.

"Patrick, Meg, good to see you," Jeremy Prentice said. For all his millions or billions, Jeremy had dressed for the Hampton Classic the same way he did every day of his life. VIP tent be damned. His Lacoste bleached-out baby blue polo shirt had seen a million washes, the alligator was nose-down, ready to jump ship. A small hole near his collarbone was starting to unravel and wouldn't survive another washing. Completing his rumpled look were khaki cargo shorts with more threads hanging from the dozens of pocket flaps than there were in the fabric's weave. As for footwear, military green Crocs completed his ensemble.

Elle had said that all Jeremey needed was a woman in his life, and I'd told her, "Why would you wish that on anyone? He'd probably make her do all her shopping at the dollar store." Then Elle had said, "Hey, you can get good stuff at the dollar store." And I'd agreed with her.

Jeremy motioned for us to take a seat across from him. "Soon as all these idiot summer people are out of our hair," he snarled, "we can get back to filming. If we don't keep on budget, there'll be hell to pay."

I continued to look at Zoe, who still wouldn't face us, and was now gnawing the cuticle on her left thumb. I was a nobody, so it didn't bother me that she wasn't acknowledging me, but I was surprised that she would ignore Patrick. The same guy who wrote every word that came out of her mouth when she played the part of wisecracking Lara Winslow.

Then I noticed something else about her left hand. On her pointer finger was a sparkling peridot and diamond cocktail ring that I knew Elle had loaned to wardrobe. I felt anger bubble, then realized there was a time and place for a confrontation. And this wasn't it. "Mr. Prentice, thanks for the offer but we should get back to our table before the Grand Prix starts."

Patrick gave me a questioning look, probably wondering why I'd elbowed him if I wasn't going to confront Zoe.

"Before you go," Jeremy said, grinning, a rare thing for him to do, "I'd like you to meet someone. You two fell for it, hook, line and sinker."

Patrick and I exchanged puzzled glances. I looked over at Zoe, who'd finally turned her head toward us. She was wearing huge dark sunglasses under her floppy hat. Something was off-kilter about her mouth. When she smiled, I saw what it was. Her front teeth protruded. Her overbite reminded me of one of the horses we'd just watched in the practice ring. *Holy smokes!*

Jeremy cleared his throat and said proudly, "Gotcha! I'd like you to meet Zoe's new stunt double, Fawn Ellis."

Fawn took off her sunglasses and I could see that she was no Zoe Stockton. It all made sense. What were the chances that after last night's revelation that Sarabeth was Catherine's identical twin, that Zoe would have her own look-alike? I glanced at Patrick's face, and saw that he was as stunned as I.

Patrick took control of the situation. All I could do was look gape-mouthed at the woman. He said, "Jeremy, do you mind stepping over to the bar, I want to talk to you about something important."

Jeremy stood. "Okay. But make it quick."

Patrick grabbed my elbow and said, "Go back to the table and wait for me. And you better save half of your dessert. You owe me."

I turned to go, but before I did, I said to Fawn, "What a lovely ring. A friend of mine has one exactly like that."

Fawn immediately put her hand on her lap.

Patrick caught on, and I started toward our table. My first instinct when I'd realized that Fawn, not Zoe, was our thief, was to get Arthur to arrest her. I knew Patrick's way was better. And I didn't want to cause any bad publicity for *Mr. & Mrs. Winslow*. I was sure that Jeremy would handle things.

Well, one mystery was solved. Now, all we had left was a horsenapping and a little ole murder. *A piece of piecaken,* I thought.

Chapter 22

I polished off my half of the dessert, saving the other half for Patrick, who hadn't come back from talking to Jeremy. He'd missed the first four riders and their horses in the qualifying round of the Grand Prix. The fourth horse and rider to compete had been Jackie Fairchild on her horse Gabriel. Gabriel was a beautiful white stallion with a black diamond-shaped patch on his forehead.

As Jackie and Gabriel had traversed the checkpoints, I'd felt like I was watching a monster truck demolition derby. Gabriel was a one-horse wrecking ball. He missed or sideswiped every jump. Every pole that could have been knocked down, was. All the while, Jackie held on for dear life. I didn't know a woman's body could be twisted in so many directions. Some jumps he'd refused to take, and at one point he'd stopped to do his business right in front of a local television station's broadcast booth. I didn't know who I'd felt sorrier for—Jackie or Gabriel. If there'd been a silver lining to the whole debacle, it was that neither horse nor rider had been injured. After Jackie and Gabriel left the course, the crowd bowed their heads for a moment of silence. Shortly afterward, an announcement was made over the loudspeaker that there would be a twenty-minute break in order to "tidy" the course.

As I gazed out at the carnage, I hoped twenty minutes would be long enough. Even though Jackie wasn't my favorite person, I didn't feel joy at her defeat and wished next year she would be able to compete with better results. Hopefully atop kidnapped and returned Black Jack. But only if Jackie didn't turn out to be Sasha's killer.

"Well, that was embarrassing," Elle said. "Too bad Patrick missed it. Where is he, by the way?"

"He ran into Jeremy," I said. "You know the two of them, once they get talkin' —"

"Wonder if he and Jeremy saw Jackie," she said. "Maybe he could use the scene in a comedic episode of *Mr. & Mrs. Winslow*."

Arthur chuckled. "I thought it was quite entertaining. Shook things up a little. How many more do we have to watch until they narrow it down to the best three?"

Elle glanced down at her program. "Says here there are a total of thirty-eight. Did you know the Hampton Classic is the largest horse

151

show in the United States? Oh, darn. Saturday there was live music, circus acts, pony rides and face-painting. We missed it."

"Gotta love a good pony ride," I said

"Listen to this," Elle said, still reading from the program. "It says here that Jackie Putnam Fairchild has won the whole enchilada three times. With her high score, which in this competition isn't a good thing, and bad timing, I'd say this wasn't her year. I bet she was upset about her missing horse."

"And Sasha's murder," I added.

"You're right, that's enough to throw anyone off their game," she said. "How much did you say the ransom was, Arthur?"

"Good try," he answered, wiping his mouth with a napkin.

"That's not the question you should ask him, Elle," I said. "More like, why didn't anyone pick up the ransom?"

"Where did you hear that?" Arthur asked. As if he didn't know.

"Was it because the cops were staked out watching," I asked. "And the horsenappers saw them and got spooked?" When her husband wasn't looking, Elle gave me the zip-it sign.

"No," he said. "We had no idea the Fairchilds paid the ransom. It's not routine to have someone on duty at the train station like they have patroling Penn Station in Manhattan. It happens all the time that the victims of a kidnapping plot don't involve the police. But then, something goes wrong, and they come with their tails between their legs looking for help when it's too late. Anyhow, I don't know what all the fuss is about. It's just a horse."

A waiter holding a tray with a bottle of Garnier Vineyards wine walked by our table. "Hey," I asked, looking at Elle. "Did you ever meet up with Bethany?"

Elle gave her husband a dirty look. "Arthur went with me to meet her at the bar. She didn't show. He refused to stay an extra few minutes because he wanted to eat his dessert."

"Glad I did," he said, sticking out his chest like a rooster about to crow. "Best piecaken I ever had. Actually, the first piecaken I ever had."

"Don't mention that to Patrick. We had a little mishap with his piecaken," I said.

"What kind of mishap?" Elle asked.

I thought now was as good a time as any to tell them what had gone down with Fawn, aka Zoe's double. After I did, Elle clapped her hands. "Oh, I'm so glad that it didn't turn out to be Zoe. So where is this Fawn? Point me in her direction. And Arthur, you better come with me in case she plans to press charges after I throttle her." Elle tried to stand but her husband put his hand firmly on her shoulder to keep her seated.

"Let Patrick and the producer handle it," Arthur said. "I'm sure they don't want it to get out to the public."

It was rare, but I agreed with Arthur.

Elle opened her mouth to protest just as her phone rang. She put it to her ear, then after a short beat said, "We'll be right there." Looking over at me she said, "It's Bethany, she's manning the table for Garnier Vineyards. She apologized for not being able to get away and said she just witnessed some kind of showdown involving Kelsie and Lee." She put her napkin to the side of her plate. "Come on, Meg. Let's go. Arthur, you stay here so you can talk to Patrick. He might need you to press charges against this Fawn creature."

Before Arthur could protest, we jumped up and scurried away. I looked back to make sure Arthur wasn't following, but it seemed he was too busy reaching across the table for pear cake. Then I saw him shovel Patrick's half into his greedy mouth.

Poor Patrick.

I guessed it was the price he paid for getting involved with me.

Two minutes later we were at the Garnier Vineyards booth. Bethany motioned for us to come behind the table. "You missed it. Kelsie was screaming and Lee was just standing there, grinning at her, which sent her into an even bigger rage, then she charged up to him with her fists clenched."

You mean, similar to what you did with Sasha, I thought.

"Noah Fairchild appeared out of nowhere and had to break them up," Bethany said. "Then Lee just stomped off."

Maybe Kelsie had a good reason to go after him. As I'd found out last night, he was a first-class jerk. "Did you talk to Kelsie? Try to find out what's going on?"

"No," Bethany said. "Because, get this, as soon as Lee was out of sight, Kelsie turned on Noah. The poor guy. Something's up with her. I've known her for years and never saw her so agitated. If she was older, I would guess she was going through menopause."

A trumpet's blare interrupted our conversation, and Bethany

said, "They must be ready to start again. Did you see that Jackie didn't make one jump? She must be mortified. Besides driving people crazy, her equestrian prowess is legendary, and it's not just in her mind. I've seen all the ribbons and trophies when Garnier hosted an event at her stables. It was years ago, when she was nice, kind, and humble, like in that country song. Then the beautiful people started coming to her stables bringing their equestrian progenies and Jackie's status in the Hamptons hierarchy soared to new heights. She's out of the competition, that's for sure. Black Jack Bouvier must be rolling in his grave."

"When did this argument happen?" I asked, getting back to why we were here.

"It was at the same time Jackie was performing in the Grand Prix," Bethany said. "Or should I say underperforming."

"Doesn't it seem strange that Noah wouldn't be glued to the Grand Prix elimination course, watching his wife navigate the jumps?" Elle asked.

"Not that strange," Bethany said. "Rumor has it that Noah's and Jackie's marriage is on the rocks. Not surprising. Not to talk ill of the dead, but I thought of something you can pass on to your husband, Elle. I've always liked Noah Fairchild, but I'd forgotten about a link between Sasha and Noah that might take some of the heat off me. Before coming to Garnier to work in the wine barn, Sasha put on her résumé that while going to culinary school she'd been an au pair for the Fairchilds. Noah was one of her references."

"I didn't know Jackie and Noah had children," I said.

Bethany laughed. "Jackie doesn't. But Noah does, with his ex-wife. Knowing Sasha, maybe she's the reason Noah's first marriage broke up. What if Sasha and Noah rekindled their relationship, Jackie found out, and either husband or wife killed Sasha?"

It was possible. Friday night, Jackie had been upset at dinner about something Noah's ex-wife had told her. And then there was that scene in the Provence Suite between Sasha and Noah, which I knew Jackie had witnessed.

Au pair! When I'd lip-read Jackie saying something about a *pear* when she and Noah had their spat on the huge screen, I'd gotten it wrong. She was asking him if he killed his *au pair*! There'd also been something else rattling around in my head about Sasha's murder—

the reports of strange things going on at Privé after hours that not only Bethany told me about, but also the dead woman herself.

"Do you have any idea why Kelsie was so incensed with both Noah and Lee?" Elle asked Bethany.

"Not really. When she was double-fisted and screeching at Lee, I did hear Kelsie mention the word *exotica*."

There it was again, the word *exotica*. The same word I'd read on the business card that Lee had dropped Friday night and then deftly scooped up. "You've never heard about this exotica before this?" I asked.

"No," Bethany said, without looking my way. I was starting to wonder if she would ever unburden her shoulders and remove the cement chip that seemed to have my name etched on it.

Bethany continued, "I don't know Lee Cutler on a personal level. But I do know that he and Sasha were in a relationship for at least a couple of years. Because on the day we fired her, Lee was the one to pick Sasha up from the winery. I've always suspected that the anonymous person who paid off Sasha's debt for stealing cases of Garnier wine and reselling them online was Lee Cutler."

Now that this argument had taken place, Kelsie, who I'd put at the bottom of my list because of her weak motive for killing her sous chef, was rising to the top. "Bethany, did you see in which direction Kelsie went?"

"It looked like she was going to the stables, and Noah was right on her heels."

Elle asked, "Did the three of them know you were watching them?"

"No. I held myself back from getting involved, just like Howard had instructed me."

"Good girl," Elle said, taking Bethany's hands in hers. "Please continue to listen to your lawyer and keep a low profile. No late-night kayak trips to Privé. No association with anyone at Privé."

"I promise," Bethany said.

For some reason, I had a feeling Bethany had her fingers crossed behind her back.

"I'm not sure what it all means," Elle said wistfully, "but I'll definitely pass this on to Arthur. In the meantime, Meg and I will look into things on our own." Elle glanced over at me and winked.

"You're the best," Bethany answered. "And Elle, thanks again for believing in me."

Bethany didn't mention my name, which was understandable. We said our goodbyes to Bethany and headed toward our table.

As we walked past the empty dessert table, I said, "Can you cover for me? I'm going to try to find Kelsie. See if I can glean anything new about these latest developments. I feel like she might open up to me."

"What will I tell Patrick?"

"Tell him I'm going to try to find him dessert. There's about fifteen gourmet food trucks out there, I'm sure one will have something, even if it's a churro."

"Oh, I love churros. Should I come with you?"

"No. Remember who your hubby is. That reminds me, what were you going to tell me in East Hampton before I got into Arthur's car?"

She stopped and looked up at me excitedly. "I heard Arthur talking to the coroner. They think they know what the weapon was used to bludgeon Sasha to death."

"Yes? Tell me."

"I don't know."

"You don't know? Ugh. And that was your big news?"

"I'm determined to find out more."

"Did you ever think of asking him?"

"Can't do that. But don't you worry. Tomorrow when he goes into the station, I'm going to hack into his notebook."

"Won't he take his laptop to work?"

"Not a laptop, a notebook. Like one you can hold in your hand. You remember those, don't you? Arthur writes down everything in his. Very old school."

"Won't he take it to work?"

"He always picks out his suits the night before, then hangs them on the standing valet in our bedroom. He also puts his trusty notebook in the inside pocket of his suit coat. In the morning while he's in the shower, I'll thumb through it. Take some photos with my phone."

"Wow, you are devious. But I like your style. Okay, I'm gonna go look for Kelsie so I can be back to catch the Grand Prix finale."

"Be careful. Kelsie might be a friend but she's also a suspect."

I gave her "the look," then hurried toward the stables, thinking Elle should take a spoonful of her own medicine when it came to Bethany.

Chapter 23

When I reached the stable door, a security guard let me in after I showed him my VIP pass and gave him some story about having an important message for Jackie Fairchild.

He shook his head. "Darndest thing. I've been here forty years. Been watching Ms. Putnam perform since she was in her teens. Putnam's her maiden name. Rarely did she ever miss a jump." He leaned in and whispered, "I'm sure it had to do with Black Jack gone missing."

Luckily for me he'd leaned closer to my left ear.

"Hey," he said, "I have hearing aids too. Irritating buggers. My wife said it was that or divorce. She'd found out all this info that there is some kind of link in us elderly people between dementia and hearing loss."

I glanced at his overly large ears with tufts of white hair springing out of them, not unlike Jo's. I reached in my bag and handed him the card to my audiologist's office. "The key to getting your aids calibrated to the perfect frequency is to have a fabulous audiologist like I have. She works with you and never gives up until you're completely happy. Sarah's the best. Don't know what I'd do without her."

He glanced down at the card. "Well, thanks, young lady." Then he stowed the card in his pocket.

"I can't help but ask, but were you working when Black Jack was stolen?"

"I was here at the time the police *think* Black Jack was kidnapped from the stables," he said. "I'm the one who comes in the morning and unlocks the doors. Horses for the Hampton Classic aren't allowed to stay overnight. We have many competitions going on over the course of the show's three days and not enough room to house all the horses. When little Jackie's new husband, Noah, came to me at ten Saturday morning, saying that Black Jack was missing, I was flabbergasted."

"Why's that?"

"Because I oversaw checking the horses in, then sending them on to their assigned paddocks. I swear Black Jack wasn't one of them.

How could Black Jack be missing when he never came in?"

"Are you sure you weren't distracted? Maybe went for coffee or something and missed Black Jack being brought in?"

"No. Never left." He pointed to the stool he was sitting on. "And here's the strange thing, when I led the police to the stall assigned to Black Jack, it sure looked like he'd been there. Buckets of food and water were turned over. His saddle was in there. But no Black Jack. Maybe I am getting senile, but I swear I didn't leave my post for a second."

"That's strange," I said. "Was Jackie, Mrs. Fairchild, here at the time?"

"No. She wasn't scheduled to come in until noon. Mr. Fairchild said he'd brought Black Jack in to save Jackie the trip so she could rest up for one of her afternoon dressage competitions."

"Did you tell the police all this?"

"I tried to. But they looked at me like I was a doddering old fool. Which I am not."

"Of course you aren't," I said, looking into his alert gray eyes.

"Look at me," he said, wiping his brow with a white hankie, "I'm babbling on and on. It's just that nothing like this has ever happened here before. Especially on my watch. And between us, I'm scared if something bad happens to Black Jack, I'll be blamed."

"Oh, I'm sure that's not the case. In fact, my best friend's husband is a detective on the East Hampton Town Police. Why don't you give him a call and tell him everything you just told me. Who knows? It might help them find Black Jack." I reached in my huge handbag, took out my cardcase, then flipped through until I found Arthur's card. "Tell him you talked to Meg."

I saw relief in his eyes. "Thank you, Meg. My name is Stanley. Stanley Pike." He reached out his hand and we shook.

"You're welcome. I better go find Jackie. I'm sure, about now, she needs some friendly solace. Take care."

"Stall forty-six," Stanley called after me as I pulled my hat lower over my eyes. Jackie wasn't really the person I was looking for. Bethany said that Kelsie had gone in the direction of the stables with Noah chasing after her.

"Thanks, Stanley," I yelled back so he could hear me clearly.

The plot of the missing horse was thickening. But did it relate to

Sasha's murder? I would let Arthur handle this one, I was off to find bigger prey. A murderer. Or two.

After I'd checked every stall, I found no sign of Kelsie, Jackie, Noah, or Lee. Only poor Gabriel the horse in stall forty-six. As I'd passed him, I reached over and patted him on his nose, crooning, "Good boy. You'll do better next year."

Instead of going out of the stable the way I'd gone in, I spied someone leaving through a small door. I followed them out, recalling Stanley's story. What he said must have been true because the only door I'd seen that was big enough for a horse to go through was the sliding double barn doors at the front of the stables where Stanley was stationed.

As soon as I stepped outside, I saw them. Not Kelsie and Noah, but Jackie and Noah. Nearby, under an arbor covered with flowering clematis, was a bench. I crept over with my head bent down and sat. Then as a ploy, I pulled out my phone, held it to my right ear, and pretended to be listening to someone on the other end. When Patrick and I had met Noah earlier, I hadn't been wearing the huge dark-lensed sunglasses Elle had loaned me. They made the perfect disguise. At least I hoped they did. It didn't matter anyway, because Jackie and Noah only had eyes for each other.

Jackie held a riding crop in her hand, the tip of it resting on Noah's right cheek. Through gritted teeth, Jackie said in a menacing tone, "A private investigator was hired. And guess what he found?"

Noah had his hands in the air, his palms facing forward. "Jackie, there's nothing to be found. I didn't have an affair with Sasha Morgan. Recently, or in the past. I didn't kill her."

"You stupid idiot. Only you would botch such an easy plan."

Noah took a step backward.

All of a sudden, as if Jackie's spider sense kicked in, she glanced in my direction. I quickly shot up, said into the dead phone, "Of course, I will tell her."

Thankful I was wearing sneakers, I scurried toward the parking lot and the long line of gourmet food trucks.

I hadn't found Kelsie, but at least I could score dessert for Patrick.

Chapter 24

The patio of the Surf Shed was near capacity. Between the music and the packed crowd, I felt transported back in time from when my NYU dorm roommates and I would take the Hampton Jitney to Montauk, party at a few popular bars, sleep a couple hours on the beach, then head back to Manhattan the next morning. Who would have known that eight years later I'd come back to Montauk forevermore.

"I'll be honest," I said to Patrick as we stood waiting for Allie Hines to join us. "I never thought you'd locate Sasha's roommate so easily."

"All I did was ask that bartender if she was here. Seems she's a regular."

"Female bartender. I don't know if she would have been so forthcoming if it was I who'd done the asking."

He smiled. "Well, there's also a male bartender. I'm sure you would have gotten the same result if you'd asked him."

"Look around. How come men can fit in anywhere, no matter what their age? And women of a certain age—not so much. Compared to all these glowing sun-kissed twenty-year-olds, I feel like an ancient dowager from the pages of Austen."

"Well, you do live alone, and you do have a cat. But at thirty-three, I don't think you're an old maid, *yet*," he said, raising an eyebrow.

"Old maid! Who said anything about an old maid. And that reminds me, I don't know how old you are. I don't even know your birthday. I even looked you up on Wikipedia."

He smiled mischievously. "You did? I guess if I must have a stalker, I'd prefer a beautiful one like you."

"Don't deflect. Birthday. Stat!"

"I'll never tell. I hate big parties. Always have. You're lucky you met me at Claire's New Year's Eve party."

"So, it was a rare occurrence? Like a solar eclipse?"

"That's pushing it. A complete solar eclipse comes around about every four hundred years."

"Answer the question, bud. When's your birthday? I know it happens at least once a year." I put my hands on my hips at the same time a pair of tipsy girls stumbled into me, forcing me into Patrick's arms. I wasn't complaining.

"See," he said, laughing. "You're totally enamored with me."

I teased, "I notice that you aren't releasing me from your steel-cage grip."

He gave me a roughish grin. "Steel-cage. Nice."

"And who said anything about throwing you a birthday party? How about a party for two in front of my fireplace. We'll have Chef Patou from Pondfare make us something special." I felt caught up in the fun of hanging out with the Surf Shed's free-spirited patrons who were commemorating the end of summer under colorful strung lights, the moon, and twinkling stars. Patrick must have felt it too because he dove in for a deep satisfying kiss. After I came up for air, I asked, "If you won't divulge your birthday, which I'll eventually get out of your publicist the next time she comes to town, at least tell me your perfect meal."

"That would be any meal with you sitting across from me."

I felt my cheeks warm. "Even one that I prepared?"

"I wouldn't go that far. But I know what I'd like for dessert, seeing mine went flying earlier. Piecaken."

I laughed. "That funnel cake I brought you was nothing to complain about. Your flying piecaken was worth the sacrifice because we caught a crook in the guise of Zoe's stunt double. I'm glad you talked to Jeremy and I didn't have to. By the way, how did Jeremy handle it?"

"Let's just say that Zoe's going to need a new stunt double. Unfortunately for our set designer, the vase that Fawn sold at the antiques show will have to be a write-off. Jeremy refuses to file a police report. And, I forgot to tell you, he wants you and Elle to do an inventory of the items stored at Windy Willows to see if anything else valuable is missing."

I spied a young woman coming toward us who I recognized from the online photos.

I whispered, "She's here."

"Good," he said, releasing me. "I was beginning to think she took a powder, instead of going to the powder room as she told me."

"Powder. Good one. Great 1930s *Mr. & Mrs. Winslow* lingo," I said as we observed Allie Hines slowly approach us like her flip-flops had been dipped in cement.

It wasn't until Allie and I were standing nose to nose that I saw that even though every feature on her face was model stunning, even more so than her deceased roommate, Sasha, she'd been crying. Her eyes were puffy and swollen. The color of the bags under her eyes matched the mauve nail polish on her short nails. When she raised her hand to wipe away a tear, I saw that her cuticles were so gnawed they were bleeding.

Patrick took charge and directed us away from the band, toward an empty picnic table next to a railing overlooking the beach and ocean. Allie sat first, then Patrick next to her. I sat across so I could read her lips. Between the loud thumping bass of the band, my single hearing aid, and the wind that was blowing my bangs in front of my eyes, I was at a definite disadvantage in understanding anything Allie might say regarding Sasha's murder. If I'd been smart, I would have turned on the recording feature of my phone and hidden it in the condiments' basket. But it was too late now.

For a couple of minutes, the three of us sat without speaking. Even though it was well after sunset, seagulls continued to divebomb the Surf Shed's patio with Hitchcockian boldness. The locals knew not to feed the gulls, but apparently that tidbit of information hadn't been passed along to the group sitting at the table next to us. The rowdy young men were taking turns tossing French fries in the air. Then they would squeal in delight as a gull caught it midair. If it wasn't for Allie, I would have charged over to their table and poured ketchup on their heads, giving the birds something to dip their fries in. I was surprised at how many out-of-towners there were at the Surf Shed. On our way back from the Hampton Classic, the line of cars heading west was bumper to bumper. Then I remembered that most of the hotels in Montauk had a four-night minimum on holiday weekends. *Patience, Meg. Patience.*

"Why am I here? You said it's about Sasha." Allie glanced first at Patrick, then me. The chin at the top of her long, graceful neck quivered, and suspicion clouded her tawny brown eyes. Her skin was a golden mahogany, and I'd sell my soul for her cheekbones. *If I had a soul,* I thought. Here we were, interrogating someone who was obviously still reeling from what happened to her murdered roommate. "I'm Meg Barrett," I shouted over the noise from the band. I reached out my hand, but she didn't take it; just glared at me until I had to turn my head away.

I focused on the ocean to my right, watching frothy-white moonlit waves crash against the shoreline fifty feet below. When the music stopped, I heard Allie say something in response to a question Patrick must have asked.

"Yes, I was supposed to pick her up Friday night," Allie said wistfully. "I wish I had. She might still be alive."

"Why didn't you?" Patrick asked, his eyes meeting hers.

Lucky for me, the band went on break. I heard her say, "Got a text. Sasha said she had to stay later and finish up some things. Said she had a few people she could hitch a ride from, and for me not to worry. So, I didn't. What a mistake. I went to bed. When I woke at five—I work at Gleeson's Bakery, here in town. That's how Sasha and I met, at pastry school—Sasha hadn't been home. Her bed hadn't been slept in."

"Did she always come home at night?" I asked. "I heard she was in a relationship with Lee Cutler."

"No, not always. But she said she'd be home Friday night, and I believed her. She was all keyed up about the big membership drive on Saturday. Plus, she and Lee were on the outs. And no, she wasn't seeing anyone else that I know of."

Patrick turned to her. "Why were she and Lee no longer together?"

"I'm not sure. She told me a little, saying the less I knew, the better. Something's been bothering her for a while."

"Was it bothering her before she started working at Privé or after?" he asked.

"Since. I've talked to the police. What's your skin in all this, anyway? I've never seen you two around, and I know all of Sasha's friends. And her enemies."

"Enemies?" Patrick asked. "Who were her enemies?"

"I'm not speaking until I know who you are and why you want to know about her."

That was a good question. I didn't have an answer and I could tell we were losing her. If we ever had her. I said, "We're friends of the detective who's assisting the case. I worked with Sasha at Privé."

I reached in my bag and handed her my business card. "I'm really broken up about this, as I'm sure you are. Such a beautiful woman. Who would want to harm her? I brought Patrick along for support. I'm sure you've seen him around. He's the screenwriter for *Mr. & Mrs. Winslow*." Wow. I didn't even have to white lie.

Allie's eyes opened wide. "The mystery miniseries they're filming in Bridgehampton. Really?"

"Really," I said. "Patrick, why don't you give her one of your cards."

"Sure." He reached into his pocket, took out his wallet, and opened it. His wallet was tattered, looking like it had gone through the wash or maybe he wore it when he went surfing at Ditch Plains Beach. A new wallet would be a good birthday present. If I knew when his birthday was.

He withdrew a white card and handed it to Allie. "Email me your comp card and résumé. I'll be sure to pass it on to our casting director."

Wow. He was good.

"That's why we wanted to talk to you," I said. "To find Sasha's killer before they strike again. You said she had enemies?"

Allie wasn't listening. She had a stricken look on her face. "What-what's this? Where did you get this!" she shrieked, drowning out the band that had just started playing. She was holding a business card in her hand. It wasn't Patrick's because his had fallen onto the table. She got up, tossed the card in the air, just as a northerly gust of air sent it straight for my face. The corner grazed my cheek, then landed on the table faceup. The wind picked it up and before I could grab it, the card disappeared through the guardrails of the fence, then floated away into the ether.

I was able to catch one word, *Exotica*.

When I looked back to where Allie had been sitting, she was gone.

Long gone.

"What was that about?" I asked Patrick. "Did you see the card? It spooked her. And it's starting to spook me."

"No, I didn't see it."

"It said Exotica."

"Like the business card you saw that Cutler had?"

165

"Yes. And a little while ago Bethany said that Kelsie had mentioned the name Exotica when she was arguing with Lee. How the heck did the card get in your wallet?" I asked.

"Haven't a clue." He opened his wallet and thumbed through it. "I think I might have solved that mystery," he said, taking out a card and handing it to me.

It was Noah Fairchild's business card that he'd given Patrick at the Hampton Classic.

"The Exotica card must have been stuck behind this one. I'll bet it came from him. It seems logical. What else was on the card that you saw Cutler drop?"

"A phone number with a Hamptons area code. Why was Allie so frightened? It has to be related to Sasha's murder. Exotica sounds like the name of a gentlemen's club. Something from *The Sopranos*."

"I've never heard of it," Patrick said. "Let's leave. We can do some digging online. I've got Charlie to walk, and you have Jo to feed."

"You know me. I've already searched. Nothing came up except a car company in Manhasset. Maybe before we leave, we should find out where Allie lives. See why she was so threatened by a business card. Any chance we might find the card down on the beach?"

Patrick didn't need to answer because a cloud covered the moon. It would be futile to search for a card in the wind and the dark. "I have a good idea. Why don't I ask Kelsie about Exotica?"

"Alone?"

"No, I'll bring Claire. She's great at getting people to confide in her. Plus, Claire knows Kelsie from our knitting class."

"I think we've done enough for one day," he said. "I tell you what. I'll go back to the bartender and tell her that Allie wrote her number on a napkin and it blew away. That way, tomorrow we can do some research on this Exotica, and you can ask Kelsie a few questions while I wait in the car."

"Now you're thinking. I must be rubbing off on you."

"Undoubtedly. We make a good team."

"We do, indeed. Wait. You're going to be waiting in the car when I go see Kelsie?" I asked.

"Either that or we could have your buddy Officer Moss go with you as backup?"

"Oh, no. Last time Officer Moss ended up in the hospital."

"My point exactly," he said with a smile. "Let's get out of here."

While Patrick went to talk to the bartender, I went out the side gate and waited for him on the sidewalk in front of the Surf Shed.

A few minutes later he approached me.

"Did you get it?"

He held up a slip of paper. "You had any doubt?"

"Not a one." I slipped my arm in his and we started walking. It was almost midnight but there were still people out and about. In a week's time Sleepy Montauk would be deserted by nine. "It's been a long day," I said.

"You got that right. More mentally draining than physically," he said. "We didn't learn much after talking to Allie. Do I still have to find her a part in *Mr. & Mrs. Winslow*?"

"By the look on her face, I don't think she would take one if you gave it to her. We do know that the name Exotica spooked her. And you did get her phone number from the bartender, you sly devil. That's something."

"It must be my trusting eyes."

"Must be. Hey, I had fun today. How about you?" I asked, pulling him under a streetlamp and giving him a kiss on his rough cheek.

"Fun. Hmmm, I think there might be a better word for it, but I can't think of one."

"And you call yourself a writer," I teased. "How about an exciting, thrilling, roller-coaster ride of a day and evening?"

He laughed. "Yes, all those things. But remember, this isn't a game. Someone was murdered, and you might be next if you aren't careful. I need you around."

"You do?"

"I do," he said softly, then he took me in his arms.

Maybe I would let go of the reins. Then I remembered that tomorrow morning, Elle planned on swiping her husband's notebook to see if she could find out what weapon bludgeoned Sasha to death.

It would be rude for me to put my hands over my ears and sing la-la-la when she told me.

Wouldn't it?

Chapter 25

I felt my phone vibrate from under my pillow. I got up on my elbow and glanced at the clock on my nightstand. Two fifteen in the morning. Jo was curled up on her side of the bed, facing me. She opened her eye, gave me a snaggletoothed snarl of annoyance, then turned to face the opposite direction. I wanted to do the same, but curiosity was killing this cat.

Thirty minutes later, I was on the road leading to Privé. I parked in a copse of trees a short distance from the service entrance and grabbed the only weapon I could think of—the horse-head walking stick with the secreted dagger that I'd bought at the antiques show. After getting out of the car, I switched on the headlamp that I used to sniff out antiques and vintage treasure hidden in the corners of attics and basements, then crept toward the farmhouse.

Elle had said that she and Bethany were trapped in the old cottage by a pair of snarling dogs. She'd told me that she couldn't call Arthur because she was worried Bethany would be arrested for trespassing. Or worse. She'd also reassured me that she was fine.

But that didn't stop my heart from beating out of my chest on the entire drive to Sagaponack.

I'd debated on calling Patrick but didn't think it was an emergency. I could handle it. The pair of dunderheads just needed me to distract the dogs so they could hightail it out of there in Bethany's kayak.

Before leaving my cottage, I'd dressed in all black, which included an oversized black hoodie that Patrick had left behind. I'd grabbed a box of Jo's cat treats from the cupboard and a bag of gluten-free chicken nuggets from the freezer. I didn't know if the dogs at Privé had an allergy to wheat, but why take a chance?

I was beginning to genuinely believe that Bethany had nothing to do with Sasha's death. If she was guilty, would she really be snooping around to prove her innocence?

As I neared the rear of the farmhouse, I saw that lights were on in Privé's kitchen. I doubted that the police would have left them on. I turned off the headlamp, stood on a crate, and peered through the window. No one was in the kitchen but the counters were strewn with cooking paraphernalia: open condiment and spice jars, every utensil under the sun, and in the sink, what looked like an animal's (hopefully not a human's) rib cage. Yuck! On the counter closest to me was some kind of menu. The heading at the top read, *Exotica*, then underneath, *The New Glutton Club*. I could only make out the first selection, Green Sea Turtle Soup with a price next to it of four hundred dollars for a cup and six hundred for a bowl. I removed my phone from my pocket and took a photo of the menu, then stowed the phone back in my jeans pocket just as Noah and Jackie entered the kitchen.

Lucky for me, they both faced the window, allowing me to read their lips. And even luckier, the casement window was open a crack. I reached in my pocket and pulled out my keys. My key fob controlled the volume to my hearing aids. Or in this case, my only hearing aid. I upped the volume to the max. I didn't want to miss a thing.

"Grab the cheese," Jackie said. "And tonight, and from every day forward, you'll be sleeping in the apartment over the stables. Once Privé and Exotica are established, you'll be out of my life forever. How did you expect to collect the insurance for Black Jack? He, and everything else I own, is insured in my name only. Thank God for that, and our prenup."

Noah looked away and Jackie punched him in the arm. He certainly was in the doghouse. And soon would be in the "big" house if I had anything to do with it. He turned back to Jackie and shrugged his shoulders sheepishly. "I never planned on getting any of the insurance money. That's all yours. I was approached by someone who wanted to use Black Jack as a stud. The old boy only had a few years left. You said so yourself."

"You ass. How much did he give you for my favorite horse? You're the reason I'll go down in Hampton Classic history as the worst Grand Prix qualifier ever. All my wins will be forgotten."

"He's just a horse."

Jackie slapped him across the cheek.

"We both win," he said, rubbing his cheek. "You get the insurance money and keep the ransom, and I get enough money to finish my project. Calm down."

"Don't tell me to calm down."

"Everything is going to be fine," Noah said.

"Shut up, Noah. You made me pay a ransom, then lost the locker key with my money. And I'm still not convinced that you didn't kill your former au pair to keep your affair on the QT. If we weren't so knee-deep in Exotica, I would divorce you tomorrow and turn you in to the police."

"Sasha and I didn't have an affair. That little witch was going to blow this whole operation. I swear, I had nothing to do with her death. How about you? Maybe you killed her. Hey, I confessed about Black Jack, didn't I? I should get brownie points for that."

"Only after I told you what my private investigator found when he followed you the day after Black Jack was supposedly kidnapped. Before we were married, I thought you married me for me. Not my money. Thought you had as much as I did in the bank because of your daddy's restaurant dynasty. But then, on our honeymoon I find out that you're dead broke. Parnell disowned you because of that little club you joined in Manhattan."

"If I didn't get cut off because of that club, I never would have had the idea for *this* club. We're gonna clear fifty grand in one night. All we had to do was to supply the food. They did all the rest."

"You're still an ass. We better get back to the Provence Suite. There's still an hour to go. I don't trust Lee to be alone with our guests."

Wow, I thought as they left the kitchen. If I wasn't holding on to the window ledge, I might have fainted for the second time in a week. So, Jackie, Noah, and Lee were involved in Exotica. Privé was just a front for an even more exclusive club—Exotica, the New Glutton Club, which was serving endangered and illegal foods. Kelsie! She had mentioned Exotica earlier today in her argument with Lee. She must have found out what was going on and had gone ballistic.

I was thrilled she wasn't part of the glutton gang. But if fear of exposing this late-night dining club was the reason Sasha was murdered, wouldn't that put Kelsie next in line for the killer to silence? I prayed Kelsie was home, snug in her bed, and dreaming of dancing petit fours and not in Privé's freezer or the morgue. Sasha had threatened everyone at dinner Friday night that she knew a secret that could destroy Privé. And look what happened to her. I knew I had to go rescue Elle and Bethany, but first, I had to see for myself what was going on in the Provence Suite.

Two mysteries had been cleared up with Jackie and Noah's *tête-à-tête*: what was going on late at night at Privé, and what had happened to Jackie's kidnapped horse. But there was one mystery that hadn't been solved.

Who killed Sasha?

Chapter 26

I sidled up to the window of the Provence Suite. Sitting at the long table were six men and two women that I'd never seen before. Facing me was a large balding man with chubby cheeks like a toddler's who was gnawing on a bone as if it was a corn on the cob. His greasy chin shined under the glow of the Lalique chandelier.

But it wasn't really the people sitting around the table that caught my attention. It was more what was sitting *on* the table. A large, unusual-looking animal head. I watched the chubby-cheeked man reach over and pet it, displacing fur with his fingertips. He said something, and the others around the table laughed.

I retched into the azaleas.

Even though I didn't want to look back at what else adorned the table, I took out my phone and shot a few photos of the guests. I also got a shot of Jackie carrying in a humongous silver-domed tray, her puppy-dog husband following close behind her.

Lee was nowhere to be seen.

I put my phone back in my pocket, or I should say Patrick's pocket, and grabbed the horse-head dagger that I'd placed on the window ledge. I clutched it tight in my hand, vowing to fight anyone or anything to rescue my best friend. Then I took one last glance inside. Jackie had placed the tray in the center of the table and was about to lift the dome. I honestly didn't want to see what was under the dome. But like a deer caught in the headlights, I couldn't tear my eyes away.

"Gotcha!" Someone with a familiar voice said into my left ear. Even muffled by the fleece of my hood, I knew whose voice it was.

Lee Cutler's.

I jerked around, stabbing the darkness with the dagger. Only catching air. Lee's dark shape took a step closer. Using all my strength, I shoved him into the bushes, then ran.

"I've got a gun," he called after me.

My lungs were on fire when I entered a thicket of trees. I paused for a second to get my bearings. My only thought was to get Lee away from the cottage where Elle and Bethany were holed up. I took off again, hoping I was heading toward my car, but realized that I was closer to the pond that separated Privé from Garnier Vineyards.

I kept running. Because of my hearing loss I had no idea if Lee was inches away or a mile. Then I heard the muffled sound of dogs barking. I stopped, reached into the inside pocket of Patrick's hoodie and removed the now-thawed bag of chicken nuggets. Using my teeth, because I was still clutching the dagger, I ripped open the bag and threw its contents behind me.

Then I took off like my life depended on it.

Because it did.

My prayers were answered when I reached the bank of the pond. Bethany's kayak was waiting. I pushed it into the water, tried to climb inside, got dunked, tried again successfully, then paddled like a maniac toward Garnier Vineyards, adrenaline giving me the power of a six-person crewing team.

Once on shore, I hopped out. I removed my phone from the pocket of my black water-logged jogging pants. Luckily, it powered on. *Yes!* I'd have to write a glowing review to the phone's manufacturer. That's if I lived to write one and wasn't shot by Lee, roasted over an open spit, then placed in the center of the table as one of Exotica's delicacies. But it was doubtful with all the junk food I ate that I'd satisfy their discerning palates.

I called 9-1-1, saying that I heard gunshots, then gave them Privé's address. Then I called Arthur, who told me that he was minutes away from Privé. He'd woken up, found Elle missing, then tracked her GPS location on his phone. After I explained what was going on, I hung up the phone.

Collapsing to the ground, I crawled over to one of the high-top tables on the winery's patio and crouched underneath. I couldn't stop shivering.

Not from my wet clothes.

But from pure, unadulterated fright.

Chapter 27

By the time I got back to my cottage I was too wound up to sleep. I didn't even go inside. Instead, I slunk down to the beach to contemplate all that had just happened. Like a homing pigeon to its roost, I made my way in the darkness to my favorite boulder, which had been formed by centuries of rough surf into the shape of an armchair. I thought of it as my mermaid throne.

I sat and listened to the gentle waves lapping the shore. Then I inhaled and exhaled a few calming breaths and reviewed what had happened at Privé following my call to Arthur.

He'd arrived before Southampton PD. All the lights had been on in the farmhouse, but Noah, Jackie, Lee, and Exotica's gluttonous guests were nowhere to be seen. Even the dogs were MIA. Lee must have reported back to Noah and Jackie that there'd been someone on the grounds who'd blown their secret club status.

Arthur rescued Elle and Bethany, and Elle immediately called me to make sure I was okay. "Arthur wants to know where your car is. He wants Bethany and me to get out of here before the police arrive. He's going to take his car and park it off the highway. Then, when he sees Southampton PD approach, he'll follow them onto the grounds, pretending he was in the neighborhood and just heard the call."

"At three in the morning?" I'd asked.

Elle went on to explain that Arthur planned on keeping Elle, Bethany, and me out of things. That was a relief. I'd then told Elle where I'd parked the Woody and that the extra key was in the magnetic box inside the rear driver's-side wheel well.

"Oh, Meg," Elle had wailed. "Will Arthur ever forgive me?"

I'd told her that he would, and to get the heck out of there and come to the winery.

We'd waited for Arthur in Garnier's gift shop. Bethany had been kind enough to pull a beachy boho skirt and top off a clothing rack for me to change into. I'd sensed a shift in Bethany's and my relationship, and I had no doubt that Bethany was innocent of Sasha's death.

I'd recited my story to them, showing them the photos I'd taken of Exotica's menu and Jackie, Noah, and their guests in the Provence

Suite. Like me, they were so disgusted by the head on the table that they didn't speak until Arthur arrived.

At first, Arthur had acted angry. But when Elle dissolved into tears, he took her in his arms and crooned, "What would I do if anything ever happened to you?"

I was gobsmacked when Arthur had said we couldn't use the photos I'd taken for evidence without implicating the three of us. Then he'd gone on to say that Southampton PD had found a myriad of illegal foodstuffs in Privé's refrigerator, all labeled with their country of origin and the animal's name. He'd also mentioned that forensics had gotten prints off the glasses and dishes around the table and would plug them into their database. He'd added, "Whoever was there was there illegally because they'd broken through the crime scene tape and were tampering in an ongoing murder investigation. The three partners' prints will be on file because they were taken after Ms. Morgan's death had been ruled a murder. Hopefully, that will be enough to charge them. Unfortunately, we still don't know who murdered the poor woman."

I stayed on my mermaid throne until the water lapped at my feet, telling me that the tide was coming in. I reluctantly got up and trudged toward the steps leading to my cottage. When I reached them, I thought of something I could do that was slightly on the shady side. Something to protect the innocent. With that in mind, I felt better about the past few hours. Justice would prevail.

It was still dark when I reached the top of the landing. I glanced over at the bench Patrick had made for me and realized things would be better once I shared my latest exploits with him. I walked across the deck, opened the French doors, and went inside. Then I collapsed on the sofa and fell into a deep sleep.

Jo's angry meows and sharp-nailed kneading prodded me out of slumber and kick-started my memory—I'd completely forgotten to tell Arthur about the conversation I'd overheard, or should I say over*see*'d, between Jackie and Noah having to do with Black Jack. The one where Noah admitted faking Black Jack's kidnapping, insurance fraud, and selling stolen property.

I asked Jo to bring me my phone because Mommy was too tired. But she refused. I got up and called Arthur.

At least one of the partners might spend some time in jail.

Chapter 28

Patrick, Bella, and I were sitting at the chef's table in the corner of Pondfare's kitchen. Pots and pans bubbled, sizzled, and spit. Line chefs chopped, fileted, and pounded. Cuisinarts were whirring, and Chef Patou was shouting, tasting, criticizing, and even throwing perfectly delicious sauces—I could tell by their smell alone—down the drain. Occasionally, Chef would reward his staff with just a slight upturn of his mouth. He was on top of each station, and though his face remained impassive, I could tell by the rosy tips of his large ears that he was in his element. At this stage of his career, Chef Patou could put his name on any restaurant marquee in the world and make it a success. But he was resolute that Pondfare would be his only home. Selfishly, I hoped he never changed his mind. I knew the sales from his cookbook alone would probably keep him and Bella in the black for years.

I had slept till noon, then called Patrick, and explained what had happened at Privé. I told him that I planned on going over to Pondfare to see if Kelsie was there because she hadn't returned any of my calls. If Kelsie hadn't heard about the illegal middle-of-the-night yuck-fest at Privé, I wanted to be the one to tell her. I couldn't use the photos I'd taken as proof of the partners' involvement in Exotica without implicating myself, but there was a chance Kelsie might come forward and tell the police what she knew.

After what had happened at Privé, Patrick insisted on accompanying me. Right as we were leaving my cottage, Elle had called to say that the health inspector and Southampton PD had closed Privé indefinitely. Even if, technically, it had never officially opened. The three partners had been brought in and scolded, but not charged with anything except tampering with a crime scene until more inquiry could be done on what laws, international and domestic, had been broken with their endangered species gourmet club. As for Noah Fairchild, Arthur was doing his own investigation based on what I'd told him about Black Jack.

So here we were, snacking on tester plates of tonight's dinner menu at Pondfare. Quite a chore, but we were up to the task.

"That's the most disgusting thing I've ever seen," Bella said, passing the paper I'd printed from my phone of Exotica's, aka the New Glutton Club's, menu to her husband.

Chef Patou grabbed his readers from the center of the table and sat next to his wife. His features, if taken separately, might fall on the ugly side. But put together, there was something magnetically handsome about him. He was like the Beast in *Beauty and the Beast*. And of course, Bella was the beauty with her olive Mediterranean skin, amber eyes, and long dark hair, which she wore braided and coiled at the back of her head. She resembled a Roman goddess from a Michelangelo frieze.

Chef Patou glanced down at the menu. "There's a history of these kinds of exotic dining clubs. In the nineteenth century at Oxford, Professor Francis Butland started the Acclimation Society. He believed that man was entitled to dominion over all of God's creatures, from insects and up. And nearby, at Cambridge University, Charles Darwin and his buddies started the Glutton Club, of which he was named president. That must be where this Exotica got the name for the *New* Glutton Club. Darwin's Glutton Club's credo was to taste species that couldn't be found on regular menus. Even today in San Sebastian, Spain, there're hundreds of txokos, or secret gastronomic societies. But they aren't known for eating endangered or poisonous foodstuffs, just using every part of the animal in creative ways, like goat's eyes in martinis."

"Stop, Pierre. We get the picture," Bella said, raising her hands in the air.

"Don't tell me Darwin sampled a Galapagos Island giant sea turtle," I said.

"Okay, I won't tell you," Chef Patou said, then shouted for one of his cooks to turn off the *damn* timer. "Eating study specimens was common practice back then." He turned to me and asked, "How'd you manage to get a copy of this menu?"

"Long story," I said. "At least they had cheese on the menu. The only thing on there that's not made from endangered or lethal animals. Although I don't know what category mammoth would fall under."

"Extinct," Patrick said, and I grinned.

Patrick hadn't been that upset about what had gone down at Privé. Mainly because nothing had happened to me, Elle, or

Bethany. Plus, as an animal lover, he was thrilled I'd exposed Exotica.

Chef pushed down his readers until they balanced on the tip of his bulbous nose. "That's not just cheese," he said. "Casu martzu is a Sardinian cheese. It goes through an extra fermentation process by using live maggots to partially decompose the cheese. It's illegal here. As is everything else on this menu."

"Maggots?" I repeated. "Ick."

He looked up. "As for the thousands-of-year-old mammoth meat, I would guess it would taste pretty bad."

"Count me out on the mammoth meat, darling," Bella said. "I have a hard enough time helping you prepare sweetbreads and the like."

"Oh, those are delicious," I said, and Patrick gave me a shocked look. See, he didn't know everything about me, either.

Chef Patou got up to taste something, then nodded his head that it had passed inspection. He sat back down at the table and said, "There's even a famous epicurean tale about Explorers Club members who met in the Grand Ballroom of the Roosevelt Hotel in Manhattan in the early 1950s. The members were dressed in formal attire and served the best wine that would complement their main entrée—a prehistoric grayish lump of extinct mammoth or giant sloth meat that had been encased in a glacier for thousands of years. Recently, a sliver of that same meat from the Explorers Club dinner was found in a jar of formaldehyde. Its DNA was tested. Turns out one of the members played his cronies for fools. The giant mammoth was in reality a green sea turtle."

"Double gross," I said. "Green sea turtle is on Exotica's menu too."

"And illegal to serve in the United States," Chef Patou added.

"So how could Exotica have mammoth on their menu? It's fake too, right?" Patrick asked.

"Not necessarily," Chef Patou answered. "There have been numerous instances of mammoths being found in thawing glaciers. One supposedly still had blood frozen in its veins, and its skin was a pinkish color. I've heard that even modern-day scientists have been known to do a taste test after finding a frozen carcass in the tundra. And of course, foxes and other animals would naturally gnaw on thawing prehistoric mammoth meat. It's nature's way. The circle of life's continuum."

"Like in *The Lion King*," I said, and Chef Patou looked at me with a blank stare.

"This glutton club business reminds me of a movie I saw as a kid called *The Freshman*," Patrick chimed in. "Mathew Broderick and Marlon Brando were the stars. It was about a private society like Exotica. I think a Komodo dragon was involved and some rare or extinct dish that cost the lucky bidder a million dollars. I was only six at the time, but I remember having nightmares about giant Komodo dragons attacking me."

"Aw, I bet you were an adorable six-year-old," I said, squeezing his knee under the table.

Chef Patou shouted for a line cook to watch the broth, then got up to do it himself.

Bella called over to him, "And to think, Pierre, we were considering joining Privé."

I didn't want to tell her that Jackie, Noah, and Lee would probably just get charged with a fine and a slap on the wrist. But I also knew about a little birdie who'd sent an anonymous email to *Dave's Hamptons* with an exclusive story and an attached photo of Exotica's menu. And this same bird might have mentioned that a murder had taken place at the same location as the illegal club. It was doubtful anyone would be dining at Privé anytime soon, if ever. I also knew that whoever this deep throat was, her arm was getting pretty sore from patting herself on the back, happy the sacrifice of those endangered animals would soon be avenged.

"What will happen now with Kelsie? She'll be out of a job," I asked Bella. "I've tried to call her, but she hasn't returned my calls."

"I saw her yesterday," she said. "Kelsie stopped here after the Hampton Classic horse show. Something's up with her. She hasn't been herself recently."

"Since the murder?" I asked.

"No, before that. I haven't had time to sit down with her and see what's up. It's been crazy around here while Pierre's been out of town."

"And what a wonderful job you've done," Chef Patou said, squeezing her shoulder.

179

Wow. Who would have thought. He did have a soft side.

Bella smiled. "I couldn't have done it without Kelsie stopping by to help out in the kitchen. Maybe it's my fault she's not herself. I don't want her to have anything to do with Privé. She'll naturally come back here to Pondfare." Bella caught her husband's eye. "And I can go back to the front of the house. The job I really love — meeting and greeting the public. And maybe even have time to make a baby Patou. Whaddya think, Chef?"

Now it was Chef Patou's turn to blush.

"So Privé being closed might be a good thing for you all," I said. Then, I had another thought. If Kelsie knew about Exotica at the Hampton Classic, why hadn't she exposed the partners, or at least gone to Privé to expose the gross gourmet club?

Because she feared who might go after her if she did. Possibly the same person who bludgeoned Sasha.

Chapter 29

I stood on Kelsie's front porch. Patrick was waiting in the car, the engine running. His head was bent, and he was going over some notes that *Mr. & Mrs. Winslow*'s new director had given him. I could tell by his frown that he wasn't a happy camper. Even though I was used to going where I wanted, chaperone-free, I realized having Patrick waiting outside couldn't hurt if Kelsie turned out to be Sasha's killer.

Kelsie lived on the harbor side of Montauk in a small cottage that she'd told me once had a water view but was now blocked by a two-story condo complex. Don't get me wrong, they were beautiful condos, probably worth a million or more each. Her story made me more resolute to never sell my cozy cottage to a developer, no matter what was offered. They'd have to drag me out feetfirst. Which might happen sooner than later if we didn't find out who killed Sasha. Especially seeing as I'd been the one sticking my nose where it didn't belong.

What if Lee had recognized me from under Patrick's hoodie? Or Noah or Jackie saw me in the window last night and didn't tell their partner because they didn't want the other to know they'd murdered Sasha and planned to get me alone to do the same.

I knocked, and what seemed like five minutes later Kelsie opened the door.

"Meg! What are you doing here?" She didn't look well. She had bluish bags under her eyes and was wearing a soiled, baggy T-shirt that read *Real Men Eat Quiche*. I guessed it was her ex-husband's.

"I'm here to see how you're doing. I stopped into Pondfare and Bella said she was worried about you."

"Come in."

I followed her into the great room. Kelsie was a minimalist. Everything was neat and in its place. The furnishings were all in neutral colors and the wood plank floor was buffed and shined to a high gloss. There weren't any throw pillows, plants, or framed photos, pictures, or dust. My guess was that after the divorce, Kelsie had wanted to rid herself of anything that reminded her of her marriage. I could relate, thinking about the antique ship in a bottle Cole had given me that was now in one of my client's cottages. All

Kelsie needed were a few minor touches to soften the place up and make it more of a home.

Kelsie plopped herself down on an easy chair and looked around the room like she was seeing it for the first time. "Sorry, you're the first person who's been here since I moved in. Always meant to do more. Maybe one day I can hire you to decorate it?"

"That would be great," I said, taking a seat on the sofa. "I'm sure with the hours you work in the restaurant industry, home décor is at the bottom of your list."

"I know why you're here. I've read that online article written in *Dave's Hamptons*."

"Did you know what was going on after hours at Privé?" I asked, then held my breath for her answer.

"No. I had no idea that those idiots were doing under-the-table stuff late at night. There goes my percentage of the business. Between Sasha's murder and this Exotica club, Privé is doomed."

I felt immediate disappointment. Kelsie was lying. In my letter to *Dave's Hamptons*, I'd never mentioned the word *Exotica*. However, I had included a copy of the menu, only I'd cut off the top portion with the words *Exotica* and *The New Glutton Club*. I said, "I was talking to Bethany this morning (true), she said that you were having an argument at the Hampton Classic with both Lee and Noah (also true)."

"Oh, that. It was just a misunderstanding about what they wanted me to serve when Privé finally opened." Suddenly, pain distorted her face. She put her hand on her stomach and stood up. "Excuse me for a minute, I'll be right back."

As she hurried down the hallway, I called after her, "Do you need help?"

She didn't answer. I waited fifteen minutes, then got up and went in the direction of where she'd disappeared. "Kelsie. You okay?" I went to an open doorway and peeked inside. It was the bathroom, but Kelsie wasn't there. I heard a soft whimpering coming from the room next to the bathroom. I hurried toward it and found Kelsie lying on the edge of the bed, curled in a fetal position. "Kelsie! What's wrong?"

She opened her eyes and looked up at me. "Meg, do you mind taking me to the hospital?"

"Of course not! Shouldn't I call 9-1-1 instead?"

"It'll be faster if you just drive me," she said, grimacing in pain.

"Do you know what's wrong?" I asked.

She didn't answer, just closed her eyes and said, "My handbag's over there on the chair. Can you grab it?"

I went to the chair and slung the bag over my shoulder, then went and gently helped her up from the bed. "I came with Patrick. Is that okay?"

"Sure. The more the merrier." Then she laughed liked she'd just told the funniest joke.

We arrived at Southampton Hospital thirty minutes later. Kelsie was admitted, then whisked away in a wheelchair. While Patrick and I sat in the waiting room, I told him what little I knew. I also told him that Kelsie had acted like she'd never heard of Exotica. "I don't think now is the right time to interrogate her."

Patrick raised an eyebrow. "Definitely not."

It was an hour before an ER resident came out to tell us that they were moving Kelsie to a room. "Ms. Stevens wants to see you," he said to me.

I glanced at Patrick and said, "Okay."

I followed behind him. After pressing his key card against a steel pad, the sliding glass doors swooshed open, and we stepped inside. Kelsie was in the first bay, sitting in a wheelchair. She looked better than she had at her cottage. "Meg. Thanks for waiting. I owe you one. No, I owe you a thousand. I have a big favor to ask. Do mind going back to my cottage and getting a few of my things: toiletries, some sweats, and my iPad?" She reached inside her handbag, which was sitting on her lap, and withdrew a set of keys, then handed them to me. "I know it's a lot to ask but I don't have anyone else, especially . . ."

She didn't finish what she was going to say because an attractive male attendant walked into the bay and asked, "You ready to see your new digs, Mrs. Stevens."

"Kelsie," she said. "You can drop the Mrs."

The attendant took hold of the handles of the wheelchair and pushed her into the hallway. Kelsie looked over her shoulder and said, "I'll be in room 314. I'll let them know you're coming."

I hadn't said I would do it. But of course I would. She'd said she had no one else. I made a pact with myself that after everything was cleared up, and the killer caught, I would try to be a better friend. I would enlist Bella and Claire and we would go for a girls' night out on the town. Maybe catch a performance by a Grammy-winning band at Stephen Talkhouse in Amagansett.

Before going back to the waiting room, while trying to ignore the moans coming from the next bay, I glanced around the curtained enclosure. I wasn't sure what was going on medically with Kelsie. Too bad her hospital chart wasn't hanging from the end of her bed like they showed in television dramas like *Grey's Anatomy*.

I went to collect Patrick and found him sleeping in an uncomfortable-looking chair. His chin was on his chest, and there was an adorable spot of drool at the corner of his mouth. He looked vulnerable, making me think of all the tragedy he'd lived through at such a young age. A lifetime's worth. I'd already googled when the movie he'd mentioned at Pondfare, *The Freshman*, came out. I deduced, if Patrick was six when he saw it, that would make him only a year or two older than me.

I nudged him awake.

He startled, glanced around the waiting room, and asked, "Is everything okay?"

I wasn't sure.

So I said, "We'll see."

Chapter 30

I'd convinced Patrick that I didn't need him to go with me to pick up Kelsie's things and make another trip back to the hospital. He'd already done enough. Plus, I knew he was anxious to get back to Charlie and let her outside. I guessed there were perks to having a self-reliant feline.

I put the key in the door of Kelsie's cottage, opened it, and walked inside. I paused and looked at the open layout. I knew from our chats at knitting class that Kelsie had been living in the cottage for at least two years—the same amount of time she'd been divorced. A home's décor said a lot about its occupant. But I couldn't tell anything about Kelsie. I wondered what someone might think when they stepped into my cottage for the first time. Compared to Kelsie's cottage, mine certainly contained a lot more "junk," as my former fiancé Michael had called it. I called it upcycled vintage treasure that made my home cozy and lived in, not a place to impress others with pricey objects d'art or uncomfortable sofas and chairs.

My footsteps echoed down the hallway. I went inside Kelsie's bedroom, found an overnight bag in her nearly empty walk-in closet, and collected a few essentials from her dresser. Then I went into the bathroom, grabbed her toothbrush, toothpaste, deodorant, and hairbrush.

In the kitchen, I found her iPad on the counter. I glanced around. It certainly didn't look like a cook's kitchen. There wasn't one *Top Chef* gadget or appliance like she used at Pondfare and Privé. Even my kitchen was more equipped, and I didn't cook a lick. I grabbed the iPad, put it in the overnight bag, then slung the bag over my shoulder. As I was leaving the kitchen, I noticed through a crack in the bifold pantry door that a light was on. I slid open the door and saw the first inkling of *cozy* in Kelsie's home. Three-quarters of the pantry was filled with cookbooks—vintage and contemporary.

Taking center stage was Chef Patou's *Nouveau French-American Cuisine* cookbook. It must have been recently used because it was sticking out from the shelf. Any kind of vibration or door slamming might cause it to fall to the tiled floor. I went over and pushed it back in place. At least, I *tried* to push it back in place. It wouldn't budge. I saw why. Something was behind it. I pulled it from the shelf, only to find a duplicate copy of Chef Patou's cookbook.

Only this one was sealed inside a large baggie. Its spine was cracked, and I saw a burgundy stain that I knew wasn't dried ketchup. Something told me not to touch it. If it turned out to be the murder weapon that killed Sasha, which I was sure it was, I didn't want to tamper with evidence. I got out my phone, took a photo, then put the undamaged copy of Chef Patou's cookbook back where it had been.

Kelsie wasn't going anywhere because she was in the hospital. I called Elle and asked if she was able to find out from her husband's notebook what the murder weapon was. "Oh, Meg. I completely forgot. With everything going on last night, or should I say this morning, it slipped my mind. I'm not a very good detective, am I? I was asleep when Arthur left for work this morning."

"No worries," I said, "talk to you soon. Hey, can you have Arthur call me. It's not important but I have a question for him."

"Oh, no. What are you up to, Megan Elizabeth Barrett?"

"Nothing. I've gotta run. Bye. Love ya." Then I hung up before she could ask more questions.

Now that I'd found the possible murder weapon, I went back down the hallway to check out the only room I hadn't looked in.

I opened the door to the sweetest, coziest baby nursery I'd ever seen. How could the creator of this room be a cold-blooded killer? On a baby blue dresser was a framed sonogram. I picked it up and scanned the grainy image. I assumed the teeny bean in the center would one day be a baby. The sonogram was dated two weeks ago. Kelsie was pregnant.

Maybe hormones had been the reason Kelsie was so volatile with Sasha?

I left the room and closed the door. "Oh, Kelsie. What have you done?" I said out loud, my words echoing back at me from the bare hallway walls.

As I was leaving the cottage, I wondered what my next step should be. Or, if I should even take a next step other than telling Arthur about the cookbook. On the way to my car, I removed a small stack of mail from Kelsie's mailbox and thumbed through it. The last envelope in the pile was from a fertility clinic.

I ripped it open. The exorbitant dollar amount at the bottom of the page for the procedure that was performed a month and a half ago wasn't quite as eye-opening as the name of the daddy donor. *Holy smokes!*

I hurried to my car, made a few important calls, then headed to Southampton Hospital.

A plan was put in place, not one that I would have come up with.

But then, if it went south, I wouldn't be to blame.

Chapter 31

Patrick and Arthur, along with a team from the Southampton PD, met me at the main entrance to the hospital. I was ushered into the hospital's small chapel, where I was told to unbutton my blouse. A microphone/recording device was attached to my chest and I was wired to go. After I left the little posse in the lobby, I took the elevator up to the third floor.

My knees were shaking in time to my chattering teeth. What if I caused Kelsie to miscarry? *Could I live with that?*

The doors opened and I stepped out. Before heading to Kelsie's room, I went over to the nurses' desk and asked the head nurse if Kelsie had any visitors. The obviously overworked nurse snapped, "We aren't wardens. We don't keep track of who comes and goes during visiting hours." Then he realized how harsh he'd sounded and apologized.

"No problem," I said, then thought that his comparison to a prison warden wasn't too far off the mark. Especially if Kelsie was arrested for murder. Even though the cookbook had been literally staring me in the eye, it was still hard for me to believe that Kelsie was guilty of killing her sous chef. I also knew from my father that on average, males committed seventy-five percent of all murders.

I followed the arrows on the wall to room 314. The door was open, and I stepped inside.

Kelsie looked over at me and smiled a weak smile. "Meg. Thank you. I don't know what I'd do without you."

"It's nothing," I said, out of breath. "Here's everything I could think of." I held up the overnight bag.

"Just put it there on the bed tray. I'll go through it in a minute."

"Can I get you anything else?" I asked.

"No. No. You've done enough. I think I'm just gonna take another nap. I'll call if I need anything. The doctor said I'll only be here for a few days. Whatever you've packed should be fine." She closed her eyes.

But instead of leaving, I pulled a chair from against the wall, placed it next to her, and sat. In a whisper, I said, "Kelsie, I have something to show you. I'm hoping there's some kind of explanation. If not, I'll be forced to call the police."

Her eyes opened wide. I reached into my handbag and took out my phone. I tapped the screen and showed her the photo of the bagged cookbook. Earlier, I'd used my phone's photo app to blow up the cookbook so that it filled the whole frame, making the dried blood on the broken spine appear even more gruesome. "Kelsie, why is this in your pantry? Did you kill Sasha with Pierre's cookbook?"

She remained mute, but tears started pouring down her cheeks. She croaked, "No. I didn't kill her. But I know who did."

I passed her the box of tissues from the nightstand. She blew her nose then whimpered, "I can't go to jail. This baby means more to me than you'll ever know. I promise to cooperate. That's why I kept the cookbook. It will have the killer's prints on it. It was my security blanket in case a promise was broken."

"What kind of promise?"

I poured a glass of ice water from the pitcher on her bed tray, then handed it to her. After she drank, she wiped her eyes, then explained everything, starting with, "It was an accident. Not murder."

Five minutes later, Arthur and one of the officers from the Southampton PD entered Kelsie's room. Arthur told Kelsie in his best, albeit slightly bristly, bedside manner what her next steps would be. As Arthur talked, the Southampton officer hooked up a small camera on top of the TV near the ceiling.

Before I left the room, Kelsie did the first thing on Arthur's to-do list. She put a call in to the person who'd supposedly killed Sasha and told them that they needed to come to the hospital immediately. If they didn't, she'd go to the police. I stepped in the hallway to give Kelsie privacy for the second thing she had to do—get wired.

My part was done. But that didn't mean I had to leave the hospital. Because I'd tipped off the police about the cookbook, and wore the wire, Arthur invited me for a ringside seat in the storage room that was being set up as command central.

Finally, I'd be able to sit back and watch the action without being in the line of fire.

But that was only if we hadn't already caught our killer, and she was lounging in bed in room 314, playing us all for fools.

Chapter 32

The room was basically a hospital storage closet and tight quarters for three adults. I thought I could name the brands of deodorant Arthur and the Southampton officer, whose name was Pete, were wearing. Arthur and Pete took a seat on a couple of swivel desk chairs that faced an open laptop. I stood behind them, watching the video feed that showed a very jittery Kelsie. Arthur and Pete were both wearing headphones. No one offered me a pair. I just prayed the camera angle would allow me to read our killer's lips.

I'd already called Patrick and told him what was going down and that he should wait in his car in case our suspect recognized him. "Any sightings in the hospital lobby?" I asked Arthur.

Arthur held up his hand for me to shush, then said something into his small microphone that I couldn't hear. Turning my attention to the video feed, I saw an undercover officer, posing as a nursing assistant, walk into Kelsie's room. I was able to read her lips when she said, "It's almost showtime. I'll be right outside the door." She squeezed Kelsie's hand, then left the room.

Now, all we had to do was wait for our guest of honor.

Three awful cups of coffee later, our supposed killer walked into Kelsie's hospital room.

It wasn't Lee.

But it *was* one of Privé's partners.

Chapter 33

Noah Fairchild strode into Kelsie's room. I could tell by the beads of perspiration on his forehead that he'd dropped everything to get to the hospital, and by the look of the dark stains under his armpits, he'd probably taken the stairs.

He reached toward Kelsie and grabbed her by the shoulders. Kelsie tried to pull away, but he held tight. "What are you playing at, Kelsie? We had a deal." Before Kelsie could answer, he got up and closed the door to the hallway. When he came back, he sat on the edge of the bed, facing away from me.

All I could do was read Kelsie's lips. "I know we had a deal," she said. "But I've been thinking. I paid you handsomely for your stud services. Thanks to you, I am going to have the baby I've always wanted. But after what happened last night, I'm not sure I can keep our secret of how Sasha died. I'm going to be a mother. I just can't risk it."

Noah said something, then Kelsie said, "Noah, it was an accident. I will tell them that. I promise. Sasha was out of her mind. She planned to expose Exotica. And when she overheard me telling you that the fertility clinic confirmed I was pregnant, she threatened to tell Jackie that you were the father. You had no choice but to throw the cookbook at her, especially after she picked up that knife. You were just defending yourself."

Noah removed his hands from her shoulders, then turned and faced the camera. I instinctively ducked, thinking he could see us. He said, "You won't say anything. It'll just be he said, she said." He balled his hands into fists, then turned back to her.

Kelsie shrunk into her pillows. "I want you to know that I saved the cookbook with your prints on it. My insurance just in case you turned the tables on me."

He said something, then Kelsie answered, "You handed me the cookbook, told me to ditch it, and leave. You said she was fine. Passed out from all the booze she drank, and you would stay with her until she woke up. So I left. You put her in the freezer without telling me. How could you?"

There was no reason for me to read anybody's lips to understand what happened next. Noah went for Kelsie's neck, just like Bethany had done to Sasha Friday night. I screamed, "Help her!" Arthur raised his hand again, then spoke into his microphone. The undercover officer that had been waiting outside Kelsie's door flew into the room with her gun drawn. She said something and Noah's hands went limp at his sides.

Arthur, Officer Pete, and I hurried out of the closet. We were just in time to see Noah being led out of Kelsie's room in handcuffs.

We got him! I texted Patrick a few minutes later.

You mean you got him, Nancy Drew, he texted back, adding a smiley face emoji, followed by a red heart — not a yellow, pink, blue, or even a green heart. A red heart.

Didn't red mean love?

Chapter 34

It was late September. Sweater weather. The scent of fall hung on the salt air as we dined under fairy lights and a plethora of stars. Stars that had aligned perfectly for Bethany. Especially after Privé's three partners, including one wearing an orange jumpsuit, signed the contract allowing Bethany to buy back her family's French farmhouse, its contents, and property, for half of what she'd sold it for.

Southampton PD had gone easy on Kelsie, believing that she had no idea that Noah killed Sasha until she'd found her in the freezer. Not that Kelsie was totally off the hook. She'd covered up what Noah had done and was being charged with "misprision of a felony." A crime, if she was convicted, that could carry a hefty fine and a three-year sentence.

Noah hadn't been so lucky. He was charged with second degree murder. Jackie refused to post his bail but did manage to come up with the money to purchase Black Jack from the breeder that Noah had sold him to. Arthur used the key that Patrick and I found at the Hampton Classic to open a locker at the East Hampton train station containing the ransom money, then returned it to Jackie.

My exposé in *Dave's Hamptons*, along with the heath inspector's charges, had been enough to make sure that Privé's doors would be closed forever.

There'd been a twist to the Exotica/New Glutton Club. All the food, except for one item, hadn't been illegal, endangered, or exotic. The main proteins served to the gluttons consisted mostly of doctored chicken, fish, tofu, and beef. The partners had purposely mislabeled things so they could rip off their guests for little overhead and a larger profit. If it hadn't been for Lee slipping in something *illegal*—green sea turtle—Privé might still be open. More to Lee's demise, the health inspector also found surplus turtle meat stored in one of his Cutler's Meat Wagons. Lee's New York food truck license was suspended, and he was persona non grata in the Hamptons. *Good riddance.*

Kelsie hadn't originally been a part of Exotica. But when Sasha told her about the after-hours dining club on the Friday she was killed, Kelsie wanted to be cut in. That was what she, Noah and Lee had been arguing about at the Hampton Classic.

The mystery of who was driving the black SUV on the morning after Sasha was killed was cleared up. A few days ago, I'd spied Sasha's roommate, Allie, getting into her black Explorer at the IGA in Montauk. When I'd approached her, she'd hurriedly hopped inside the car, then rolled up her window. I'd shouted through the glass that I'd come in peace and just wanted to ask one question. Reluctantly, she'd rolled the window down a crack.

"Allie, why were you so scared when you saw the card with the word *Exotica* printed on it?"

She hesitated, then said, "Late at night, a few weeks before her death, Sasha followed Lee to Privé. She thought Lee was cheating on her, but it turned out that he and the other two partners were serving illegal food to a group of rich people dressed in formal attire. She was totally grossed out about a disgusting animal head that she'd seen on a platter. Sasha swore me to secrecy until she figured out what to do. Then she started getting texts from an unknown number, warning her to keep quiet or she would end up like the head on the platter."

I told Allie something of a positive nature that I'd learned from Arthur about the aforementioned animal head. It hadn't been real. Noah had it specially made by a creature effects artist that he'd worked with on one of his previous films.

"Too bad Sasha hadn't known that," Allie had said, a tear trailing down her cheek.

"One more thing. Where you at Privé early Saturday morning on the day we found Sasha?"

"Yes. I went before my shift at the bakery. I talked to Sasha's boss. I told her that Sasha hadn't come home, and I was worried. She told me she hadn't seen her, saying Sasha was fine when she'd left the previous night."

Kelsie was a big fat liar, I'd thought. Sasha had been far from fine; her head had been bashed in with a hardcover six-hundred-page cookbook by a man who would do anything for the mighty dollar. As Allie pulled away, I recalled thinking that maybe Kelsie should be in a cell next to Noah. Pregnant and all.

I let go thinking about the past and watched Elle stand up from the table at Maison Garnier topped with dozens of lit votive candles. She extended a hand that held a flute of Garnier Vineyards' best champagne. "I propose a toast. To Bethany. May your beautiful new restaurant be a huge success."

We raised our glasses and Bethany laughed. "I only wish Tom was here. But I'm sure he's looking down on us. It's hard to believe that Maison Garnier will open its doors tomorrow. Thanks to Meg's interior design —"

"And for her catching a killer," Elle added.

"Yes. That too. But seriously," Bethany said, looking over at me with appreciation. "We barely had to change a thing to get this place up and running. All I did was switch out the Limoges bone china for sturdy white hotel dinnerware like you might find in a French bistro. Maison Garnier will be serving family-style meals, at affordable prices, using only local produce and meat. Our new chef will be preparing meals like my grand-mère, and her grand-mère, cooked back in France."

"It was a team effort, on both counts," I said, squeezing Patrick's hand and looking over at Elle and Arthur. I could already tell that Bethany's style of management was the opposite of Privé's partners. Case in point: she'd hired me to turn the old cottage into a cozy place her waitstaff could go between shifts to relax and rest their tired feet.

Bethany had allowed me to keep the contents from the cottage that I'd stored in my guest room. But I hadn't kept everything. I'd returned to her a box of old Garnier family photos and letters written in French that were dated prior to World War II. I'd also handed over a magnificent oil painted by a famous French resistance artist. The landscape painting depicted the original Maison Garnier farmhouse in the forefront and rows of rolling grapevines in the background. Bethany had hung the painting in a place of honor inside the restaurant. She'd been more than grateful about what I'd found, just as I had been about the furniture and goodies I got to keep.

When it came to Bethany, I had a feeling I shouldn't have judged a book by its cover, like I had with Kelsie. A lame analogy, especially thinking about the murder weapon, but it seemed to fit. And I looked forward to forging a friendship with Elle's childhood friend.

"To Bethany and Maison Garnier," the four of us called out.

I took a sip of champagne, then glanced at my companion. Butterfly wings fluttered, then pounded, in my chest. Champagne wasn't the only cause of my giddiness. It was more the conversation that Patrick and I'd had an hour earlier. We'd been sitting on the bench he'd made, watching the ocean get swallowed up by the last light of the day. It was a serious, deep conversation that ended with Patrick taking my hand, looking into my eyes, and saying, "I know I have a lot of scars that need healing. And so far, you've been better for me than any shrink or antidepressant. Catherine was a wonderful woman and an exceptional mother, but she was also human. We had our things. Every marriage does. It's taken a long time. But I now realize that she would've never wanted me to suffer this long. I was a good dad and a good husband. My penance has cost me three years of my life. I can accept that. I can't accept the cost of losing you because I have such a hard time sharing my feelings. Know that I'm in it for the long run. Please have patience."

"Take all the time you need," I whispered, squeezing his hand. And I meant it. "I'm not going anywhere."

Then we'd kissed. A long, soulful kiss.

After we pulled apart, I'd asked, "So, when's your birthday, Mr. Seaton?"

Without hesitation, he'd answered, "January twenty-ninth." Then he'd followed with, "What are you grinning about, Ms. Barrett. Or more importantly, what are you planning?"

"Why, nothing," I'd white lied.

Chapter 35

A light blinked over the kitchen door.

"Can you get it?" I asked, calling over to Patrick, who was sitting in front of a roaring fire on a cold November day. Charlie was at his feet, and miracle of all miracles, Jo was on his lap.

"I'm a little tied up," he said, looking down at Jo. He tried to eject her from his lap. All Jo did was get up, stretch, then settle down again, leaving plumes of fur in her wake. Patrick let out a sneeze of cyclonic proportions.

"Bless you," I said. "Jo, treat!" She hopped off lickety-split. "Sorry, Patrick, you'll have to give her one. As you can see, I'm elbow-deep in bread dough. You should've done this part. You know the only step I like is the one where I punch the dough. It's so satisfying."

He grabbed Jo in his arms, stood, and put her on the floor. After another sneeze, Patrick reached in his pocket, and tossed her a treat. It was a homemade dog treat meant for Charlie, but Jo didn't care. "As long as you're not picturing my face when you're doing your pummeling," he said, moving toward the door.

"Never," I said, laughing.

Patrick opened the door and I felt frigid air snaking its way into the kitchen. Last night we'd gotten a light dusting of snow. I wasn't complaining. Being snowed in with Patrick made my cottage seem even cozier.

"Hi," I heard Patrick say. "Come in."

I turned to see my ex, Cole, and his dog Tripod standing in the open doorway.

Cole took a step inside. "I think Meg is expecting . . ."

Before Cole could finish his sentence, Tripod came bounding over. He placed his lone paw on my shoulder and knocked me flat against the refrigerator. Then he went to town licking my cheek with his slobbery tongue. Well, that answered one question I was curious about. Would Tripod remember me? I knew I'd never forget him. Especially seeing as he'd saved my life.

After Cole, Patrick, and I went over the logistics of things, Patrick and I walked Cole to the door.

And guess what? It wasn't even awkward.

Patrick held the door open. On the way out, Cole gave me a peck on the cheek, then shook Patrick's hand. He walked toward a waiting Uber. Halfway to the car, Cole turned and waved. A shaft of sunlight broke through the dark clouds and caught the gleam of his gold wedding ring.

"You okay?" Patrick asked as we stood in the open doorway.

"I really am. Between you and me, I've had a lot of sleepless nights knowing that Tripod wasn't able to accompany Cole on any of his long sailing voyages because his girl . . . wife was allergic to dogs."

"Do you think he'll be back for Tripod after their year in Australia?"

I thought about it, and said, "I hope not."

After I closed the kitchen door, I turned to look at Tripod. He hadn't changed a bit, except he seemed shaggier than ever. My best guess was that he was a cross between a St. Bernard and a golden retriever. Maybe I could order a doggie DNA kit to find out for sure. Whatever he was, he was more than welcome to the family.

I watched Tripod sniff Charlie. She backed away at first, then decided Tripod wasn't a threat, but still eyed him warily. I could tell they would soon be friends. Next, Tripod headed over to the ginormous doggie bed I'd bought and nestled down and made himself at home.

He was home. Maybe for a year or maybe longer.

Jo seemed almost gleeful at the appearance of her old paramour. She snuggled next to his furry belly and closed her eye.

Patrick sat down on the reading chair by the fire and Charlie sat at his feet.

Could it get any better?

That's when Patrick called out, "What's burning in the oven?"

Recipes

Jeff Barrett's Coq au Vin

One of my all-time favorite dishes, this classic is updated to be more flavorful and easier to execute than is typical.

Serves 6–8

2 tablespoons olive oil
½ pound slab bacon, cut into ½-inch cubes
3–4 pounds chicken thighs and drumsticks, skin on, seasoned with salt and pepper. (If you have time and a meat cleaver, lob off the "knob" end of the drumsticks. Makes for a more elegant serving.)
1 large red onion, halved and sliced
4 cloves garlic, finely chopped
8 ounces carrots, cut into diagonal slices approximately ¼ inch thick.
2 tablespoons coarsely ground black pepper
1½ teaspoons salt
1½ cups brandy or cognac
3 cups chicken stock (preferably homemade, low- or no-sodium), plus more if necessary
1½ bottles red wine
10 fresh sprigs of thyme, tied into a bundle
8 ounces fresh mushrooms (any will do), sliced
8 ounces frozen pearl onions
4 tablespoons softened butter
3 tablespoons flour

Preheat oven to 300 degrees.

Set a large "Dutch oven" (such as Le Creuset 9-quart) on medium heat, add the oil and the cubed bacon. Brown and render the bacon, about 5 minutes. When browned, remove bacon to a plate with a slotted spoon and set aside.

Add the chicken pieces to the hot fat in a single layer, skin side down first. Brown nicely on all sides until golden. When browned, remove to a platter and set aside, leaving the hot fat in the pot. You likely will need to do this in batches.

Add the onions and stir. Allow them to soften a bit, around a minute or two. Then add the garlic and carrots. Stir to brown but be careful not to scorch the garlic by browning too much. Add the ground pepper and salt. Stir.

Pour in the brandy. Turn the heat up to high and let the alcohol cook off and the brandy reduce by about half. Then add in the chicken stock. Bring to a boil and cook for about 10 minutes to reduce. Add in the browned chicken and bacon and all their juices. Return to a boil. Add in the red wine and thyme sprig bundle. Return to a boil.

When it is boiling again, place the Dutch oven, uncovered, into the 300-degree oven. Bake for a total of 3 hours. After the first hour, check to make sure the liquid is still covering the chicken. If the liquid has reduced too much, add more chicken stock. After two hours, place a lid on the Dutch oven.

Near the end of the cooking time, brown your mushrooms in one tablespoon butter in a sauté pan.

After three hours, remove the Dutch oven to your stovetop. With a slotted spoon, carefully remove all the chicken pieces to a platter, leaving the sauce and vegetables in the pot. Remove the thyme sprig and discard. Bring to a boil.

Combine the remaining butter and flour in a small bowl with a fork to form a paste. Whisk in the butter/flour paste into the boiling sauce in the Dutch oven to thicken.

When it reaches a boil, add in the mushrooms and frozen onions. Stir to incorporate. Add in the chicken and cook on medium heat for another 10 minutes. Check for seasoning.

Serve over toasted, buttered baguette or steamed potatoes.

Meg's Compound Butter Recipes

All of the following compound butters are prepared in the same way. Make sure that all the ingredients have reached room temperature. Blend all ingredients in a bowl with a spatula until combined well. If you want, you can store in a bowl or roll into individual rolls using waxed paper and twisting the ends. Refrigerate for at least two hours for the best results. Makes approximately ½ cup. Serves 8.

Note: The compound butters will last in the fridge for up to a week or six months in the freezer.

A loaf of bakery bread, along with a log of homemade compound butter, would make a fabulous hostess gift. And the best thing, no cooking required!

Garlic Herb Butter

8 tablespoons (1 Stick) unsalted butter, slightly softened
1 tablespoon minced garlic
1 tablespoon flat-leaf parsley, finely sliced
1 tablespoon chives, finely sliced
½ tablespoon freshly squeezed lemon juice
¼ teaspoon kosher salt

Jalapeño and Lime Butter

½ cup softened unsalted butter
½ teaspoon salt
¼ teaspoon ground black pepper
1 jalapeño pepper, finely chopped
1 tablespoon fresh lime juice
1–2 tablespoons freshly chopped cilantro

Lemon and Herb Butter

½ cup softened unsalted butter
½ teaspoon salt
¼ teaspoon ground black pepper
2 teaspoon lemon zest
1 tablespoon fresh lemon juice
2 cloves garlic, crushed
1–2 tablespoons freshly chopped herbs of your choice: basil, dill, thyme, or rosemary (if using dried herbs, use 1–2 teaspoons)
* You could also add red pepper flakes to taste.

Walnut & Blue Cheese–Flavored Butter

½ cup softened unsalted butter
¼ teaspoon salt
¼ teaspoon ground black pepper
¼ cup walnuts or pecans, chopped
⅓ cup crumbled blue cheese (you can also use goat cheese)
1 teaspoon onion powder
1–2 tablespoons fresh chopped parsley or 1–2 teaspoons dried parsley

Patrick's Molten Chocolate Cakes

Makes 6 servings

7½ ounces bittersweet chocolate, coarsely chopped
½ cup plus 3 tablespoons unsalted butter, cut in large pieces
3 eggs
3 egg yolks
¼ cup plus 2 tablespoons sugar
pinch of salt
5 tablespoons sifted flour

Preheat oven to 325 degrees.

Butter and lightly flour six 6-ounce ramekins. Place on baking sheet.

In a metal bowl over a pan of simmering water, place 5 ½ ounces of the chocolate and the butter.

Heat until smooth, stirring frequently.

Remove the bowl from the heat and let mixture cool slightly.

In another bowl, beat the eggs, egg yolks, sugar, and salt at high speed for approximately 10 minutes, until pale and thick.

Reduce the speed and gradually add the flour, beating constantly, until mixed.

Add the chocolate mixture and beat for an additional 5 minutes or until thick and glossy.

Pour half the batter into the six ramekins equally.

Divide the remaining 2 ounces of chocolate and place in the center of each ramekin (approximately 1 tablespoon of chocolate per cup).

Top with the remaining batter in each ramekin.

Bake for 12 minutes or until the cakes are set around the edge but the center is not quite set.

Remove and cool for 5 minutes.

Run a sharp knife around the edge, cover with an inverted dessert plate, turn over and remove the ramekin.

Garnish as desired with whipped cream, confectioners' sugar, raspberries or fresh mint.

Meg and Elle's Think-Outside-the-Box Guide to a Cozy Home

Elle: To clean artificial flowers or greenery, pour salt in a paper bag, add the flowers or greenery, then close the bag and shake vigorously. The salt will get rid of all the dust and grime.

Meg: Buy an inexpensive grocery store flower bouquet, then break the bouquet up and place the individual flowers in vintage bottles, Ball jars, or small vases. You can scatter them around your home or put them in a grouping in the center of your table.

Elle: Buy vintage books at thrift or vintage shops, then frame individual pages from the books—an inexpensive way to have one-of-a-kind art.

Meg: Make sure you bring a measuring tape with you when shopping for your books, that way you can see if the print from the book will fit in a store-bought or vintage frame. Here are the standard sizes for most frames: 3 x 5, 4 x 6, 5 x 10, 11 x 14, 16 x 20.

Elle: Spray the outside of inexpensive clear glass candleholders and vases found in thrift stores and garage sales with *frosted* spray paint in different hues made specifically for glass. You can find the spray paint in your local craft or home improvement store.

Meg: Placing candles in the freezer three hours before your guests arrive will make the candles burn longer.

Elle: Showcase your antique china serving dishes on a buffet by elevating each platter or bowl using cake and dessert stands in varying heights.

Meg: A tip from Patrick is not to throw out leftover wine after a dinner party. Fill an ice cube tray with the wine and use the cubes in your cooking sauces.

Elle: Here are some inexpensive and fun ways to make place cards for your dinner guests: take a colorful autumn leaf and write your guest's name on it with a marker; use a pine cone and stick the place card between the spines; saw slits in the top of wood spools to hold a photo of your guest or a place card with their name.

Meg: Elle, you're giving me great ideas. How about putting a green plant in a mini terra-cotta pot and writing the person's name on the pot with a Sharpie; or loop wire around a bottle to form a card holder and add flowers to the bottle. A bunch of twigs tied with a gift tag with the person's name written on it would also be cool. The choices are endless, and you'll leave your guests feeling incredibly special.

Elle: To keep clutter at a minimum, paint the inside of a pair of cupboard doors with chalk paint and use it to write reminders and shopping lists.

Meg: To spruce up a boring ceiling, add a medallion around your light fixture or chandelier.

Elle: When shopping for antique or vintage furniture, give the furniture the sniff test. If it is too smelly, you should keep on walking. Also give furniture the wobbly test. Rock the piece left to right and front to back. If it moves, I advise passing it up.

Meg: My advice when it comes to shopping for vintage and antique wood furniture is to look for solid wood or real wood veneer pieces. They are the easiest to paint and repair. I know from experience that laminate, composite, and fake veneer pieces are hard to work with.

And remember, a modern home can meld perfectly with that little touch of vintage or antique.

Wishing you great finds!

About the Author

Kathleen Bridge is the national bestselling author of the Hamptons Home & Garden Mystery series and the By the Sea Mystery series. She started her writing career working at *The Michigan State University News* in East Lansing, Michigan. A member of Sisters in Crime and Mystery Writers of America, she is also the author and photographer of an antiques reference guide, *Lithographed Paper Toys, Books, and Games*. She teaches creative writing in addition to working as an antiques and vintage dealer. Kathleen blissfully lives on a barrier island in Florida. Readers can visit her on the web at www.kathleenbridge.com.

Made in the USA
Middletown, DE
06 October 2021

49768780R00128